Praise for

THE BLACK COUNTRY

"Devilishly dark . . . It isn't often that a mystery-thriller enthralls so completely . . . but as usual with Mr. Grecian, there is more to this tale than complex plotting . . . A displaced eye, a crumpled note, cryptic limericks and lost ribbons: Like our detective heroes, we follow these trails into the white-blinding snow to its brilliant and unexpected conclusion. Whether you read the tale in the dark night of winter or the haze of a summer sun, be prepared for the chill. The days are dark in Black Country." —*The Huffington Post*

"Grecian creates an eerie atmosphere from start to finish, and without giving anything away, the killer here is creepy and unexpected."
—Bookreporter.com

"Riveting . . . an intelligent historical thriller."
—*Booklist* (starred review)

"Startling and spooky . . . [a] bold melding of horror with historical elements." —*Publishers Weekly* (starred review)

"[Grecian] presents with fine precision the gray and gritty atmosphere of late Victorian England." —*Kirkus Reviews*

THE YARD

"Grecian has a talent for capturing gory details . . . extremely vivid (and strangely moving) . . . Bounding from the workhouse to the lunatic asylum to the stinking streets, [Grecian] does outstanding descriptive work on the mad and the maimed, the diseased and the demented . . . If Charles Dickens isn't somewhere clapping his hands for this one, Wilkie Collins surely is." —*The New York Times Book Review*

continued . . .

"[A] mix of historical facts and vivid fictional creations. It's great fun . . . Grecian's debut is the promising start of a new series and should be one of the most acclaimed and popular mysteries of the year."

—*The Huffington Post*

"Exuberantly grisly."				—*The Guardian* (U.K.)

"Grecian powerfully evokes both the physical, smog-ridden atmosphere of London in 1889 and its emotional analogs of anxiety and depression. His infusion of actual history adds to this thriller's credibility and punch. A deeply satisfying reconstruction of post-Ripper London."

—*Booklist*

"A brilliantly crafted debut novel with unforgettable characters. An utterly gripping tale perfectly evokes Victorian London and brings you right back to the depraved and traumatic days of Jack the Ripper."

—Lisa Lutz, author of *The Spellman Files*

"Lusciously rich with detail, atmosphere, and history, and yet as fast paced as a locomotive, *The Yard* will keep you riveted from page one. It's truly a one- or two-sitting read."

—Jeffery Deaver, *New York Times* bestselling author

"Grecian successfully re-creates the dark atmosphere of late Victorian London."				—*Kirkus Reviews*

"A winner, filled with Victorian arcana and eccentric characters and more humor than one expects from such a work."		—*The Rap Sheet*

"This excellent murder mystery debut introduces a fascinating cast of characters. Grecian displays a flair for language as well as creating vivid (and occasionally gruesome) depictions of places and events."

—*Library Journal*

"All the gruesome sights, sounds, and smells of a depraved Victorian London are vividly depicted . . . not for the squeamish. Suspense is competently handled, as are the multiple points of view which make up the narrative. The characterization is particularly adept, and there's even the occasional thought-provoking comment on industrialization and metropolitan Victorian society . . . Add to it all a few genuinely funny moments courtesy of absurdity and human nature, and you have *The Yard*: a gripping police procedural mystery and cracking good read. Recommended."   —*Historical Novel Society*

"I enjoyed every minute of *The Yard* . . . If you like gritty crime stories with a psychological thriller edge then you're in for a treat!'
—*Popcorn Reads*

THE
BLACK
COUNTRY

ALEX GRECIAN

BERKLEY BOOKS, NEW YORK

THE BERKLEY PUBLISHING GROUP
Published by the Penguin Group
Penguin Group (USA) LLC
375 Hudson Street, New York, New York 10014

USA • Canada • UK • Ireland • Australia • New Zealand • India • South Africa • China

penguin.com

A Penguin Random House Company

Berkley trade paperback ISBN: 978-0-425-26773-8

The Library of Congress has cataloged the G. P. Putnam's Sons hardcover edition as follows:

Grecian, Alex.
The black country / Alex Grecian.
p.   cm
ISBN 978-0-399-15933-6
1. Murder—investigation—England—Fiction.   2. Detectives—England—Fiction.
I. Title.
PR6107.R426B53   2013   2013003820
823'.92—dc23

PUBLISHING HISTORY
G. P. Putnam's Sons hardcover edition / May 2013
Berkley trade paperback edition / May 2014

PRINTED IN THE UNITED STATES OF AMERICA

10 9 8 7 6 5 4 3 2 1

Cover photographs: Street © Michael Trevillion / Trevillion Images. Man © Mark Owen / Arcangel Images.
Cover design by Sara Wood.

For Graham,
who is not allowed to read this
until he's much older

Rawhead and Bloody Bones
Steals naughty children from their homes,
Takes them to his dirty den,
And they are never seen again.

—*Black Country children's rhyme*

THE
BLACK
COUNTRY

PROLOGUE

It was an unusual egg. Not at all like other eggs Hilde had seen. It was slightly larger than a robin's egg, white with a thin spiderweb of red, visible under a paper-thin layer of snow. A bit of dirty pink twine curled out from under the egg, and Hilde reached out, nudged it with her fingernail. The egg turned, rolling over in its nest of straw and feathers and bits of old string. Hilde could see now that the worm-thread was embedded in mud on one side of the egg and on the other side of the egg was a large colored dot, slate blue, darker than a robin's egg ought to be.

She adjusted her position in the tree, resting her behind against a big branch to free her hands. She looked down at the ground, but there was nobody to see what she was doing or to tell her no. Carefully she reached into the nest and plucked out the unusual egg. It was slippery, not as firm as the eggs she had handled in the past, and its surface gave a little under the pressure of her fingertips.

She held it up to the pale sun, turning it this way and that. It glistened, a dappled branch pattern playing over its surface. She brought it closer to her face. The blue dot in the center ringed a smaller black spot and reminded her of something, but it was out of context and it took her a long moment to place it.

And then she did and it was an eye, and the eye was looking at her.

Hilde reeled back and dropped the eyeball. It tumbled down through the branches below, bouncing once, then twice, off the trunk, and disappeared into a pile of soft snow-covered underbrush. Her foot came loose from its perch on the branch and she felt herself slip. Her weight fetched up against a smaller branch to the side, but it didn't hold her. She felt the adrenaline rush too late as she grabbed for the nest and it came loose in her hand. Her dress snagged and tore, and all of her sixty-three pounds caromed off the branch and slammed back into the tree trunk.

Still holding the useless bird's nest, Hilde fell to the ground, screaming all the way.

1

THE VILLAGE OF BLACKHAMPTON,
THE MIDLANDS, MARCH 1890

Inspector Walter Day stepped off the train and directly into a
dirty grey snowbank that covered his ankles. He was a solid
block of a man with dark hair swept straight back from his
face, and he smiled at the fat flakes that eddied in the train's ex-
haust. The ride from London had been longer than expected, and
he was tired and thirsty and nervous, but he took a moment to
breathe in the fresh air. He set his suitcase down and raised his face
to the sky, stuck out his tongue, and tasted the cold wet pinpricks of
melting snow.

"Ow bist?"

Day turned to see a stout man in a blue uniform striding toward him. The man's cheeks were red and raw, and ice glinted in his thick handlebar mustache.

"I'm sorry?" Day said.

"You the inspector, then?"

"I am. And you'd be Constable Grimes?"

"I am," Grimes said. He put his hand out before he had reached Day and hurried to make up the distance, his arm held out like a lance between them. "Welcome to Blackhampton, sir. Quite excited to be workin' with the Yard. Been a dream of mine."

Day was flattered. This distant sheltered village still respected the detectives of Scotland Yard, saw them as a force for good. London was a different matter. Jack the Ripper had ravaged London and left his nasty mark on a city that had since become cynical and scornful of its police. Scotland Yard was in the process of rebuilding, but it was a daunting task. Day had only been with the Yard for six months, much of that on the new Murder Squad, twelve men tasked with hunting murderers like Saucy Jack. The commissioner, Sir Edward Bradford, had told Day he could spare him for only two days, so two days it was. He hoped it would be enough.

"We'll try not to let you down." Day took a few steps in Grimes's direction and shook the constable's hand.

"Let's get your luggage," Grimes said, "and I've got the carriage here to take you straight round to the inn. Cozy place, I think you'll find. They do it up good there."

"Thank you. I've just got the one bag here. But we're waiting for my sergeant."

"Sergeant? Was told to expect a detective and a doctor."

"The doctor will be along tomorrow. He had pressing business in London."

"So we've got an extra man, do we?"

"It seems you do."

"Well, we'll find room for him."

Day wondered whether there was a territorial issue. One detective might be of assistance to the constable. But two men from the Yard might seem like a threat. The local law was already outnumbered.

"I'm sure we'll depend on you completely," Day said.

"No worries there."

"Dash it all!" Sergeant Nevil Hammersmith's voice preceded him, muffled by the noise of the train's engine. "It's cold." Hammersmith hove into view carrying a small canvas bag. He stepped down from the train and shook his head at Day. The sergeant was tall, and rapier thin, and his unkempt hair hung over his eyes. His coat was unbuttoned, and a large wet spot decorated the front of his shirt.

"I'm sure that doesn't help with the cold," Day said. "The wet, I mean. Makes it colder yet when the breeze hits you."

Hammersmith looked down at himself. "I don't think it's helped the shirt, either."

"Did we spill?" Constable Grimes said.

"Train lurched," Hammersmith said. "When it entered the station."

"Perhaps the innkeeper will be able to get that tea stain out," Day said.

"What say we get you out of this wind and somewhere warm?" Grimes said. "Got any other luggage, Sergeant?"

"Just this."

"I admire a gentleman who travels light."

Before Day could pick up his suitcase, Grimes grabbed it and led the way past the depot through shifting snowdrifts. Hammersmith was left to carry his own bag. He raised an eyebrow at Day, who shrugged. The constable's notion of their pecking order was clear enough. Day put a hand on Hammersmith's arm and let Grimes walk ahead so that they wouldn't be heard.

"What is it?" Day said.

"What do you mean?"

"Something's troubling you. I can tell."

"This snow is half ash from the furnaces," Hammersmith said. "It's grey."

"Only half grey," Day said. "Still white beneath the surface. There's good to be found in everything."

"That's fine talk for a detective of the Murder Squad."

Day smiled and looked past the station to the snowy field and, far beyond it, the pit mounds, the huge tanks of steaming wastewater, the tiny engine houses, and the iced-over stream that wound past them all. Here and there the snow made way for long furrows of mud and hopeful clusters of green spring grass. He pulled his coat tighter around his body. He waited, and Hammersmith finally nodded and pointed past the evidence of a thriving coal village. A dark line of trees stretched across the horizon.

"A forest," Hammersmith said. "Coal mines. Furnaces. The water. We only have two days to find three missing people in all this. It's impossible. There are too many places to look."

"We'll find them. If they're dead, we'll find bodies. If they're alive . . ."

"If they're alive, they'll be moving about and we might never find them."

"We're not the Hiding Squad, after all," Day said. "We weren't sent for because anyone thinks they're alive. And if murder's been done, two days ought to be enough time to prove it."

"If they're not found when we have to go back, you could always leave me here."

"I'm not going to leave you anywhere. The squad hasn't enough men as it is and we have cases piling up at the Yard. I'm frankly surprised Sir Edward sent us here at all."

Constable Grimes waved to them from the running board of a carriage parked at the station house. "You men comin'?"

Day and Hammersmith trotted across the springy boards of the platform floor and down the steps to the waiting carriage. The driver stuck his mouth in the crook of his elbow and emitted a series of short barking coughs. He shook his head as if dazed by the effort, then smiled and waved at them.

"That's Freddy," Grimes said. "He drives the carriage, but you'll see him tendin' to most everythin' else needs doin' round here."

"You fellas need an errand, you look ol' Freddy up and I'll run it," Freddy said. He appeared to be barely out of his teens, red-haired and freckled, with a gap between his two front teeth. Even sitting, his right leg was noticeably shorter than his left and rested on a block of wood that was affixed to the floor in front of the driver's seat, but the boy's grin seemed genuine and infectious. Day smiled back and nodded.

Something drew Freddy's eye, and he pointed to the sky behind the inspector. "Look there," he said. "Magpie."

Day turned to see a small bird with a black head and a white belly flutter up past the far side of the depot. It banked and wheeled back on its own flight path, then straightened out and flew on.

"Bad sign, that," Grimes said.

"Wait," Freddy said. "Look."

Three more magpies erupted in a flurry of beating wings and joined the first. They glided overhead and away toward the distant woods.

"Four," Grimes said.

"Is that significant?" Day said.

"Maybe. Maybe not. One is for sorrow, of course. So it's good to see the other three."

"One bird brings ill fortune?"

"Ah, you know. One for sorrow, two for mirth, three for a wedding, four for a birth. Old rhyme. Not sure I give it much credence, but there's some round here what does."

"Four for a birth, eh?" Hammersmith said. He smiled at Day.

"None round here's expecting, far as I know," Grimes said.

"My own wife is due to give birth soon enough," Day said. "Back in London."

"Congratulations to you," Grimes said. "Could be that's what the birds was tryin' to tell us."

The three police clambered into the carriage. They heard a "haw" from Freddy, and the wagon rolled smoothly forward.

2

———◆◆◆◆———

The American waited inside the train's rear passenger car until the two policemen were gone. He gave the porter a sixpence coin and stepped out onto the platform. The cold air on his cheeks felt invigorating after the closeness of his forward compartment. He took in the grey landscape with his grey eyes and checked the pocket of his grey leather duster to be sure the folding knife was still there. He smiled when his fingers touched the cold metal handle. The American's smile was lopsided and horrifying. Even with his lips closed, a puckered hole from his left ear to the corner of his mouth exposed sharp yellow teeth behind the flesh of his cheek.

A sign swinging from the station's awning welcomed the American to Blackhampton. He was in the right place. It was possible he'd bought old information, possible the soldier had moved on from Blackhampton, but *this place felt right. He could almost smell his quarry. He'd never been so close. The American sniffed and wiped his nose on the sleeve of his duster.*

He swung his knapsack and rifle case over his shoulder and walked away from the empty station, following the fresh wagon tracks in the snow.

3

ay and Hammersmith sat together facing Grimes, who
had taken the backward-facing bench, leaving the better
seats for the visiting policemen to see out through the
windows on either side. Hammersmith hunched forward on the
seat and cleared his throat.

"Tell us about the missing family," he said.

"Are you sure you wouldn't rather settle in first?" Grimes said.
"You've had a long trip."

"There's a child missing, no?" Hammersmith said.

"Every hour we delay diminishes our chance of finding the boy
and his parents," Day said, "if they're alive."

Grimes shook his head. "Been gone for days. I'm afraid it's bodies
we're looking for." He looked away from them at the shifting scenery outside, but not before Day saw the sadness in the constable's

red-rimmed eyes. Day remembered his own time as a village constable, the responsibility he'd felt for his people. He sympathized
with Grimes. "We'll stop at the inn," Grimes said. "There are people who want to meet you, want to help. I'll introduce you round, let
you get a feel for the way things work here. Might be questions you
want to ask, though I'm sure I've asked 'em already."

"We were told you'd found some evidence," Day said.

"'Twas little Hilde Rose found it."

"You've talked to her."

"I have, sir."

"Wonderful. Good work. Of course, we'll want to talk to
her, too."

"I suppose you will," Grimes said. "If her father'll let you within
a mile of the girl."

"He's protective?"

"He's set in his ways."

"How long after the disappearance was the eyeball found?"

"Well, you see, I'm not at all sure about that. It might have been
the very next day, but it might have been as much as three days.
Hard to pinpoint when they went missing. The weather's made
school a bit of an off-and-on thing round here, and the children
weren't missed right away."

"Children? I thought it was just one child."

"Oh, it is, but he has three siblings."

"And they've been accounted for?"

"Yes."

"Well, how long do they think their brother's been missing?"

"Not to mention their parents," Hammersmith said. "Didn't they
miss their parents right away?"

"I'm sure they did, but they have conflicting stories, and they're not all able to tell time very well. The oldest kids say they thought their father had taken an extra shift at the mine. He's a night guard."

"And their mother?"

"Is not truly their mother. She's the second Mrs Price. Was their nanny before the first Mrs Price run off. No love lost there. They say they simply didn't notice whether she was around or not."

"That seems unlikely."

"Be that as it may, sir, it's what they're tellin' me."

"Are they staying with someone?"

"The housekeeper's got them under control for the moment. I suppose we'll have to find a new place for 'em if their parents don't turn up soon."

"Any other staff currently at the Price home?"

"None. We're not a posh estate here."

"Of course."

The three lapsed into an uneasy silence, and Day watched the scenery roll by outside the carriage. As they drew closer to Blackhampton proper, the train tracks, which crisscrossed the countryside and jounced the carriage as it eased over them, thinned out and were replaced by high ridges covered with a thin rind of snow. Hammersmith pointed past Day out the window.

"Slag," he said. "What remains after the smelting process."

"Where?" Day said.

"The hills. The villagers pile the slag about, and after a few winters it becomes fresh soil. Good for gardening. Vegetables, potatoes, that sort of thing."

Day smiled. Tiny rivulets of melt-off curled through the maze of slag mounds, bordered by stone footpaths. Children, bundled in coats and mittens and boots, ran about, jumping over the water, throwing snowballs, and shaping small round snowpeople.

"What kind of bush is that?" Day said. He pointed to a large woody thicket that seemed familiar.

"Not a bush," Grimes said. "That's a tree. Or the top of one, at least." He indicated a strange-looking house several yards behind the bush. "It's all sinking."

Day craned his neck to see the house as it disappeared from view around a bend in the road. It was a single story with a sloping red roof and lined all about with small windows. There was no door on either side of the house that Day could see.

"Do they enter by the back door?"

"Doors are underground now," Grimes said. "That place was two stories tall once. House and tree was above a seam what's been mined already, so everything tends to sink down into the tunnel. People livin' in it—that'd be the Baggses, mother, father, five children, and the lady's sister—they go in and out through a window."

"So even though that looks like a bush . . ."

"It's an oak tree. It'll be dead by spring, its roots down past the dirt layer."

"Will it keep sinking?"

"Aye, until it falls the rest of the way through."

"Then they shouldn't be living in that house, should they? Won't it collapse beneath them?"

"It's their house, innit? Their choice, I suppose. Frankly, it's a common problem round here."

"But why would you tunnel under your own homes?"

"You've got it turned round in the case of that house. Been mining this area for generations. Some of the shafts under here are hundreds of feet deep, and some're just below the surface. Nobody knows where they all are anymore, but we've got to live and work, don't we?"

"You've built on top of the tunnels."

"Sometimes. Built where we could build. No real way to avoid the mines."

Grimes pointed to another building, small and faded red, set back from the road on a hill and barely visible through the swirling snow. "That one's built better for the mines beneath it, but the road up to it can be a mite tricky in weather like this. We had an early spring here, nice and warm, but then a late storm hit. Snow shut the road down yesterday."

"It's a barn."

"No. Though 'twas a barn at one time. Now it's a schoolhouse. Put it up on stilts what go right down into the tunnels and rest on the floor."

"So it won't sink like the other buildings?"

"Oh, it'll still sink. Even the floors of the tunnels've got tunnels beneath 'em, but it'll take it a wee bit longer and we'll move it to a new place and put it up on new stilts when it starts to go. We don't take chances with our children round here." He smiled at them, proud of his village's commitment to the future.

"But I'll wager you put them to work in the mines," Hammersmith said.

Grimes's smile disappeared. "I don't do that, no," he said. "That'd be their parents' decision, wouldn't it?"

The two men glared at each other, and Day kept his eyes glued to the window beside him. In his experience with Hammersmith, the sergeant could be hostile whenever he spotted something he deemed an injustice. At times, his attitude made him difficult to handle, but Day admired his unwavering sense of right and wrong. There was never a doubt in Hammersmith's mind, which wasn't something that Day could say for himself.

The carriage rolled across a wide field. Half-sunken houses and crumbling stone walls dotted the landscape. Far in the distance, Day could see furnace towers, flames leaping high against the dull grey sky. As they drew near the village, Day saw a grouping of at least a dozen old converted train cars, set side by side and painted in bright colors. Green and red and yellow and cornflower blue, curtains in the windows and wooden fences painted the same colors as the cars bordering tiny square lawns. They looked warm and dry and homey, but curiously unpopulated. It seemed to Day that there ought to be more people out and about.

But there was only a long line of dust-covered men slouched past the carriage. Miners headed home after a long day. Their skin was brushed with black, and their hair was matted grey. It was impossible to tell how old any of them were.

The carriage passed the village well and pulled up next to a neat stone two-story building with a thatched roof and two tall chimneys that billowed smoke. An enormous tree grew next to the inn, centuries old by the look of it, its branches spreading out over the roof, its roots invisible under the covering of snow. Day wondered what might happen if it ever sank into the village's mines.

"Here we are," Grimes said. "The best inn in town. The only inn, of course, but it's a good one nonetheless."

"Does it get much business? The inn? Blackhampton can't have all that many people passing through."

"I suppose you're right. Besides you, there's just one guest at the moment. But when they converted the old inn, someone must have felt the need to build another one."

"So the inn's new?"

"As new as things get around here. Perhaps fifty years old? I'm not certain."

Day opened the carriage door and jumped to the ground before the horses came to a full stop. Hammersmith followed. Day grabbed his suitcase before Grimes could get to it, but he noticed that Hammersmith left his bag on the carriage, waiting to see if he would be given the same courtesy Day had been given at the train station. Day watched Grimes hesitate before picking up the sergeant's luggage.

"You go ahead, Constable," Day said. "I'd like to talk to Mr Hammersmith alone, if you don't mind."

"Again?"

"We'll just be a moment."

Grimes frowned, then shrugged and pushed open the inn's front door with his free hand. A wave of warmth and human voices washed over them before Grimes disappeared through the door and it swung shut behind him.

"You wanted to talk to me, Inspector?"

Day sighed. "You've already antagonized the local police, Nevil."

"I haven't either."

"But you have. You've taken an instant dislike to Mr Grimes, and he to you, and it won't help us in the least."

"He doesn't like me?"

"Well, he doesn't seem warm toward you. And you must admit that you dislike him, don't you?"

"Why wouldn't he like me?"

"You haven't been kind toward him."

"I didn't realize. If that's true, I'm sure it's not his fault. He does seem eager enough to find the missing child."

Day stepped back and looked out over the snow-covered fields. From far off, the sounds of the forges came echoing down the grey wind.

"Were things as bad as all that," Day said, "when you were a child?"

Hammersmith looked around and pulled his overcoat still tighter to his torso. When he sighed, Day could see the breath steam from his nose and rise against the sky.

"This place does take me back," Hammersmith said.

"Did you grow up near the Black Country?"

"No, nowhere near here. But the sounds, the scents . . . I hear the smelters and I'm back there again, back in a hole, alone in the dark, waiting for the coal carts to come up through the tunnels."

"How old were you? When you started in the mines?"

"Oh, three or four. I forget. Too young."

Day opened his mouth to speak and closed it again. He watched his unspoken words drift away like smoke and he avoided Hammersmith's eyes. After a long moment of silence, he tried again. "I suppose there's not much difference between one coal mining village and another?"

"The houses here," Hammersmith said. "Their homes are different."

"That's something, then. Something different. Remember, you're a policeman, not a miner."

"Aye." Hammersmith nodded. "It has been a long time."

"And you are not the person that you once were."

"Maybe not. But the child is the father of the man."

"Is that a saying?"

"From a poem I read."

A figure reeled at them from out of the dusk. The man wasn't wearing a coat, but he had woolen mittens on his hands and he waved at them as he passed by. His face was cherry red, and he staggered, went down on one knee, and righted himself, a fresh glaze of snow on his trousers. He smiled and blinked and shuffled off out of sight.

"Drunk," Hammersmith said.

"I can think of worse ways to keep warm in a place like this," Day said. He clapped his hands together and stamped his feet. "I miss my wife, Sergeant. I'd like to finish this case and get home. I very much fear that my child will come into the world before we return."

"You have time. Claire's got weeks to go, and we'll be leaving Blackhampton on Friday."

"True enough, I suppose. Still, I worry."

The two men stood side by side in the snow, quietly studying the crystalline landscape. The setting sun reflected through a million tiny prisms and sparked an electric red wire on the horizon. Behind them, out of sight over the hills, the train they'd arrived on sounded its bell and chuffed slowly away.

"The child is the father of the man," Day said. "I quite like that."

4

⎯⎯◦∘◦⎯⎯

Anna Price shivered and hugged herself against the cold breeze from the open door. A few brave snowflakes circulated through the room as Constable Grimes slammed the door shut, and Anna edged around the small crowd to get closer to the fire. When Peter touched her shoulder, she jumped, but before she could turn around, he said, "Where's the other policeman? The one from London?"

"Mr Grimes has his bag," Anna said.

The children watched Constable Grimes cross the room, stamping snow from his boots, a black suitcase dangling from one meaty hand.

"So he has luggage," Peter said. "I don't care about luggage. Where's the detective?"

"If he has the detective's luggage, then the detective must be close behind him. Use your head, idiot."

Peter ignored the insult. He was practically thirteen years old, but his sister often treated him like a baby, even though she was a year younger. "He could be out there talking to her even now," he said.

"How would he even know to talk to her?"

"He's a detective, isn't he?"

"But he's just now got here."

"What if he does talk to her?"

"She'll be quiet."

"There's evidence."

"What evidence? A shriveled eyeball? That means nothing."

"And there's Hilde. He'll talk to Hilde."

"God, you're such a numpty," Anna said. "Let him talk to Hilde. All she knows is that she found an eye and then she fell down onto her great round bottom and broke it."

"Be nice," Peter said.

"Yes, let's do be nice. Let's be as considerate as we can be to the constable's new friend from Scotland Yard and, while we're about it, let's tell him all we know. Then we can continue to be nice to all the people in prison for the rest of our lovely nice lives."

"You're in a fine mood today."

"Oh, I'm sorry," she said, "but this is all such a mess, and now we have this new policeman to muck about in it and make everything ever so much more difficult for us."

"Well . . ."

"Well, what?"

"There's the reverse of that to consider, isn't there?"

"The reverse of what? Oh, please do speak in complete sentences, would you?"

"That was a complete sentence."

"But it made no sense whatsoever."

"Only because you're too busy pouting to use that pretty little head of yours."

"Do you really think I'm pretty?"

"Do shut up," Peter said.

"Tell me," Anna said.

"All right, if the detective can make things difficult for us by stomping about in it and asking questions, then can't we also make it difficult for him by answering his questions?"

She almost hugged him. Instead, Anna smiled for the first time in weeks and clapped her hands. "Of course. I mean, of course we would have lied to him if he'd asked us anything, but it didn't occur to me . . . We can lead him round in circles by the nose, can't we?"

"Right. We'll be ever so helpful."

"I've never felt more helpful in my life."

"And when he tires of chasing his own tail, he'll retreat back to London and everything will return to normal."

"As normal as it can ever be again."

"Right. Not very normal at all, but at least the fuss will die down."

"I'm almost looking forward to meeting him now."

And, as if he had been listening to them speak, a man opened the front door and entered the inn. He was tall and earnest-looking, his shoulders broad and his eyes wide. His hands were clean and his back was straight, and it was clear that he had never set foot inside a coal mine. He appeared to be taking in everything around him, as if memorizing the room, and she took a step back to avoid his gaze. The detective stepped aside and held the door, and a moment later, a second man entered. Anna gasped. There were two of them. One detective was bad enough, but two was simply too much. This second man was thinner and quite handsome in an oblivious sort of way. He seemed more intense than his companion and, after shaking the snow from his damp hair, he peered about the room as if he suspected everyone of wrongdoing.

Anna sucked in her breath and the second man turned and looked directly at her. Then his gaze moved on to some other random spot in the room, and she slowly let the air out of her lungs in a long sigh.

The fire at her back felt almost unbearably hot.

5

⸻◆⸻

Hammersmith surveyed the inn's great room. There was a long bar across from him on the back wall and two large fireplaces, both of them lit with cheery fires that cackled and whispered at each other across the long room. To his right, a stag's head over the far fireplace stared back at Hammersmith and, beneath it, a roast dangled on a chain, twisting and swinging as it cooked, a big copper pot set under it to catch the drippings. Dark lamps hung from the high vaulted ceiling, but windows filtered the fading sunlight that had seemed grey outside, and here the walls glinted with orange and yellow and green from glass panels set above the bar. There was an inner door between the bar and the farthest fireplace that presumably led to a dining room and a kitchen, and on the other side of the bar, next to the fireplace on Hammersmith's left, was a wide arch with a staircase leading up to a gallery above. Everything was scratched and faded wood, scarred leather, and smoke. The room was huge, plenty of space for the handful of villagers gathered at the farthest fireplace. They stole glances in his direction and murmured amongst themselves. The air hummed with their excited energy. Hammersmith shuffled his feet back and forth across the rug to get the snow off and then he hurried after Day, who was talking to a heavyset bearded man.

"You'd be the sergeant," the bearded man said when Hammersmith joined them at the bar. The man's shoulders were broad and rounded, and he stooped forward as if the weight of his gleaming pink head were nearly more than he could carry. He reached across the bar and pumped Hammersmith's hand up and down. "Name's Bennett Rose," he said. "This is my place. Mine and the wife's." He turned back to Day. "Like I was sayin', we only put aside two rooms, one for Mr Day and one for the doctor what's comin' tomorrow. But we've got plenty others. Only got one other guest right now, so it's no trouble to make up another room."

"It seems nobody here expected me," Hammersmith said.

"That might be my fault," Constable Grimes said. "Could be I read the cable wrong. But we're glad enough to have you here. The more eyes out there lookin' for the missin' family, the better."

Hammersmith tried a smile, but he feared it looked insincere.

Bennett Rose reached to untie his apron, his thick fingers fumbling with the knot under his belly. "The missus would be glad to meet you herself," he said. "But she's not feelin' well."

"I'm sorry to hear it," Day said.

"Lotta people round here have taken ill since the Price family disappeared."

Hammersmith pointed to the gathering of people at the fireplace. "These people look healthy enough. Who are they? You say you've only got one guest."

"And he's one of 'em there. The big gentleman watchin' us. The others are here to get a look atcha." Rose pointed here and there among the gathered crowd. "The vicar and his wife, the school-teacher, and—"

Hammersmith produced a small pad of paper and a pencil from his breast pocket. "Names, please," he said.

"Ah, yes, well, the vicar's Mr Brothwood. He's the older gentle-man, right over there. Miss Jessica's our schoolteacher. She's got two of the Price children here with her. The boy is Peter. The girl An-na's a year or two younger than he is."

"It's their brother that's missing?"

"That's right. Little Oliver."

"Isn't there a fourth child in the family?" Day said.

"There is," Rose said. "I haven't a clue where Virginia is today, but I'd imagine she's probably back home with the housekeeper."

"What about your daughter? The girl who found the eyeball? Is she here?"

"That'd be Hilde. She's my youngest. She's in our rooms up-stairs, tendin' to her mother."

"We'd like to talk to her," Hammersmith said.

"You might wanna put your bags away first and get somethin' warm in your bellies. I'll have some of that roast sent up to your rooms. Or I've got some groaty dick back in the kitchen, still pipin' hot from the oven. Hilde's not goin' nowhere."

"Thank you," Day said. "Something to drink would be nice."

"Of course," Rose said. "What kind of host am I, not offerin' it already?" He pulled three mugs out from under his side of the bar and set them on the long counter. He walked to the other end of the counter and came back with a tall thin glass, as big around as a stout rope and at least three feet tall. He filled it with beer from a keg on the wall behind him and handed it across to Constable Grimes. "Run that out to Freddy, would you? Must be freezin' his knickers off out there in the carriage."

Grimes took the glass and carried it across the room and out the door into the snow.

"That has to be the tallest glass I've ever seen," Day said.

"Gotta be that tall if you're to hand it up to a carriage driver, don't it?" Rose said. "Otherwise, the poor gents'd allus have to be clamberin' down and back up just to get a bit of refreshment."

"Ingenious," Day said.

Rose filled the three normal-size mugs with beer from the keg. He handed two of them to the men from London and set the third mug at the end of the counter in anticipation of Grimes's return.

Day raised his mug in a silent toast to the innkeeper and gulped half of the beer at once. He set the mug on the counter and wiped his mouth with his sleeve. "Your daughter Hilde," he said. "Doesn't she have friends?"

"Course."

"But she likes to play by herself outdoors."

"What're you gettin' at, Mr Day?"

"The report we have says that she was playing alone, climbing a tree, when she found the evidence. It might help us to know more about her habits."

The innkeeper suddenly leaned across the bar and grabbed Day's wrist. An excited murmur passed through the people watching from the other end of the room. Hammersmith's hand went immediately to the nightstick at his waist, but Day shook his head. Hammersmith left his hand there, hovering above his belt, waiting.

Rose's voice was low and hoarse, barely above a whisper. "Let's talk honest, while Mr Grimes is outten earshot. You can see my Hilde when I says you can see her. That might be never. Folks round here know what's happened, and we'll deal with it ourselves. Not a one here wanted Grimes to send for you lot, but here you are and you're under my roof and that makes you my responsibility. But that don't make me your friend. And it don't give you free rein here."

Day nodded. Rose let go of his arm and took a step back.

"What did happen?" Day said. He sounded unfazed. It was as if Rose's outburst hadn't occurred. Hammersmith knew that the inspector could be infinitely patient when he was asking questions.

"I'm sorry?"

"You said you know what's happened to the missing family. What was it, then?"

"You wouldn't believe me if I told you."

"Try me."

"We can take care of our own, and we can bury 'em, too."

"Then you think they're dead?"

The innkeeper blinked. "Hilde found an eye. Said so yerself."

"That doesn't mean they're all dead."

"Just ain't found the bodies yet."

"Where have you looked for them?"

"Dunno. Ain't looked very hard since everybody knows what we'll find when we find them."

"Pretend we don't live in this godforsaken hellhole and give us a fact we can use," Hammersmith said. Day looked at him, eyes wide, but there was a small smile on his lips.

"It's a good village we got here, mister."

"I'm sure it is," Day said.

Rose nodded. His shoulders slumped and the hostility drained from his face. "Oliver, the missing boy, he was a fine boy, too. This whole village is in mournin'. You've got no part of that. And this place is dangerous for you."

"Why is it dangerous?"

"There's somethin' at work out there. It's not here for you, it's for us. But all the same, don't be wanderin' about by yerselves."

"You have Scotland Yard here to deal with anything you think you have," Day said. "So let us help you."

"Why did Grimes bring us here if you don't need us?" Hammersmith said.

"That'd be a question for Grimes hisself," Rose said.

"What's all this?" Constable Grimes said. His cheeks were bright red from the cold outside and he'd left a trail of slush behind him, but the two detectives hadn't heard him reenter the inn. "You've a question for me?"

"How many able-bodied men can you muster for a search tonight?" Day said.

"There's not much daylight left," Grimes said.

"Will you not listen to me?" Rose said. "I've told you there's danger. Nobody should be goin' out there tonight."

Hammersmith turned on him. "It's time you listened to us. Right now there are people who need us in London. But we're here and we'll be here for the next two days. We're not leaving until we've found that little boy and his parents. If you won't help us do that, then you'll at least stay out of our way."

Rose sniffed. "You think I don't want the boy found?"

"You've made it clear that you don't."

"Then I've made the wrong thing clear. What I'm tryin' to tell you is that the boy's dead as sure as we're standing here. There's nothing you can do for him, except find his tiny body out there. But if you're not careful, you'll end up dead, too."

"Is that a threat? Because if it is—"

"Oh, stop this, the lot of you."

Day turned at the sound of a reedy voice behind his left shoulder. A painfully thin older gentleman stood there, dressed all in black except for a thick woolen oatmeal-colored sweater that had bunched up under his ribs. He extended a hand, and Day shook it. "Mr Rose means well," the old man said, "but I'm afraid he's liable to run you off if he can."

"And why would he do that, Mr . . . ?"

"Brothwood. Pleased to make your acquaintance."

"Of course. The vicar."

"Indeed."

"And why would Mr Rose try to run us off?"

"Please, Mr Scotland Yard," the vicar said, "come and meet the others. I promise we'll do our best to explain everything that we can."

Brothwood gestured toward the farthest of the two fireplaces, where the handful of villagers watched them. Day nodded. "Lead the way, Mr Brothwood."

6

D ay and Hammersmith followed Brothwood to the small
gathering near the fireplace. Grimes went with them, but
hung back, quiet, apparently content to observe. Aside
from the vicar, Day counted six other people there. An old woman
bobbed her head at him. She wore a simple dress with a subdued
floral pattern. Her hair was white, but she had it carefully done up
at the top of her head. From the pattern of lines across her face, it
seemed to Day that she must have smiled a lot in the ordinary course
of things, but as they came near, the old woman's eyes darted around
the common room and she took an involuntary step back, away
from the policemen. Day suppressed an urge to reach out and pull
her away from the fire, which threatened to lick the hem of her
dress. Another woman, much younger and slimmer, stood next to
the old woman. Her long hair was copper-colored and shimmered

in the firelight. Her eyes twinkled (although that, too, might have been a trick of the light), and she allowed the faintest smile to pass over her lips by way of greeting. Two children stood behind her, close to the fire. The boy was perhaps twelve years old, the girl a bit younger, but just as tall. They were both slightly built, with rounded shoulders, fair hair, and clothing that was a bit too small for them. Neither of them looked directly at the policemen, but the boy took a step in front of the girl, as if to protect her. A young man who stood warming his hands at the fire smiled at them. The man was short and thin, with long floppy brown hair and wire-framed spectacles. He wore a waistcoat but no jacket, and his shirtsleeves were rolled up almost to his elbows.

Apart from the others, filling a large armchair at the periphery of the fire's light, another man sat regarding Day carefully. He had long shaggy hair streaked with grey. Ropes of muscle bunched and rippled under his clothing as if he were constantly tensing up and then reminding himself to relax. The man's green eyes sparkled with secret knowledge, and he gave Day a nearly imperceptible nod after sizing him up.

The man stood, pushing himself up out of the armchair, and offered his hand to Day. He was enormous, much taller than the men from Scotland Yard, and he clearly outweighed them by at least fifty pounds. His hand, when Day shook it, was hard and calloused, and Day felt the man holding back, as if he might accidentally crush Day's fingers like a handful of dry twigs. Day got a sudden sense that the giant had killed men with those outsize hands.

"Good of you to come," the man said. "We can use the help."

"I'm Inspector Day. And this is Sergeant Hammersmith."

The man let go of Day's hand and nodded. "My name is Campbell," he said. "Calvin Campbell." There was the trace of a Scottish brogue in his voice, but it was faint and mixed with something else. He gestured toward the group of people on the hearth. "We, all of us, want to help find that boy. Anything we can do to help, that's why we're here."

"And the parents?" Hammersmith said. "I assume you want to find them, too."

"Yes, of course. All of them."

Now that introductions had been initiated by Calvin Campbell, the big man faded back to the outskirts of the group and the vicar took over, accustomed to politicking. The others moved forward and surrounded the police. All except the two children, who hung back, close to the fire.

"Mr Campbell is a visitor here," Vicar Brothwood said. "A guest of the inn, like you. And this is my wife, Margaret."

The vicar held his hand out, palm up, toward the old lady. Margaret Brothwood smiled and nodded at them, but the smile was strained and didn't touch her eyes. She had a small folded piece of paper in her left hand and she worried at it, pressing it and rubbing the paper with her thumb.

"I wish we had a bigger turnout to greet you," Brothwood said. "So many are ill at the moment. Dr Denby is being kept busy."

The bespectacled young man smiled ruefully and nodded. His floppy hair bounced over his eyes. "I wanted to meet you anyway," he said.

"You're the doctor here?" Day said.

"I am indeed. I'm afraid half the village is sick in bed, but if there's anything I can do to help, I'm at your . . ." Denby paused and held his hand up, palm out. His shoulders quaked with a sudden silent coughing fit. Day waited. Finally, the doctor stood up straight and smiled. "Forgive me. I am, of course, at your disposal."

Day frowned. "You're quite all right, I hope."

"Perfectly."

"When you say half the village has fallen ill—"

"Not precisely half, but a great many of them."

"What are they sick from?"

"I don't know yet. It's all I can do to treat their symptoms. Blackhampton simply isn't equipped for a plague."

"A plague!"

"I don't know what it is. *Plague* may be too strong a word, but what else would you call it when a hundred people fall ill at once?"

"Is it possible, Doctor, that the missing family are among the ill?" Day said. "That they've holed up somewhere to convalesce?"

"I suppose it is possible. But I think I would have been notified. I haven't visited the Price home in a great long time."

"I see."

"I do hate to be rude, but I must be off. Many homes to pop in at before bed."

"Will you tell us when you've reached a conclusion about the nature of the illness?"

"I will. Although I can't see how it could possibly help you to know."

"It may not help. But I'd like to know anyway. And I understand how busy you are, but we may need your assistance when we find the Prices."

Dr Denby smiled and nodded and walked away across the room. Day noticed that the doctor moved carefully, as if each step pained him. He grabbed a hat and overcoat from the rack by the door and exited in a flurry of snowflakes. Day turned back to Vicar Broth-wood, who touched the young red-haired woman on the elbow by way of introduction.

"This is our schoolteacher, Miss Perkins," he said.

"Please call me Jessica, Inspector Day," the young woman said. She put a gloved hand in Day's, then turned her attention to Hammersmith. "It's lovely to meet you, too, Mr Hammersmith. Though one might wish for better circumstances."

Day thought her gaze lingered on Hammersmith a second longer than was necessary, and he looked down at his feet so that neither of them would see him smile. He had noticed that women often looked at Hammersmith a bit too long to be merely cordial, but in his experience the sergeant was unaware of their attention. Hammersmith was almost fanatically focused on his work. Day gestured past the schoolteacher at the children behind her.

"And who might these young people be?" Day said.

"This is Peter," Jessica Perkins said, tearing her attention away from Hammersmith, who was busy taking notes in the tiny cardboard-covered tablet he carried with him everywhere. "And this is Anna Price. It's their parents who have . . ." Jessica paused, obviously trying to think of the best way to finish her sentence without upsetting the children.

"They've gone missing, sir," Anna Price said.

Her brother nodded.

"Well, we're here to find them," Day said. "Don't you worry."

He immediately regretted saying it. His words would be taken as merely polite by the adults gathered there, but the children would accept it as a promise.

The boy, Peter, nodded, but his sister Anna didn't move or

change her expression. She locked her gaze on Day and stared until he had to look away.

"Why don't you two go and see if Mr Rose has a ginger beer for you?" Jessica said. She put a hand on each child's shoulder and pushed them toward the bar. They went without complaint and without looking back.

"We'll need to talk to them," Day said.

"Of course," Jessica said.

"Perhaps you would help my sergeant with that?"

Jessica looked briefly at Hammersmith and then back at Day. "If you'd like."

"Yes, thank you. They might be more comfortable with you there. Sergeant, check if they've seen anything, would you?"

Hammersmith shot Day a puzzled look, but followed the schoolteacher to the bar, where the children were already pulling themselves up onto stools. Day wanted to question the villagers as quickly as possible. The teacher seemed likely to want to impress Hammersmith and she might encourage the children to talk to him. Day doubted they would learn much from the small welcoming party here, but there was always the possibility that someone knew something useful. He took his own little notebook from the pocket of his waistcoat and found the stub of a pencil. The notebook was a match for Hammersmith's, but had never been used. He opened it to the first page and creased the cardboard cover back on itself.

"Let's start with you, Mr Campbell," he said. The giant had settled back into his armchair and had leveled his gaze at Day. "We have the village vicar, the schoolteacher, the doctor, and you. What function do you serve in Blackhampton?"

"I'm only a visitor here," Campbell said. "Like you are."

"I'm sorry," Vicar Brothwood said. "I thought I'd mentioned that."

"Perhaps you did," Day said. "Why Blackhampton, though? Why visit this place in particular?"

"Why not Blackhampton?"

"I'm having some trouble placing your accent, sir. Where are you from?"

"I've traveled."

"Yes, I'd wager it's been some time since you've seen Scotland."

"A long time."

"You've been to America?"

"Spent time there."

"Liverpool?"

"Spent time there, too."

"And now the Midlands."

"I'm passing through. Staying here, same as you."

"What's kept you here? What's your interest? Why do you care about the missing family?"

"We all care. Everyone here does." Campbell turned his attention to the fire. He slid out of the chair and squatted on the hearth. Day watched as Campbell grabbed the poker from the rack beneath the mantel and poked at the logs. Orange sparks leapt out, burning tiny holes in Campbell's trousers. Campbell didn't react, didn't move back, kept turning the logs, and talked into the fire. "I've lost people I cared about. It's a hard thing, and I hate to see it happen to anyone."

"Do you know the family?" Day said.

"Only by reputation."

Day frowned at the Scotsman's broad back. Campbell wasn't

telling him everything, but his posture and the tension in his shoulders told the inspector that he had finished talking for the moment. Day decided not to press him. He could come back to him later. Right now he wanted a broad overview, as much information as possible before he began ordering things and narrowing down the possibilities. He turned to the others. "What can you tell me about the Prices?"

"Sutton Price is the night watchman on the main seam," Vicar Brothwood said. "He wasn't at his post three days ago when the morning shift came on."

"An alarm was raised?"

"Not right away. Nothing else appeared out of the ordinary and there was work to be done."

"When was the alarm raised, then?"

"That evening, when he didn't arrive for his shift."

"Someone . . ."

"Yes, someone was sent to his house to inquire after him."

"And what was discovered?"

"Three of the Price children and their housekeeper were at their evening meal. Mr Price was nowhere to be found and had not been seen since the previous evening."

"And Mrs Price was also missing?"

"Yes. Along with her boy."

"Her boy?"

"The oldest boy, Peter, is not properly her own. Nor are the girls. Oliver is her only child."

"Ah, yes. As I understand it, the missing woman was the second Mrs Price."

"Exactly so."

"Whatever became of the first Mrs Price?"

"She simply disappeared one day a few years ago," Brothwood said. "When was that, dear?"

He looked at his wife, who muttered something unintelligible and turned her attention to her feet. She was still worrying at the small piece of paper in her right hand. Her face looked grey.

"Just so," her husband said. He turned back to Day. "We're not sure when that was. Not with any certainty. Some years ago. I might say perhaps three or four, but don't hold me to it."

"And she has not been seen since?"

"Never."

"Was there a proper interval between the marriages?"

"I wouldn't say so. In fact, I refused to grant him the second marriage. They traveled to Wolverhampton to get it done."

"You didn't approve."

"Oh, it wasn't a matter of approval. It was simply too soon. Mathilda might well have turned up—Mathilda was the first Mrs Price—and then where should we be? Two Mrs Prices at once, and us with a village scandal. I was simply being prudent, nothing more."

"She's a lovely lady," Mrs Brothwood said. Day was surprised. It was the first thing out of her mouth that he'd been able to understand and it was spoken with force.

"The first Mrs Price, you mean?" Day said. "Or the second?"

"I apologize. I spoke out of turn."

"No, please. Which lady did you mean to indicate?"

"Hester."

"The second Mrs Price, then."

"Of course. Mathilda Price was a monstrous woman. Everyone knew it. I don't know why we pretend to be surprised that she ran off. She was unfit to be a wife or mother to anyone, let alone those darling children. How they turned out so well, I'm sure I don't know."

"Now, dear," Mr Brothwood said.

"Of course," his wife said. "I apologize again." She turned her head so that Day couldn't see her face, only the firelight that flickered through a few stray wisps of hair that had come free of the pale bun atop her head.

"We're all quite upset, of course," Mr Brothwood said.

"Of course," Day said. "What about you, Mr Campbell? Did you know either of the Price wives?"

Campbell didn't look up at him, continued stirring the logs. "I told you I know the family by reputation only," he said.

"How long have you been in the village?"

"Two weeks, perhaps."

"That's right," Brothwood said. "I'd say he's been here two weeks."

"What brought you here? What's your business in this place?"

"Am I your suspect, then?" Campbell's voice was tired and harsh from the smoke. There was no anger in it that Day could detect.

"I have no suspects at the moment, Mr Campbell. I don't even know that a crime has been committed. The more information I have, the better able I am to do the job here. I never know what might be useful."

"I'm an ornithologist."

"I'm sorry?"

"A bird-watcher."

"He studies birds," Brothwood said. "We have several splendid specimens near Blackhampton."

"You study birds?"

"I do," Campbell said. "I sketch them. Would you like to see my notebooks?"

"Not necessarily. You've been out there in the woods, watching birds?"

"I have."

"Perhaps you wouldn't mind taking me out there."

"We can go now."

"The sergeant and I should eat something. And we'll need supplies."

"I checked the woods," Grimes said. Day was startled to hear him speak. The constable had been so quiet that Day had nearly forgotten about him. "I checked the woods, the tunnels, the river-bed. I've checked everywhere."

"By yourself?" Day said.

"After the eyeball was found, I spent the entire day out in those woods."

"We should check again. I've no doubt you did as thorough a job as possible, Constable, but you have more people at your disposal now."

"It's growing dark out there."

"No time to waste."

"Then I'll ask Mr Rose to get together some lanterns for us," Grimes said.

He left the knot of people by the fire and crossed to the bar. Day watched him go and lean over the bar next to Hammersmith and the Price children. He murmured something low and emphatic to Rose. Rose nodded, wiped his hands on his apron, and left through the door to the back rooms. Day caught Hammersmith's eye and raised a questioning eyebrow. The sergeant shrugged and shook his head. He hadn't learned anything useful yet.

"I'm afraid we ought to get back," Mr Brothwood said. "My wife and I wouldn't be of much use to you, tramping through the woods in the dark of night. But we remain at your disposal should you need anything else."

The vicar's wife fidgeted, her eyes flicking here and there about the room, never settling anywhere for more than a fraction of a second.

Day had no illusions about his abilities as a detective. He knew that he wasn't the most intimidating man in any room; he had no steely resolve or grim determination. He wasn't tireless in his pursuit of justice (that would be Sergeant Hammersmith's strong suit). But he was very good at listening to people. He paid attention when they talked. And when they didn't talk. He understood what their bodies and their eyes told him and he understood what people wanted to tell him, despite what they actually said. Mrs Brothwood clearly had something she desperately needed to say, but her husband's presence prevented her from speaking. Day would have to find a way to get her alone for a few moments.

"Mrs Brothwood, would you—"

He was interrupted by the sound of the front door crashing open and the late winter wind swirling into and through the big room. There was a rustling of wings, and a huge dark shape filled the doorway.

7

Something flew over their heads, circled the room, and perched on the rail of the gallery above them. Bennett Rose emerged from the back room with a lantern in his hand and ran to the front door, slamming it shut against the wind. He turned and scowled up at the gallery and the feathered shape there.

"Oh, this is not good," he said. "Not a bit. I'll need some help."

He went to the counter, where he set the lantern down, then found a long stout plank somewhere behind the bar. He took it to the back door and slotted the plank into brackets on either side of it, barricading the way into the kitchen. Meanwhile, Grimes and the vicar Brothwood walked slowly to the front door. They seemed to jockey with each other for position until Grimes conceded to his elder. Brothwood stood behind the door and gripped the knob. He fixed his gaze on the bird in the gallery. Mr Rose returned to the counter, rummaged about, and pulled out a handful of rags, sizing them against one another. Hammersmith froze on his stool, unsure what to do. He didn't understand what the fuss was about. He glanced at Day, who raised his eyebrows, but neither man moved. The customs here were alien, and it was hard to know what was proper.

"Mr Rose," Hammersmith said. "Isn't that an owl?"

"You mean that creature up there?" As if they might be talking about some other bird in the room.

From the tone of Rose's voice, they might have been talking about an ancient nightmare that had invaded the inn with great tentacled limbs, intent on dragging them all down to hell. The bird swiveled its head so that it was looking at Hammersmith, its yellow eyes shining out from the shadows above the landing, and hooted. *Who who who whooooo.* Hammersmith nodded to himself. Yes, it was an owl.

"It doesn't look likely to hurt anyone," he said.

"Not worried about it hurting anyone," Rose said. "Only worried about what it means and getting it to leave."

He set four glasses on the bar in front of Hammersmith, the schoolteacher, and the two Price children, and filled them from a wooden pitcher of water on the sideboard behind the bar. The pitcher was old and beaded with droplets, the glasses dull and chipped, their edges worn smooth by countless drinkers.

"Perhaps if we got behind it, we could scare it back outside," Hammersmith said.

"That'd be disrespectful," Rose said. "We'll be ready when it decides to move."

Hammersmith shrugged. He picked up his glass and raised it to his lips.

"Wouldn't drink that," Peter Price said.

His sister nudged him and grimaced at Hammersmith. "My brother prefers ginger beer," she said. She pushed her own glass away from her. It left a glossy trail on the bar. "So do I."

"I like water," Hammersmith said. He took a long swallow. Water dribbled down his chin from the many chips in the rim, and he wiped it with the sleeve of his shirt before taking another drink.

Peter shuddered and looked away. Hammersmith made a mental note that the boy seemed to have an aversion to water. He recalled a disease of some sort that made people avoid water. It might be something to mention to the doctor when he saw him. He set the glass down and wiped his chin again.

"What about the owl?" he said.

"It's a bad sign," Rose said. He seemed irritated at being kept there, at having to talk to Hammersmith. He wiped the streak of water off the bar, moving his whole arm, putting his weight into the minor effort, then turned and used the rag to cover one of the panels of colored glass above him.

"It's just a bird, isn't it?"

"It means death. We've got to make it leave, but it's best if we all act calm and give it a way out."

"An owl in the house is bad luck," Jessica said. "Any bird is. And if it lands near you, you're meant to die within a day."

Hammersmith watched as Rose moved smoothly about the room, quietly covering the rest of the windows with his rags. "You believe that?" he said.

"It's happened before," Jessica said. "We have our ways."

"I didn't mean to make light. But, really, it's just a bird."

As if it took offense, the owl left its perch on the rail of the gallery and took flight. It sailed down over the great room, hovering over each of the villagers gathered there. Everyone ducked and covered their heads, making themselves small. Day, alone among them, stood up and watched the bird glide past him. He uncorked his flask and raised it to Hammersmith. Hammersmith slid off his stool and held his ground as the owl approached him. It was brown underneath with fingers of white feathers that reached up and over its head. It flapped its wings and put out its talons and gripped the back of the stool, settling there for a long moment, regarding him with its broad flat face, its yellow eyes wide and intelligent.

Who?

The vicar Brothwood swung the front door open, and the owl turned its head to an impossible degree, saw the night sky outside, and took off again. Like a dream, it flapped slowly toward the vicar and then banked sideways and passed through the door and out. Brothwood slammed the door shut and leaned against it.

"Oh, that's bad," Anna said.

"That's awful," Jessica said.

"It is?" Hammersmith said. "I thought it was rather magnificent."

Anna regarded him for a long time before responding. "You're going to die now," she said. "The owl landed on your chair. That's a sign that you're to die." She shrugged. "I'm sorry, but that's the way it is."

Hammersmith glanced around the room, but no one would look at him. Brothwood slunk back to the fire and put an arm around his wife. Grimes positioned himself at the door and watched out through the tiny pane of glass set high in the wood, as if protecting the place from more birds.

Rose looked at Hammersmith, his eyes wide and his forehead creased with concern. "I'm sorry, sir, but she's right."

"It picked your chair," Peter said. As if that was all that needed to be said.

"Well, I don't mean to offend," Hammersmith said, "but I don't share your beliefs."

Rose nodded. "Nothin' to do about it. Don't matter whether you believe or not, it's the way of things." He moved away down the bar, tore the plank out of its brackets, and stalked through the back door, presumably to contemplate Hammersmith's impending death alone. Hammersmith blinked and shook his head.

He looked at Day, who was busy with the knot of villagers, the vicar and his wife saying their good-byes. Mrs Brothwood shook Day's hand and held it for a moment, but Hammersmith couldn't see that she spoke at all. Then the vicar's hand was around her shoulders, hurrying her away toward the front door. They passed by Hammersmith without looking at him, nodded to Grimes and left. Day glanced down at his hand, then put something in his pocket. He turned his attention to the big man with the grey hair, Calvin Campbell, but their conversation was held in low tones and Hammersmith couldn't hear what was being said.

Hammersmith shook his head and sighed. Back to work. He swiveled on his stool and looked at the Price children. They looked back at him. He had never been good with children, never comfortable with them. Even when he was a child himself. He had spent long stretches of time alone in cramped tunnels far underground, listening for sounds that would let him know that the ponies were coming up from the mines, laden with coal. The sounds of the ponies' hooves and the rats skittering in the darkness were his only company. When he had spent time with other children, he had been quiet, had listened to them jabber and laugh together, joke and complain, and it had all seemed alien and pointless to him.

He lifted his glass and took another swallow of water, then picked his notebook and pencil up off the bar.

"What were we talking about?"

Anna rolled her eyes. "Yes," she said. "If you want to waste what little time you have left talking to us, go ahead."

"Right," Hammersmith said. "Thank you, I will." He looked at his notes. "You haven't supplied me with many facts yet. You think your stepmother's run away, but you don't know why. And you think I should be suspicious of Calvin Campbell because you don't know him. So let's talk about things you do know."

"Sergeant," Jessica said. "Surely the children aren't suspects."

"Of course not."

"Then perhaps you could be friendlier?"

"I apologize. I'm not used to speaking to children." He smiled at Peter and Anna, and cleared his throat. "I'd like to know about your sister, if you don't mind. Her name's Virginia?"

"No," Peter said. Anna turned and looked at him. "I mean, yes," he said. "Of course. Virginia is our sister."

The boy seemed peculiar to Hammersmith, but then everyone in Blackhampton seemed peculiar. "Where is she?" he said.

"Who?"

"Virginia. Your sister."

"Oh, her."

"She's at home with the housekeeper," Anna said.

"Your brother seems to be more nervous than you are."

"He's like that."

"You seem calm enough."

"I'm like that."

"Are you worried about your parents?"

"Hester isn't my mother. She's only our stepmother and therefore not really our parent at all."

"What about your father and your brother?"

"Oliver isn't my brother. He's Hester's child."

Hammersmith stared at her, waiting for her to say something more. She was deflecting his questions, not answering. But Day had taught him that sometimes all it took to make the other person talk was a moment of silence that needed to be filled.

"Of course we're worried about them," Peter said.

Hammersmith wasn't surprised that Peter was the one to break the silence. He made a note on the blank sheet of paper: *Separate the Price children. Talk to Peter alone.*

"Why did you leave Virginia with the housekeeper instead of bringing her with you tonight?" he said.

"She was sleepy," Anna said.

"How old is she?"

"Five."

"I'd like to talk to her."

Anna shrugged. "Come to the house, then," she said. "But I don't think you'll have time."

"Why is that?"

"Because you're going to die tomorrow. The owl chose you."

"Right. Then I'll come to your house first thing in the morning."

"Why do you even want to talk to her?" Peter said.

"I want to talk to everybody."

He made another note: *Children very protective of Virginia. All the family they have left.*

"May we go home now?" Anna said. "We're tired, too. And we're sad about you."

Hammersmith nodded and closed his notebook, slipped it back into his pocket, along with the pencil.

Jessica Perkins went to the door and opened it wide enough that Hammersmith could see past her. The sun had set and light from the distant furnaces sparkled on the crust of snow. Jessica closed the door, rubbed her hands together, and smiled at the sergeant.

"More snow coming," she said.

"Wonderful," Hammersmith said. "I was hoping for more snow."

Jessica shook her head. "I certainly wasn't. It's supposed to be spring. All those poor trees just started growing their leaves out." She snapped her fingers at the children. "Anna, Peter, button your overcoats. It's getting colder out there."

"I'll be fine," Peter said.

"Button your coat, Peter," she said.

The boy clicked his tongue, but he did as she'd instructed.

When the children were ready, she waved good-bye to Hammersmith and the others and stepped out into the frigid night again. She gestured for the children, and they hurried out behind her and down the path to the avenue and she closed the front door behind them.

For a moment the room was cold and silent, then Bennett Rose entered the room through the back door carrying two more kerosene lanterns, holding them high, swinging them by their wire handles. He thunked them down on the bar in front of Hammersmith and leaned over so that his face was mere inches from Hammersmith's.

"I filled 'em so you'll have enough light out there for a good while," he said. "The woods ain't as bad as they could be, ain't as bad as the mines after dark, but they ain't safe. You watch where you step and you pay attention."

He moved back a bit, but then frowned as if remembering something. He motioned Hammersmith close and ducked his head. When he spoke, it was in a low whisper.

"You stick close to your inspector," Rose said. "Stick close and watch out, each for the other. You're doomed, of course, but he still has a chance."

Rose broke off and looked down at the bar as Day approached. It was evident in his expression that the inspector had heard Rose's warning.

"We appreciate the warning, Mr Rose," Day said. "And I'm grateful for your concern. But you let us do our jobs, sir."

Rose was quiet for a long moment, and then he nodded. He wiped his hands on his apron and disappeared again through the door at the back of the room.

"Did you learn anything from that lot over there?" Hammersmith said.

Day opened his mouth to respond, but was interrupted by a quiet voice.

"Excuse me?"

The men turned to see a girl on the landing. She was clutching a small wooden box, which she held out for them to see.

"I can show you my eye if you'd like," the girl said.

8

The girl hobbled the rest of the way down the stairs. She was perhaps eight or nine years old, lace at her throat and wrists, her hair done in a short blond bob. Dirty white bandages covered a splint on her right leg that ran from hip to toes, and she was leaning on a cane made from the varnished branch of a river birch. She smiled at them, bowing her head slightly in lieu of a curtsy.

"I don't mean to interrupt," she said.

Day rose from his chair and went to the stairs. He held out his arm for the girl to steady herself and led her to the gathered men.

"You'd be Hilde Rose?" he said.

"Yes, sir. You're the detectives from London?"

"We are," Hammersmith said. "Very good to meet you, young lady." He stood and offered Hilde his chair.

"Likewise, I'm sure," she said. "I've been awfully anxious, waiting in my room. Papa said for me not to come down when you arrived, and I was going to wait, but I know that if I do I shall never sleep a wink tonight."

"Should you be walking about on that?" Day said.

Hilde looked down at her bandaged leg. "It's not so bad," she said. "I was quite lucky that it was a clean break. Dr Denby was able to set it, and both legs are the same length again. Otherwise he might have amputated, and I shouldn't want that."

Day shuddered. "No, I don't suppose you would. Please sit. You've got something to show us?"

Using Hammersmith's arm to balance, Hilde maneuvered herself onto his chair. She held out the box, and Day took it.

"You won't keep it from me forever, will you?" she said. "It's ever so odd, and I'm the one who found it."

Day smiled. "May I?" he said. He cracked the lid and swung it back on its delicate brass hinges. Hammersmith stepped closer and peered over Day's shoulder. Inside the box was a small shriveled eyeball, a thread of dried optic nerve curled around one side of it.

"It's blue," Hammersmith said. "Did any of the missing people have blue eyes? Is this the little boy's eye?"

"I don't know," Hilde said. "I don't remember their eyes. But it can't belong to anyone else, can it? I mean, nobody else round here's missing an eyeball or I think I would have noticed."

"How big was it?" Day said. "Before it withered, I mean?"

"It was the size of an eyeball, I suppose. I thought it was a tiny egg."

"But was it the size of an adult's eye or a child's?"

"I've never seen an eyeball that wasn't in a person's head before."

"Yes, of course. I don't suppose you have."

"It's not much of a clue," Hammersmith said.

"The good doctor might be able to tell us more about it to-morrow."

"Dr Denby would help you," Hilde said.

"Yes," Day said. "But we're talking about our doctor friend from London."

"Oh, please don't let him take it to London," Hilde said. "I'll never get it back."

"I don't think that will be necessary," Day said. "He'll join us here soon enough. In the meantime, is there anything you can tell us about the missing boy, Oliver? Was he your playmate?"

"He's only a baby."

"Then you didn't know him?"

"Of course I *know* him. I said I don't *play* with Oliver. He always follows Peter about, and it's quite annoying."

"Peter?"

"His older brother."

Hammersmith cleared his throat and reached for his notebook and pencil.

"What can you tell us about the Price family?" Day said.

"Well, there's Oliver, of course. Virginia is next youngest. She's five. Then Anna and Peter. But they're not all properly brothers and sisters. Peter and Anna and Virginia all had the same mother. But Oliver is different and not properly a part of the family, except that they have the same father, which is nearly good enough, but Virginia doesn't think so at all."

"And you play with the elder siblings."

"Peter and Anna are far too old to play with me. Anna is very nice to me, though. Peter and I will be married when I'm old enough, only he doesn't know that yet."

"I see. Then Sutton Price is father to all four children and has two missing wives, yes?"

"Yes, sir."

"And the most recent missing wife would be Hester Price."

"Yes."

"She is mother to Oliver, also missing, but not to the other three."

"No, sir. Their mother's dead and gone. Or gone, anyway. Oliver's mother was nanny to the others before she married Mr Price. Now she's their stepmother."

"They do seem particular on that point," Hammersmith said.

"Her name was Mathilda, is that right? The first Mrs Price, I mean."

"I think her name was also Mrs Price before the new Mrs Price come along, sir."

Day looked at Hammersmith, who shrugged and nodded.

"That does make sense," he said.

"Indeed. Very well, Hilde. Thank you for your help. Would you mind if we keep your souvenir for a day or two if I promise to return it before we leave Blackhampton?"

"You really will give it back?"

"I really will."

"Okay. I had better get to my room before Father returns and scolds me."

"How is your mother? We heard she's feeling a bit ill."

"She's sleeping. Dr Denby says he'll come first thing to look after her again."

Hilde rose from the chair with some difficulty and tottered on her good leg before getting the cane under her and limping to the staircase. She looked back at them, a shadow of doubt flitting across her face. She bit her lower lip.

"You won't lose it now? The eye, I mean."

"We won't lose it."

She smiled and moved slowly up the stairs. Hammersmith waited until she had passed from sight and sighed. "Well," he said, "we do seem to have evidence of a murder, but I don't see that it helps us a bit."

"Nor I. Perhaps the doctor will be able to work some miracle of chemistry on this eyeball."

"You don't think Hilde Rose had anything to do with the crime?"

"Don't be ridiculous. She's a child." Day snapped the box shut and set it on the table.

9

———⊰◦◦◦⊱———

Jessica let the siblings run ahead, not too far, but they had been cooped up inside all day and needed to release some energy. They could easily be mistaken for twins. Peter was twelve years old, and if his father had been anyone but Sutton Price he might already be working the mines. He was a bright lad, quiet and independent, but quick to find solutions. He rarely completed his schoolwork, but he performed brilliantly at quizzes. His sister Anna was more decisive and studious. She was only eleven, but she was as tall as Peter was and she mirrored her older brother in nearly every way. If he was the creative light of the Price family, Anna was the practical rock that grounded him.

"That's far enough, children," Jessica said. Peter in his black overcoat had disappeared in the darkness.

When she caught up to them, she found that they were hunkered over the top of an old pit. Peter was leaning forward on a slag pile while Anna hung back a bit, urging her brother on.

"Say it," Anna said.

"I will," Peter said.

"Then say it."

"I'm working up to it."

"You're not going to say anything."

"Am, too."

"Then say it."

"Peter, come away from there," Jessica said.

Anna looked up at her as she drew near them and smiled as if to convey that she was uninvolved in any wrongdoing. Peter glanced in her direction and then leaned farther over the edge of the pit, clearly in a hurry now to carry out his sister's challenge.

"Rawhead and Bloody Bones," he said.

Jessica rushed forward and slipped on a patch of ice as Peter continued chanting down into the pit, his voice louder now that he was committed to the dare: "Steals naughty children from their homes!"

Jessica landed on her bottom on the hard ground and stifled a scream. She was wearing a corset, a petticoat, a dress, and a heavy woolen overcoat, so the fall didn't hurt her in the slightest, but her face flushed with humiliation. Anna rushed over to help her teacher up, but Jessica waved her hand at Peter, who was still at the lip of the pit, still staring down into the dark.

"Peter, stop that right now!"

Peter didn't even glance in her direction. "Takes them to his dirty den," he said. His voice was strained now, and the words were nearly choked off by the time he mouthed *dirty den*.

Jessica struggled to her feet as Anna scurried about, picking up the books Jessica had dropped. Jessica let the girl tend to the books. She marched forward, more careful now about the ice underfoot, and grabbed Peter by the back of his collar. He came easily away from the pit, but Jessica almost lost her footing anyway and rocked forward as she recovered her balance. For a moment, she was staring down into the maw of the pit. Compared to the utter blackness down there, the night sky seemed blue and full of life, stars and moon and white frozen breath. But it seemed to Jessica that she could see the slightest orange glow somewhere down there in the tunnel, as if a small fire had been lit in response to Peter's call. The thought that something might be coming through the mines toward them made Jessica shudder. She drew back from the pit and pressed a knuckle to her teeth.

She whirled Peter around and gripped him by his shoulders. The boy was so thin as to be nearly weightless, all elbows and knees. She saw now that he was crying, quietly, tears dragging down his cheeks, sluggish in the cold. She pressed his face against her coat and stroked his hair. He needed a haircut, she noticed. She wondered, not for the first time, how well the children were faring without their parents, how well the housekeeper was caring for them. If Mr and Mrs Price weren't found soon, a decision would have to be made about where to put Peter, Anna, and Virginia. It was likely they'd be split up and raised in different households. Jessica felt her throat closing and forced herself onto a different train of thought. It would do Peter no good if she started crying herself.

"Here you are," Anna said. She had brought the books and was holding them out to her teacher.

"Thank you, Anna," Jessica said. She let Peter go and stepped back, taking the bundle of books from the girl. Peter turned away from her and wiped his eyes. Jessica pretended she hadn't seen him crying, busied herself with ordering the books in their small stack. Anna brushed the back of Jessica's long coat where she had fallen.

"Come, children," Jessica said. "Let's have no more of this nonsense."

She led them away from the mouth of the pit, listening to make sure they followed. Beneath the footsteps of Peter and Anna, Jessica thought she heard something else, and she almost turned back, but forced herself to keep moving. She spoke into the night, without looking at either child, hoping her words would cover that strange soft sound before the children heard it, too.

"I know what the other students are saying," she said. "But there is no such thing as Rawhead and Bloody Bones. It's a silly thing that was made up to scare children. Children much smaller than the two of you, anyway, and I'm surprised you would put any stock in the notion."

She waited for them to catch up to her and walked on between them toward the Price house on the hill. She felt the darkness of the pit behind her and increased her pace.

"I promise you, you'll see your mother and father again. And little Oliver as well."

She glanced down to either side and saw Anna nod. Peter was ramrod straight, marching forward with no sign that he heard her at all.

"You'll see them soon," Jessica said.

But she could hear the lack of conviction in her own voice. *It was nothing,* she thought. But however hard she tried to push it out of her mind, she knew what she had heard. Something had moved down in the tunnel, something had responded to Peter's voice, had shuffled toward them from somewhere below and had dislodged a rock from the tunnel wall. She had heard the rock clatter and echo, however faint or far away.

She set her jaw and led the children onward through the scatter of snowflakes and ash in the night air, and she did her level best to put thoughts of childhood monsters out of her head.

Rawhead, indeed, she thought. *Nonsense.*

She shivered again and hurried the children away down the path.

10

⸺◦∞◦⸺

The bowls Bennett Rose brought his guests were full of something thick and brown and hot, with thumb-size chunks of beef floating amidst cubes of onions and leeks. It was exactly what was called for on a dark snowy evening in a strange place. Sharing the tray with the two bowls was a half a loaf of good bread and a pair of beer steins filled with dark ale. Rose instructed them to leave the tray in the hall when they were finished, where it would be picked up by the scullery girl in the wee hours.

"You can always wait and tackle them woods in the morning," Rose said. "I expect you'll sleep hard tonight."

"There's no time to waste," Day said. "We'll eat and freshen up a bit and be right down."

"I'll tell the others you'll be ready to go in a bit," Rose said. He smiled and bowed and left the room, closing the door behind him.

Hammersmith took a bowl and sat in the room's single straight-backed chair.

"You eat," Day said. "I'm more thirsty than I am hungry and I want to unpack now while I have the energy. By the time we get back tonight, I suspect I'll want nothing more than sleep."

"I'll wait for you."

"No, eat."

Hammersmith shrugged and sniffed the bowl. He levered a spoonful into his mouth and frowned.

"Where's your suitcase?" Day said.

"In my room."

"I never saw you go to your room."

"I was there long enough to set my suitcase down. I'll worry about unpacking it later."

"Your clothing will be wrinkled."

Hammersmith smiled, and a moment later, Day laughed. Hammersmith's clothes were always wrinkled, whether they came from a suitcase or a closet.

"Well, try not to spill any of that on your shirt."

"I make no promises. Pudding stains go quite well with tea stains."

"It's a pudding?"

"Rose said it was groaty dick," Hammersmith said.

"Groats?" Day said. "That's bird feed."

Hammersmith shrugged. He tore off a hunk of his bread and used it to soak up some of the stock. He popped the soggy bread into his mouth. Broth dribbled down his chin and narrowly missed the front of his shirt. He leaned forward so that it would drip into the bowl and then wiped his chin on his sleeve, realizing too late that he'd only altered the location of the stain rather than avoiding it. He sighed and set the bowl aside. "I was watching," he said. "Looking your way when the vicar's wife gave you something."

Day held up a finger and went to the door. He opened it slightly and looked both ways down the hall, then shut the door again. He reached for his stein. He took a deep swallow of beer and licked the foam from his upper lip. Then he reached into his pocket and pulled out a small piece of paper, creased and wadded and still damp from Mrs Brothwood's sweaty hand. He pushed aside the washbasin and laid the paper on the vanity. He carefully unfolded it, teasing the edges so that the soft paper wouldn't tear. There was scratchy handwriting on one side, ten words, broken up into three short lines, hurriedly written in violet ink. Day took the scrap of paper by one corner and flipped it over. The back side was blank. He turned it back over and both men leaned in close to read:

She is under the floor.
   He means no harm.
      Please.

They both read it silently, and then Day read it out loud. His voice was hushed but clear in the small room.

"She is under the floor. He means no harm. Please."

He backed up to the bed and sat down on the edge of it.

"What does it mean?" Hammersmith said.

"Should we assume it's the missing Mrs Price?"

"I think if it were all of them, the whole Price family, she would have worded this differently, wouldn't she?"

"But under the floor? What floor?"

They both looked down at the smooth wooden planks beneath their feet. Day shook his head.

"We were in the common room, near the hearth," he said.

"Mrs Price is under the hearth?" Hammersmith said. "That makes no sense."

"No, you're right. I don't think that's what the note means," Day said. "That's where we were when she gave this to me, but she can't have written it there, can she?"

"Why not? Before we arrived."

"Her husband would have seen. And so would Calvin Campbell, and the schoolteacher, the children, Bennett Rose. There were a lot of people in that room. They all would have seen her write it."

"Maybe they did see her."

"I don't think so," Day said. "She was nervous. She handed this to me carefully, as she took my hand to say good-bye. She didn't want anyone else to see. If she wrote it in front of them all, why keep it a secret afterward?"

"So she meant this for you."

"For us."

"She wrote it somewhere else and brought it with her."

"She may not have even made up her mind about whether to give it to us. She might have waited to decide until she met us."

"Then the floor she mentions could be anywhere. Why not be more specific? It's not much of a clue, if you don't mind my saying so."

"I think she would have given us more information if it had

occurred to her. It must have seemed quite obvious to her as she wrote it. She was in a hurry to write this before being discovered doing so and she was thinking about a place so familiar that it didn't enter her mind that we wouldn't know it, too."

"But we're not from here."

"Exactly."

"We don't know this village."

"So she didn't just mean a place in the village, she meant the place where she was when she wrote this, the place where she's most comfortable and at home, a place that needs no explanation for her."

"Her home."

"The rectory."

"Mrs Price is hidden under the floor in the rectory."

"It's as good a theory as we've got."

"Unless the note means nothing. It could be the ravings of a madwoman."

"But if that's the case, then we have no clues at all. So let's assume it means something unless and until we discover that it doesn't."

"We don't even know that this is meant to be Mrs Price. Or, if it is, where the other two are. Mr Price and the boy."

"No."

"And who is the man she mentions? 'He means well.'"

"Yes. But she says 'He means no harm.' It could be Mr Price."

"That doesn't tell us where he is. This is a maddeningly imprecise note, Mr Day."

"But I don't think she means Mr Price. She was nervous, positively jumping out of her chair."

"Well, three people have disappeared from her village."

"She was standing next to her husband the entire time. She kept the note a secret from him."

"Her husband."

"The vicar. Mr Brothwood."

"This is getting us nowhere."

"Not entirely," Day said. "We'll want to examine that rectory. And we'll want to do it without letting Mr Brothwood know that his wife gave us this note."

"We don't owe her anything."

"No, we don't. But we have no reason to make her life more difficult. She's clearly already upset about all this. We'll tread carefully."

"Not so carefully that the little boy dies while we're being polite to the vicar and his wife."

Day sighed. "Of course not. Sometimes, Mr Hammersmith, your single-mindedness is just the slightest bit maddening."

Hammersmith grinned and pulled another chunk of bread off the roll on his plate.

"Is it good?" Day said.

"Hmm?"

"The groaty dick."

"Oh, I'm not sure. I didn't notice right off, but it has a curious aftertaste. And I feel a bit dizzy."

"It's been a long day, and it's colder here than it was in London."

"True enough, but I've been drugged before, and this has the same feel about it."

"Drugged? You've said nothing about being drugged as we've sat here discussing mysterious notes and rectories."

"It may not be drugged. I'm only mentioning the possibility that there may be something in the groaty dick."

"And if there is? Rose poisoned us?"

"I think perhaps someone did."

"Are you all right?"

"I'll be fine. I had a bite or two, that's all, but I recommend you eat only the bread."

"I feel all right. I don't think there's anything in the beer."

"Good. It was probably meant to disguise the taste of the drug. The bitterness."

Day rummaged in his suitcase and brought out his Colt revolver. He checked the chamber and nodded.

"We'll go downstairs and confront Rose," he said.

"What if we don't?"

"You mean, let him think he's drugged us?"

"Just that."

"He'll know he's failed when we continue to tramp about his village alive and well."

"I don't think he meant to kill us."

"It wouldn't make a lot of sense, would it?"

"London would only send more men if we both died or disappeared."

"Perhaps the poison is only in *your* food. They don't seem to like you here."

Hammersmith reached and picked up Day's bowl. He sniffed it and dipped a spoon into its murky brown depths.

"Don't," Day said. "If it's got the drug in it—"

"A bite won't hurt me. I have the constitution of an ox."

Hammersmith tasted Day's pudding. He spit the bite back into the bowl and smacked his lips. "That's thoroughly unpleasant," he said. "He's overdone it. I don't suppose he's ever poisoned anyone before."

"And, as you pointed out," Day said, "the beer might have masked the flavor of the drug."

"So we were both meant to succumb."

"It would appear so."

Hammersmith stood and gripped his truncheon. "This does seem to be a clear indication of Mr Rose's guilt, sir."

"Sit down, Sergeant. I've changed my mind. I don't want to arrest him just yet."

"But I do want to arrest him."

"For slipping something in our food?"

"Well, yes. That seems sufficient grounds."

"But without a reason."

"Well, sir, we can ask him his reasons once he's in custody."

"Or we can wait and see why he wanted us out of the way," Day said.

"What if he's got the Price family hidden away somewhere?"

"It doesn't seem likely. There's something else going on here. Let's see what happens."

"Of course, he could be trying to kill us, after all," Hammersmith said. "And he could decide to try again when he sees it didn't work this time."

"Then we'll arrest him," Day said. "Eat your bread to soak up the drug in your stomach. Eat mine, too."

"Thank you, but if you wouldn't mind turning your back for a moment?"

"Of course."

Day turned and pretended to examine the chest of drawers against the window. Hammersmith took a deep breath and stuck a finger down his throat, immediately choking up a small amount of liquid back into the soup bowl. He wiped his lips on his shirtsleeve again and took a long swallow of beer to wash the taste of vomit out of his mouth.

"You are a hardy sort, aren't you?" Day said.

"I do wish people would stop drugging me," Hammersmith said. "I'm going to have to start preparing my own food and I'm a terrible cook, so that's hardly better than submitting to all the poisoning going on around me."

"It's your second time. I can't imagine it'll happen again. You're already bucking the odds."

"Let's hope you're right."

Hammersmith dropped to his hands and knees and pulled the chamber pot from under Day's bed.

"There are still chamber pots in the rooms here?" Day said.

"I assume indoor water closets haven't yet come to Blackhampton. At least, not all of it. Still, this ought to do," Hammersmith said. He poured both bowls into the big pot and looked around for a place to dump it out.

"Huh," he said. "They've blocked the window."

"The chest of drawers. I thought putting it in front of the window was merely an unfortunate use of the space."

"It was done to keep us in here."

"Further evidence that the drug wasn't meant to kill us. If we were dead, we wouldn't try to climb out the window tonight."

"Probably not. At any rate, I can't dump the contents out the window, so I'm afraid you'll have to put up with the scent of groaty dick in your room."

"It's not altogether unpleasant," Day said. "If I have to put up with a scent, I mean."

Hammersmith shoved the chamber pot back under the bed. He and Day sat and ate the bread, washing it down with the strong ale. Hammersmith yawned. "We were supposed to fall asleep quickly," he said.

"The question is why?"

"Our host is hiding something from us," Hammersmith said.

"Then I think it behooves us to find out what that might be." Day stood and held out his hand, and Hammersmith handed him his plate. Day chuckled. "You still managed to get a bit on your sleeve there."

"I know. I did it practically on purpose. I think you planted the notion in my head."

"I'm devious that way." Day put their plates and glasses on the tray with their bowls and opened the door long enough to set the tray in the hall. He came back into the room and closed the door.

"We should be very careful in those woods tonight," he said. "They'll think we're sleepy, so we'll watch them for mistakes. But no unnecessary chances."

"Agreed."

"I mean it, Nevil. You are not invincible. You have a tendency to leap before you properly think a situation through."

"I'm touched that you worry about me."

Day shook his head and smiled. He searched his pockets until he found his flask and took a deep swallow from it. He held it out to Hammersmith.

"Take a drink. It'll kill the poisons."

"No, thank you, sir. I'd prefer tea."

"Of course. But brandy will keep you healthy."

Hammersmith took the flask and raised it in a mock salute to Day. He took a swallow and handed the flask back. The two men stood and looked around the room.

"Well," Day said. "Are you ready to go and risk our lives in the woods behind an unsettling village in the middle of the night?"

"It's what I live for," Hammersmith said.

"Then after you, Mr Hammersmith."

He swung the door open and waved the sergeant through, then stepped out into the hall and closed the door behind him. The two men stepped over the tray of empty bowls and steins and walked to the staircase. Without a look back, they headed down into the flickering darkness of the inn.

11

Fires banked forty feet into the air, throwing the landscape into sharp contrast and spreading shadows of the four men across the snowy fields. Constable Grimes led Day, Hammersmith, and Calvin Campbell past the furnaces, which worked night and day, smelting ore and creating the slag that bordered every path. Day and Hammersmith had seen the furnaces from the train windows when they arrived, but the effect was much more dramatic in the dark. Everything was indigo and white, and as they drew nearer the forest, shadows capered beyond the tree line, a fairy dance for the unaccustomed audience.

Day let Hammersmith and Campbell walk ahead. The two men seemed to have found an easy camaraderie based on their shared fear for the life of little Oliver Price, but Day wasn't ready to trust the stranger yet. He held out his hand in front of Grimes to slow the constable down.

"Tell me about him." Day nodded in the direction of Campbell's back.

"Nothing much to tell," Grimes said. "He's been around the village for a week or two. Staying at the inn. Studying birds of the region, he says."

"Rose doesn't like him."

"Rose likes him well enough," Grimes said.

"He didn't want Campbell with us out here."

"No," Grimes said. "You misunderstand. It's nothing to do with Mr Campbell. He's probably harmless enough."

"Then what?"

"I think Mr Rose was trying to protect you."

"But you just said that Campbell's harmless."

"Not from Campbell. It's only that most of the people round here are superstitious. Rose is the same as any. He didn't want you out here tonight."

"I'd say he didn't. He drugged Sergeant Hammersmith and me."

"Drugged you?"

"Put something in our supper to make us sleep."

"I'm sure he didn't mean to harm you. He doesn't always think. They're good people here, they really are, but they're closed off."

Day didn't say anything. He waited.

Grimes sniffed and looked at the trees ahead of them. "You understand I'm not one," he said.

"One what?"

"Like the others in Blackhampton. I don't believe in the . . . I don't think the same things about it all."

"Rose thinks he knows what happened to that family, doesn't he?"

"Not just him. Lot of the folks here do."

"That's why you sent for us?"

"I had to. I couldn't find that family myself. And nobody else wants to help."

"So where does Rose think they are?"

"Down below."

"In the mines?"

"Yes."

"What makes him think that?" Day said.

Grimes said nothing.

"Should we be down in the tunnels," Day said, "rather than out here in the woods?"

Grimes shrugged. "I didn't say I thought they were in the tunnels."

There was another long silence. The two of them walked on. They drew up alongside Hammersmith and Campbell, who had stopped at the tree line where the snow abruptly ended.

"Let's get in there," Campbell said.

Day nodded, and Hammersmith produced a box of matches. He withdrew a long wooden match and lit each of the men's lanterns. Day looked around at the faces of the three other men. Hammersmith wore his customary expression of determination. Campbell's face was partially hidden in shadow, and the light from his lantern cast yellow highlights under his cheekbones that made him seem cadaverous and deadly. Day looked at Grimes. The constable's eyes were wide and his nostrils flared. He had the appearance of a high-strung horse ready to bolt.

Hammersmith plunged into the forest, his lantern held high ahead of him. Campbell followed close behind. Day grabbed Grimes's elbow and held him back.

"What is it?" he said. "What's got you so frightened? What's got the innkeeper poisoning the police? There's something you're all tiptoeing around out here."

"It's nothing," Grimes said. "Let's go."

"Tell me what Rose has told you."

"Let go of me!" Grimes pulled away, and his lantern swung in a wide arc. Day staggered, but caught his balance. The constable shook his head and stared down at the footprints they had made in the snow. "I apologize," he said. "Disrespectful of me."

"Tell me," Day said.

"Rawhead and Bloody Bones," Grimes said.

"Rawhead and . . . What does that mean?"

"Rawhead and Bloody Bones. He what waits in the mines and takes people. That's who has the boy and his parents. What Rose and the others think, anyway."

"Who is Rawhead?"

"It's a children's rhyme. A monster. Nonsense, really."

"But Rose, the other villagers here, they think the monster's real?"

Grimes nodded his head and said nothing. Day opened his mouth to ask another question, but before he could speak, Grimes hurried past him and disappeared into the dark forest.

"Rawhead and Bloody Bones," Day said. He sighed and thrust his lantern into the shadows, and allowed himself to be swallowed by the trees.

12

Claire Day had thought ahead and packed a pair of sturdy boots for her husband, along with a short-brimmed hat and a quilted vest. Wearing them now, Walter Day looked out ahead at the dark tangle of low briars and the patches of snow and ice that had gathered despite the canopy of branches above and he counted himself lucky.

As he did every day.

He allowed Constable Grimes to lead the way into the dark, wild country. He followed Grimes closely, but kept careful track of Sergeant Hammersmith and Calvin Campbell, who were spread out ahead of him. There was always the possibility that the villagers might lead Day and Hammersmith into the woods and lose them or, worse, do them harm. Of course Grimes had sent for Scotland Yard in the first place. It was a good indication that he wanted to find the missing family. But there was something about Campbell that Day didn't trust. He was the only stranger in the village, and yet he seemed more concerned than almost anyone else about the Prices. And, most especially, about finding little Oliver Price. Day felt certain the birder knew something that he wasn't sharing.

Grimes crunched his way through brambles and around trees, and Day kept up as well as he could. His vest had several pockets, and he had filled them with matches, a compass, a good folding knife, his flask, and his Colt Navy. He was a trusting person, but he wasn't foolish.

Snow-covered branches swept low across the path and reached out for him, knocking his hat off and sending a rivulet of freezing water down his collar. A deer rushed across the path in front of him and he stood still, listening to it as it crashed away through the underbrush.

A hand on his shoulder startled him and he jumped, then felt a moment of embarrassment. He turned, and the giant Campbell leaned toward him.

"The path will end soon," Campbell said.

"Doesn't it go far?"

"No."

"Did you see the deer?"

"Something must have spooked it."

"What could have spooked it?"

"A wolf."

"There are wolves here?"

"Oh, most definitely."

"If Oliver and his parents are out here . . ."

"If they're out here, they're dead."

Day nodded and sighed. "Still, we'll find them."

He turned and saw Grimes tromping toward them, leaves crunching under his heavy boots. Hammersmith followed close behind the constable.

"The path splits here," he said. "It might be best if we separated to cover more ground."

"I don't think it's a good idea to divide our manpower," Day said. "More of us might be lost." He meant himself, of course, but he didn't want to say so and risk looking vulnerable.

"Two groups of two, then?"

"I'll stay with Mr Campbell," Day said. If Campbell had a secret, he might be dangerous. Best to keep an eye on him.

"Yes," Grimes said. "It might be better for Mr Campbell and myself each to stay with one of you Londoners. I'll go with the sergeant. But we'll stay close to each other, both groups. Shout out if anyone finds anything."

"We're off this way," Campbell said. He walked away to the left before the others could say anything.

Day gave Hammersmith a pointed look, hoping that he had communicated the need for caution, then turned and plunged into the woods after Campbell. When he looked back again a moment later, the other men were gone, swallowed up by the dense skeletal winter wood.

Campbell's broad back filled the view ahead of Day. He looked down and saw that they were leaving footprints in the snow, black on grey, and was comforted by the notion that Campbell would not be able to turn him around and lose him in the trees. If that was his goal, Day would be able to trace his own steps back to the tree line.

They veered to their right so as to keep the other search party nearby, Campbell leading the way. Finally, Campbell stopped and turned and glared at Day.

"What do you know?" Campbell said.

Day stopped walking and took a step backward. He felt the comforting weight of the Colt Navy at his side. He was confident that he'd be able to draw it before Campbell could reach him.

"I'm not sure what you mean."

"You know me?"

"I know the name you've given me."

"Nothing else?"

"What should I know about you?"

"Nothing. Nothing that has any bearing on the disappearance of Oliver Price."

"Do you know where he is? Where the family is?"

"I do not, sir."

"Mr Campbell, I'm here to find a missing family. To rescue them if possible, to avenge them if they're already dead. Your behavior makes me more suspicious with every moment that passes. If you've killed those people or hidden them away, I'll find out. And I'm not alone. If you plan to kill me here and leave my body in these woods, you'll have to kill Mr Hammersmith, too. He won't be easy to kill. And neither will I."

"I have no wish to kill you."

"Good. I have no wish to be killed."

"Please believe me when I say that I mean no harm to anyone, that I only want to find Oliver alive and well."

Campbell bit his lower lip and looked off to the side. He raised his head and opened his mouth to speak, but his eyes rested on something over Day's shoulder and a look of alarm suddenly appeared on his face.

Day whirled around and scanned the woods. He saw nothing but dark trees and thickets. He turned back in time to see Campbell disappear. The big man faded back into the trees and was gone without a sound or any trace.

"Campbell," Day said. "Campbell!"

There was no response. Day drew his Colt Navy. He stood in place and turned in a circle. There were trees behind him, in front of him, on every side, and they all looked the same. Grey and brown and black and, occasionally, a bit of the starry night sky high above. There was no indication of which direction to go. He realized that the comforting trail of footprints in the snow had been false. Here there was only damp underbrush; no snow had made it down through the canopy to the ground. It had all been caught by the branches above and melted away.

What had frightened Campbell? Was there something in the forest or had it been an act meant only to distract Day long enough for the big man to leave him? Had he abandoned Day or was he setting the inspector up for an ambush? Could Day count on Grimes to find him? Or was Grimes cooperating with Campbell? Had Hammersmith been abandoned, too?

There were too many questions. Anything was possible, and Day decided that conjecture was useless. The best he could do was be cautious and be brave. He thought of Claire and his unborn baby.

He drew his compass from a pocket in his vest and opened it, waited until the needle pointed north. When he had got his bearings, he started walking.

13

As he lay half asleep in his bed, Peter Price caught sight of movement from the corner of his eye and turned his head. A spider lowered itself from the ceiling above his chest on a glistening thread. It was the size of Peter's fist, and he could see each of the wiry hairs on each of its writhing legs. For a moment he lay unmoving, simply watching the thing draw closer, and it seemed to him that its gestures were deliberate, as if it were communicating something lovely and terrible to him.

Then he sprang from the bed and lit a candle. In its unsteady glow, he searched the air above the bed. He pulled the covers from the mattress and threw them on the floor, picked them back up and shook them out. Nothing. There was no spider. Just to be sure, he patted himself down and ran his fingers through his hair.

The sound at the door was soft, and had he been asleep, it would not have awakened him. He padded carefully across the room, carrying the candle and watching for spiders the whole way. He opened the door a crack. His sister Anna stood in the hall, small and shapeless in her nightgown. Her bare feet stuck out below the hem of the gown, and Peter noticed, for the first time, that her toes had the same squared-off appearance as his own. He wondered whether little Oliver's toes had looked like that.

"Did I wake you?" Anna said.

"I wasn't sleeping."

"May I come in?"

Peter nodded and moved out of the way, and his sister stepped inside, closed the door behind her. She hurried across the room and sat on the edge of Peter's bed, drawing his rumpled blanket over her lap. She stared at the window over the foot of the bed, but Peter was sure there was nothing to see. Candlelight reflected against the darkness there, swaying and jumping across the rippled glass.

"Is Virginia asleep?" Peter said.

Anna nodded. "Asleep and snoring," she said.

"Why does all of this bother us so much more than it does her?"

"She seems to have put it entirely out of her mind."

Peter shook his head and leaned against the wall. He set his candle on the low table by the door. He glanced at the floor, looking for spiders, but saw only bare polished wood. He didn't look up at his sister when he spoke.

"How can we do that?"

"Forget, you mean?"

"Yes."

"She's very young. She's only a child."

"Aren't we children, as well?"

"We're practically adults."

"And yet we still shout at Rawhead in the pits."

"Everyone does."

"Everyone who's a child."

"I didn't say we were adults yet, only that we're practically grown. We're still allowed to do childish things."

"Except forget about Oliver."

"Or what was done."

"Have the policemen found anything? Have you heard?"

"Where would I hear? I've been in all the same places as you today."

"Sometimes you find out about things."

Anna nodded solemnly. "I do pay more attention than you. But nothing's been said. I imagine they're out in the woods or perhaps down in the mines, looking for everybody."

"Maybe they'll find Father."

"Maybe they'll find Mother."

"Don't be ridiculous. Mother's long gone. At most they'll find Hester, and nobody wants her back."

"I'm sure Father does."

"Do you think they left together?"

"Left us?"

Peter shrugged, unable to repeat the possibility that they'd been left behind.

"No," Anna said. "Hester might leave us. I hope she did. But Father would never."

Peter let out a breath that he hadn't realized he was holding.

"If they're in the woods . . ." he said. "The policemen, I mean, they might find something."

"So what if they do? I don't think they will. It was well-hidden."

"It was hardly hidden at all."

"Well, anyway, if they do find it, they still won't know anything."

"They might deduce things."

"There's no use crying about it."

"I never cried. I'm perfectly relaxed."

"I didn't say you were crying. I said there's no use in it."

"Well, I wasn't crying anyway."

"If they find it in the woods . . . If they find anything out there, it will lead them nowhere, and we oughtn't get worked up about it. There's nothing we can do, unless you want to go tramping back through the woods in the dark."

"No," Peter said. He was the oldest and he wasn't supposed to believe in Rawhead and Bloody Bones, but that didn't mean he wanted to explore the forest at night.

"Then I suppose we should sleep."

"I can't."

"Virginia can. We should, too."

"Anna?"

"Yes?"

"Don't you think there's something wrong with Virginia?"

"You shouldn't say that. She's your sister."

"You're my sister, too, and I don't think anything's too terribly wrong with you. Except when you get up to something stupid."

"Virginia will be fine once this is all over and the policemen have left and Father has come home and it all goes back to normal."

"Do you think it will? Go back to normal, I mean?"

"It has to, doesn't it? I mean, it's just one little boy. Everything can't change because of one little boy, can it?"

"I suppose not. He was very little."

"Very little. Hardly a speck."

"Yes. What about what Hilde found?"

"The eye?"

"She showed it to me," Peter said.

"She fancies you."

"She does not." But the idea that Hilde Rose fancied him was new to Peter, and he wondered if it was true.

"She does. She never showed it to me."

"It was blue." He hoped that Anna would allow him to change the subject away from Hilde and her romantic inclinations.

"Oliver's eyes weren't blue, were they?"

"I think they were green."

"I think so, too."

"And Hester?"

"No, her eyes weren't blue. I would have noticed. Father's weren't, either. But I think Mother's eyes might have been blue."

Peter was quiet for a time, watching the candlelight reflected in the window. When he spoke, he wasn't sure Anna would hear him across the room, but she looked up at him.

"Do you remember her?" Peter said.

"Mother? Yes, of course I do."

"Virginia's forgotten her, I think."

"Well, she was a baby when Mother . . . Well, anyway, she mustn't be blamed for being young."

"Oh, I wasn't blaming her."

"You shouldn't let it bother you. We can remember her for them. For Virginia and Oliver, I mean."

"She wasn't Oliver's mother."

"Hester hardly counts as a mother. I say we should share our mother with him. The memory of her, I mean."

"Anna . . ."

Anna swallowed and her eyes went wide. Peter looked down at his bare feet, confused and embarrassed. She had spoken about Oliver as if none of the ugliness of the past several days had happened. Peter felt alone in that instant, but if Anna wanted to put it out of her head, he would let her. He looked up when Anna cleared her throat. Her face was red.

"Of course I don't know what I meant by that. Not at all."

"It's all right. Really, it is."

"Anyway, I don't think Mother did have blue eyes, now that I think about it."

Peter smiled. The feeling of isolation lifted a bit. "So whose eye did Hilde find?" he said.

Anna shrugged. "Perhaps it belonged to someone else. Perhaps the eye doesn't matter in the slightest."

"Wouldn't that be odd," Peter said. It wasn't a question, and Anna didn't answer.

She stood and crossed the room to where Peter still leaned against the doorjamb. She brushed a lock of hair from her face and smiled at him.

"Don't worry, Peter dear. Soon this will end. The policemen will return to London and Father will come home. He'll know what to do about Virginia."

Peter nodded and attempted a smile, but he knew Anna wasn't fooled by it. He was the worrier and Anna was the logical one. Between them, they had to take care of their little family, what was left of it. Even if Father did return, that wouldn't change.

Anna opened the door and looked both ways down the hall before scooting out and closing the door behind her. Peter listened for her footsteps, but couldn't hear whether she returned to her room or went the other way to the stairs. He knew that she sometimes slept on the rug by the fireplace when she had nightmares.

Peter returned to his bed. He arranged the covers and crawled back beneath them. There was still no sign of a spider. He left the candle burning on the table beside him and watched the ceiling until he settled into a deep and dreamless sleep.

14

Day pushed through brambles and stepped carefully over fallen logs. He was conscious of the fact that he didn't know the local animals, had no idea whether there were actually wolves in the woods. But he hadn't encountered anything dangerous, except the cold and the wet. He marched ahead, cautious but confident. He felt he should be coming to the tree line any time now. Lone snowflakes drifted down past him from above. Twigs crunched underfoot, and he slipped on a pile of wet leaves, but caught himself before he fell. He had no idea how much time had passed. He felt certain that he hadn't been wandering in the forest for long, but he had read about men who got lost in the woods and were never seen again, men who spent their remaining hours tramping about in circles, wandering ever farther into the wilderness.

He hoped that the others were looking for him, that this was all a mistake. Hammersmith would come looking, he knew, but if Campbell had purposely left Day behind, then Hammersmith might be in danger, too, and Day had no way of warning him.

He turned and sat heavily on a fallen log. He took his compass out and checked it again, glad to see that he had been walking in a straight line. He put it back in his pocket.

A furtive noise, a rustle of leaves and a crunch of snow, caused him to glance up, and he saw a flash of burnt orange as a fox raced past him and disappeared in the underbrush. Day smiled despite himself and looked at the break in the trees where the fox had come from.

Standing in the trees there, nearly invisible back in the gloom, was a man.

Day scrambled to his feet. The man tipped his hat and faded back into the shadows. Day rushed forward and plunged into the trees. He looked about frantically, but there was no sign of the other man. Had he hallucinated someone else out here in the forest?

Day crouched and examined the ground where he thought the man must have been standing. There, at the edge of a clump of brown leaves, was the outer rim of a boot print. Someone was out there, someone was watching. Day stood up and looked all around without seeing any sign of another living soul. He cupped his hands around his mouth and shouted.

"Hullo!"

He held his breath and listened, alert for the slightest sound, but heard only the echo of his own voice.

"Hullo! I saw you! Help me!"

Again he listened. He heard something, some slight noise behind him, and he turned and stared into the darkness. Two yellow pinpricks of light stared out at him from under a bush. He stepped toward them and they vanished. An instant later, he saw the blur of the fox's tail disappearing deeper into the bushes.

He made his way back into the clearing and sat again on the fallen log. He found his handkerchief in one of the inside pockets of his vest and wiped his face. He was certain the man had been no trick of the light or figment of his imagination. But the man's appearance had been hideous, and Day was struck by the notion that he had not seen a man at all, but rather some spirit, an apparition conjured by the forest. How else to explain what he had seen?

The man had been dressed all in grey, from his hat to the hem of his trousers. Even the man's eyes seemed to be grey, though it was hard to be sure. The most disturbing detail of the man's appearance was that, through the flesh of his jaw, Day had clearly seen a portion of the man's skull, his exposed teeth bared in a wicked grin.

He felt suddenly sure he had seen the local children's nightmares come to life.

Rawhead and Bloody Bones.

15

Hammersmith followed the broad back of Constable Grimes through the forest. He moved his lantern up and down, watching for branches and roots, ice and slippery leaves. Hammersmith wasn't comfortable in the trees. He had been raised in coal mines and mountains, and more recently he had spent his time in London and its sprawling suburbs.

But there was a child missing somewhere in the vicinity of Blackhampton, and so he put aside his discomfort and watched for signs of the boy and his parents. It was difficult because the lantern light didn't penetrate far into the gloom, but the two men walked slowly and carefully, alert for the slightest anomaly in the underbrush.

They had traveled this way in silence for perhaps an hour when Hammersmith made up his mind to clear the air.

"Constable," he said.

"Have you seen something?"

"No, I haven't. But I may owe you an apology of some sort."

"Whatever for?"

"It was brought to my attention that I may be oversensitive on the subject of child labor and the mines."

"Oh. Parents putting their children to work, you mean?"

"Actually, you said that. I implied that the village itself encouraged that sort of thing."

"The village itself?"

"When I was a child—"

"Ah, you worked the mines yourself? But it was a different time then, wasn't it?"

"It was."

"The entire world's changed since you and I were children."

"Child labor still exists."

"That it does, Sergeant, but it's no longer the prevailing way of things, is it?"

"I wouldn't think it is."

"Then we agree. Of course, putting children to work in the mines is no longer legal. Some parents do still bring their children with them, but those children have nothing to do with hard labor. They perform menial tasks, such as a woman might."

Hammersmith didn't respond. It was clear that he and Grimes were very different people who happened to wear the same uniform. Still, Hammersmith's attempt at an apology, no matter how clumsy and unsatisfying, appeared to have worked. Grimes seemed a bit more relaxed. The men from Scotland Yard might have another two days to spend in Blackhampton, and having Grimes on their side would go a long way toward a productive investigation.

Hammersmith opened his lantern's shutter wider. A more focused light was useful, but he felt hemmed in by the winter woods. He listened for signs of life, but heard nothing that didn't sound like a small animal. He assumed a lost little boy would cry out for help at the sight of a lantern bobbing through the trees. He didn't want to think about the alternative, that the boy was dead.

He stopped every few feet and shuffled through the leaves at the side of the narrow trail with the toe of his boot. He doubted he would find any footprints so long after the family had disappeared, but he held out hope that he might discover a dropped handkerchief, a paper pastry wrapper, anything at all. Grimes tramped on, though, without looking around, without waiting to let Hammersmith catch up. Hammersmith was conscious of the fact that he might get lost, and by the time the sun rose there would be new search parties out in these woods, looking for the London policeman and diverting time and attention from the missing Price family. He kept the back of the constable's blue jacket in sight and never stopped moving for long.

They had been searching for quite some time when Hammersmith spotted an odd shape deeper in the brush.

"Over here," Hammersmith said. "What's that?"

Grimes turned and came back to where Hammersmith stood on the path. The glow from their lanterns spread out in a wobbly circle across the ground.

"What've you found?"

"I'm not sure. Does that look strange to you?" Hammersmith pointed into the trees. The ground cover grew thick here, and it was hard to spot anything amongst the dead grey branches and wet black leaves. Grimes held his lantern up and peered into the dark. He stifled a yawn with his free hand.

"I don't see nuffin'."

"There. Right there. Do you see it?"

"Right in there?"

"That's it."

"Dead animal, I'd say. Doesn't look like a person, no ways."

"I'm going to take a closer look."

Hammersmith handed his lantern to Constable Grimes and crouched down. He pushed aside a handful of thin low-hanging branches and shuffled forward until he had to kneel. The knees of his thin uniform trousers were immediately soaked through. He realized that he hadn't felt any sensation in his feet for some time. They were numb. Unlike Inspector Day, Hammersmith had not packed any boots but the standard black Wellingtons he was accustomed to wearing. They were excellent for walking a beat, but they weren't at all suited for tramping about the countryside in snow and ice. He braced himself for the cold and settled forward, putting his weight on his hands. He crawled through the brush, out into the darkness, keeping his head down. The glow from the dual lanterns didn't penetrate as far as he'd hoped. He was as good as blind.

"Hoy, Mr Hammersmith, you've drifted off to the left a bit there, sir."

Hammersmith adjusted course, surprised that Grimes's voice sounded so close. He really hadn't gone as far off the path as he'd assumed. His legs already felt frozen from the knees down. It was quite clear to him that a lost little boy might not survive a single night in the wilderness, and Hammersmith found himself hoping once again that Oliver Price was somewhere warm and dry with his parents.

He raised his head and a sharp branch scraped across his face, from his hairline to his chin. He dropped again and covered his head. Snow plopped down from above as the branch sprang back into position. Hammersmith dabbed at his cheek and felt something wet, but couldn't tell if he was bleeding or wet with snow.

"It's right there, Mr Hammersmith. No, there. Reach out with your right hand."

Hammersmith groped about him until his fingers touched something wet and slimy. It was fabric of some sort. He grabbed the nearest edge and backed quickly out of the narrow tunnel he'd made with his body, dragging the cloth.

"Here you go, man," Grimes said. "All's well."

Hammersmith felt Grimes's hands on the back of his jacket, pulling him along, lifting him up. He stood and shook twigs out of his hair, wiped his eyes with the back of his free hand. The lanterns were swinging side by side from a nearby tree branch.

"That's a lad, that's a fine lad." Grimes brushed Hammersmith's clothing, clumsily patting the leaves and mud off his uniform. Hammersmith grinned and ran a hand through his unkempt hair.

"I'd like to wait for daylight before attempting that again," he said.

"No need, sir," Grimes said. "If there's to be a next time, I believe it will be my turn. But if you don't mind, I hope there won't be a next time."

"Don't blame you a bit."

"Nasty scratch you've got there, though."

"It's nothing. Let's see what we have."

Grimes took the dripping wad of fabric from Hammersmith, who rubbed his hands together and blew into them, trying to warm his fingers. Grimes held up the cloth and stretched it out between his hands. He moved so that the lantern light shone directly on, and through, the fabric. It was an article of clothing. Hammersmith identified a short sleeve, bordered by torn lace. Amid the dark streaks and blotches that stained the cloth, he picked out traces of a subtle floral pattern. It was impossible to make out colors, but the black marks were clearly not any part of the natural design of the thing.

"It's a dress," Grimes said.

"A child's dress."

"It's awfully small."

"Does it look familiar to you, Mr Grimes?"

"Familiar in what way?"

"Have you seen anyone wearing this?"

"I'm sure I don't have any idea who might have worn this. Maybe in better light . . ."

"Well, it's certain Mrs Price never wore this."

"Not within the past twenty years, I'd say."

"What about Oliver?"

"Oliver's a boy."

"But could it be a baptism gown or nightshirt or somesuch?"

"Ah, I suppose it might be. But the lace? And the flowers?"

"Rather feminine."

"Indeed."

"Those black spots and this." Hammersmith pointed to a large dark patch near the midsection of the little dress and moved his finger down to the hem where a chunk of lace had been torn out.

"That's blood, sir. I'd stake my career on it."

"I agree."

"And that means we're looking for someone else entirely."

"Mr and Mrs Price, little Oliver, and a girl."

"What is happening in my village, Mr Hammersmith?"

"Something evil. The children here may be in great danger."

"Rawhead."

"I'm sorry?"

"That silly rhyme comes to mind. Nothing, really. Blackhampton's always been so quiet. One of the things I like about it, really."

Hammersmith nodded, but there was nothing more to say. The case had just become even more urgent. Grimes folded the dress, squeezing out the excess water, and they each took a lantern from the branch behind them.

"Should we keep looking?" Grimes said.

"I believe we'd better. It's more important than ever."

Grimes closed his eyes and sighed. Hammersmith didn't wait for him to follow. He plunged back down the path, headed farther into the forest. A moment later, he heard Grimes at his heels.

They had not gone more than five or six yards into the woods when Hammersmith stopped and held up the lantern.

"What is it?" Grimes said.

"Listen."

The two men stood quietly, their breathing shallow, and waited. Grimes motioned to get Hammersmith's attention and pointed off to their left. Hammersmith heard the muffled crack of a twig breaking and then the wet slap of a leafy branch.

"Who's there?" he said.

A voice answered from the darkness beside the path, almost at their elbows.

"It's me, Campbell. Say something else. Guide me to you."

"We're here, sir. Right here. Do you see the lanterns?"

"Ah, there you are."

Campbell stepped out from under the trees and let out a deep breath. His shaggy grey hair was mussed and full of leaves, and the shoulder of his jacket was torn. A long streak of mud ran from his left hip to his ankle. He shook Hammersmith's hand.

"I slipped down an incline of some sort. Didn't see it in the dark and then got hopelessly turned around. It's a lucky break for me you hollered out when you did or I'd have been lost in there forever."

It was the most Hammersmith had heard the big man say, but he understood. It was easy to lose one's composure under the dark silent trees.

"Where's Inspector Day?"

Campbell blinked and looked all round them at the path and the trees, as if Day might suddenly swing down and land among them.

"I'd actually hoped he was with you."

"You left him?"

"I thought I saw something in the woods and circled round to investigate. When I returned to the spot where we were standing, Mr Day was gone. I struck out in pursuit, but got turned around myself."

"What did you think you saw?" Grimes said.

"It was nothing."

"It must have been something if you left Inspector Day in the woods," Hammersmith said. "Let's find him before he freezes to death out here. And then I'll want to have a word with you, Mr Campbell."

16

———❊———

The American stood back in the trees and watched the other men on the path. He knew Cal Campbell. He also knew the policeman from London. He had sat behind him on the train. There was another man dressed in the uniform of a policeman, and the American guessed that he was the local lawman. He and Campbell seemed to be friendly. The American's rifle was slung over his shoulder, and he reached up, fingered the trigger, ran his tongue over his teeth and through the hole that separated his jaw from the rest of his face. Its pink tip left a silvery trail in the broken lantern light.

He pulled the rifle off his shoulder and sighted down the barrel. He lined up each of the men in turn and mimicked pulling the trigger. But there were too many of them and he was too close. He felt confident that he could kill at least two of them quickly, but the third might reach him *before he could line up the last shot. He slung the rifle back over his shoulder and moved farther back into the trees.*

There was plenty of time. No need to rush things. He had waited more than twenty years and he could wait another day. He would need to find shelter for the night, though. The woods were too cold and too crowded with policemen. The American had seen a building on the hill that seemed deserted. A perfect place to stay the night.

17

Day stopped in midstride and listened. He had heard something nearby, something almost subliminal. The grey man with the hideous face was still out there in the woods, and Day had no idea whether the man was dangerous or a friend. He was being careful.

The sound came again. A tiny high-pitched whistle. A chirp. He crouched and brought his lantern down close to the forest floor. There, nearly invisible, black and white against the ice and mud and grey thickets, was a round ball of fluff, its beak open to the sky, the pink maw of its throat as big around as Day's little finger.

He stood and scanned the closest trees, looking for a nest. He moved the lantern in a circle and turned slowly, careful not to step on the baby bird at his feet. He saw nothing.

He squatted again and patted his jacket.

"I know I have . . ." he said. "Aha."

He supposed he was talking to the bird, but he knew it didn't understand. It just sat there in its damp makeshift nest in the mud, its beak trembling at him. He reached into a pocket and pulled out a half-eaten biscuit from the train. It was hard and he broke it apart, letting the crumbs fall to the ground, and fished in his palm for the nuts and raisins that had been baked into it. He found three raisins and one piece of a walnut. He decided the walnut might be too difficult for the bird to deal with and let it fall through his fingers. He scooped a palmful of slush from the top of a log and dropped the raisins into it. The bird chirped again and opened its beak.

"Patience, little one," Day said.

He scanned the woods, alert for the grey man and for the bird's parents. But he was alone.

In a few moments, he fished the raisins out of the handful of water and squeezed them gently between his thumb and finger. They still seemed shriveled and dense, but the bird was shaking with hunger or anticipation, and so he poked a raisin into its beak. The raisin immediately disappeared down the bird's eager throat. Its beak never closed. He gave it another one and waited to see if there would be any problems. He didn't think magpies probably ate raisins in the wild, in the woods. But this one seemed to have an insatiable appetite for them, and so he poked the last raisin into its beak.

He sat cross-legged in front of the bird and watched it. The raisins had changed nothing. It sat trembling in the leaves, occasionally chirping, its beak open.

He found his flask in another pocket and opened it, tipped some of the brandy into his mouth. He held the half-empty flask out and showed it to the bird.

"I don't suppose you'd care for a bracer, would you? No, I thought not."

He smiled and plugged the top of the flask, put it back in his pocket.

"What happens to you if I go on my way, little chum?" he said.

He looked at the trees again, hoping to see a nest or an anxious adult bird, but of course he saw nothing. His visibility extended perhaps four feet into the trees.

"Will you learn to fly? Will your mother come to feed you?"

He sighed.

"We both know something will eat you. Or you'll simply die here in the snow and then bugs will come when things warm up out here. Bugs are something, too, I suppose. So, yes, you will be eaten. That's how it works, isn't it? You've left the nest too early and now you'll be a victim of . . . of what? The forest, the world, the natural way of things?"

He reached down and gathered up the ball of fuzz. It was ridiculously lightweight. He turned it over and noticed that there were no feathers on its belly. The skin was nearly translucent, and he could see its heart beating, see its dark organs arranged within the compact globe of its body. He touched a fingertip, gently, to the smooth grey-pink casing and felt its pulse against his own.

"Are you supposed to have feathers there?" he said. "Are you sick? Were you kicked out of the nest?"

The bird closed its beak and kicked out with a twiglike leg. He turned it back over in his hand so that it could sit upright.

"Well, you'll freeze to death out here, at any rate. Not a good idea to leave home without your feathers on a night like this. I'd best do something about you."

He tucked the bird away into the empty pocket that had held the biscuit and he stood up. He checked to make sure there was room enough for the bird and arranged the flap of his pocket so that it could get air. He bent, carefully, and picked up the lantern by its handle, checked the trees once more for a nest, and continued on his way, listening for the random chirp of his new companion.

18

When Hammersmith, Campbell, and Grimes returned to the inn, it was just before dawn and smoke was already pouring upward from the twin chimneys. Grimes left the other two at the door with a promise to return after washing up and getting a bite to eat. Inspector Day had not been found, and the men were anxious to recruit more bodies to aid in the search. Campbell opened the inn's door and waved Hammersmith through to the common room, where they were surprised to find Inspector Day sitting before one of the two fires, sipping at a steaming mug of cider, still wearing his quilted vest and heavy boots.

Day stood and greeted them warmly when they entered the room. Hammersmith was speechless, and Campbell seemed happier to see the inspector than either of them would have expected.

Bennett Rose, looking sleepless and bleary-eyed, emerged from the door at the back of the room and counted heads, then returned a moment later with two cups of hot tea and a plate of tiny sweet cakes. The men stripped off their wet overcoats and hung them on hooks near the fire. They stacked their boots on the hearth, where they steamed. Hammersmith noticed a small wooden box filled with straw on the stones near the fire. He glanced at Day and saw the inspector watching him with a mischievous smile.

"What happened to your face, Sergeant?"

Hammersmith touched his cheek and winced. "I'll tell you all about it," he said. "But how are you here ahead of us?"

"I've been here for hours," Day said. "Or perhaps it only seems like it's been hours."

"But I lost you in the woods," Campbell said.

"Yes, about that," Day said. "Why did you leave me?"

"I apologize. I thought I saw something and wanted a better look. I expected you to stay where you were, but you left me."

"What did you see?"

"I'm sorry?"

"In the woods. What did you see that caused you to run off?"

"It was nothing."

"What did you think it was?"

"There was nothing there, so what does it matter?"

"Was it a man with a hole in his face? More than a scar, a great gaping maw where his jaw might ordinarily be expected?"

Behind them, at the kitchen door, Bennett Rose gasped and dropped a cup. It clattered on the stone floor and rolled for an instant before shattering against the wainscoting. Rose dropped to one knee and began mopping up tea. Hammersmith jumped up and went to help, and Day noticed that the sergeant was covered in muck from head to toe.

"You do look as if you've had an adventure," Day said.

"We've spent half the night looking for you."

"I had my compass, my knife, a good pair of boots. You needn't have worried."

"We thought you were lost."

"I was. But then I wasn't. As soon as I heard the whoosh of flames from the furnaces, I knew I was close to the tree line, and I simply followed the noise out." Day swiveled in his seat as Hammersmith returned to the fire. Bennett Rose was already on his way back to the kitchen, holding the fragments of the broken cup in the palm of one hand and a sopping dishcloth in the other. "Mr Rose," Day said, "why were you surprised just now?"

"No time for talk, sir. I should take care of this mess."

"Was it because you recognized my description of the man in the woods?"

"Man in the woods, sir?"

"Mr Rose, you surprise me. For an innkeeper, you're a terrible liar."

Rose shook his head and hurried away through the kitchen door. Hammersmith turned to Day and raised an eyebrow.

"Shall I follow?" he said. "I may be able to make him talk."

"No," Day said. "Let him be. He wants to tell us what's troubling him, but he hasn't quite got his courage up yet. Let him sleep on it and he may tell us about it in the morning."

Hammersmith glanced back at the kitchen door. "It's morning now, isn't it? In the technical sense, I mean." But he walked reluctantly to where Day and Campbell sat by the fire. He took a brocade-covered chair across from the inspector.

"I believe you've just now ruined Mr Rose's chair, Sergeant," Day said. "He may decide not to talk to us, after all."

Hammersmith held his arms out in front of him and looked down at himself. "I'm dry. The mud should brush out of the upholstery without difficulty."

"Ah, of course. You think of everything."

"You seem a bit tetchy."

"Not at all. But you did leave me in the woods, after all."

"Actually, I believe you left us in the woods."

"Quite so."

"I only came back to refill the oil in our lanterns."

"You were going back out tonight?"

"Couldn't leave you there."

"I'm touched."

Hammersmith pointed to the little wooden box by the fire. He raised an eyebrow.

"Have a look," Day said. "But be quiet. He's only just settled down."

Hammersmith stood and walked to the hearth. He looked down into the top of the box and then crouched to get a closer look. "It's a bird," he said. "Did you bring back a souvenir from the woods, Mr Day?"

"I'm thinking of promoting the little fellow to sergeant already."

"Looks more like an inspector to me."

"Well, we'll see how he does. He'll have to work his way through the ranks, same as anyone else. I rescued him. Rose gave me that box for him."

Hammersmith stood and shook his head. "Kind of him."

"Actually," Day said, "Mr Campbell might be able to help us with our new ward."

"How is that?" Campbell said.

"You're the resident expert on birds. What should we do for him?"

"What have you done for him so far?"

"I gave him raisins from a biscuit in my pocket. And I like to think I saved him from being eaten by a fox."

"I'm amazed he didn't choke on raisins. They must have been awfully firm."

"They were."

"Baby birds generally have their food chewed for them."

"He's remarkably hardy, I think. I'm quite proud of him."

"You should be. But you might moisten anything you give to him in the future."

"I'll keep that in mind."

"Fascinating as your bird may be," Hammersmith said, "we found something, too, Grimes and me." He reached into his jacket and frowned. He opened the front of the jacket wider and checked the other side. "There it is. Forgot where the pocket was. Look at this."

He pulled out a small cloth bundle and unwrapped it. The stains had been folded on the inside surface to help preserve them. He found the seams at the tops of the shoulders and held the child's dress up for Day to see. Day sat forward and peered at it, moving his head to take advantage of the light from the fireplace. He didn't touch the dress. Campbell stood and looked over Day's shoulder.

"Is that blood?" he said.

"I think it might be," Hammersmith said.

"The missing child is a boy," Day said, "and I presume the missing woman is too big to wear this."

"A nightshirt perhaps?" Campbell said.

"I thought of that," Hammersmith said.

"But a flower pattern around the hem here."

"Yes."

"Curious."

"The doctor will be here soon," Hammersmith said.

"Good thing, too," Day said. "And good of you to find something for him to do, Sergeant."

Hammersmith smiled grimly and folded the dress, putting it back in his pocket. "I rather think it's him who will put us to work," he said.

"Who is this doctor?" Campbell said.

"Dr Kingsley," Day said. "A colleague of ours."

"To help if we find the boy alive?"

"Well, that, yes. But the doctor is, in his way, another detective of the Yard. He often finds clues in the evidence we bring him."

Campbell stood and wiped his mouth on the back of his hand.

"I'll turn in. If you chaps are going back out there in the daylight, whatever time, I'll go with you, if you'll have me. The boy's not dead. We'll find him, and your doctor will help him."

Campbell nodded at each of them in turn, and they nodded back and watched him cross the room and mount the stairs. He turned at the landing and disappeared from view.

"Mr Hammersmith," Day said. "What do we know about Mr Campbell?"

"Very little. I'm not sure he's much of an expert on birds. I might have given the same advice about our baby there. He seems quite anxious to find the boy, but seems dismissive of the parents."

"He does. I wonder why."

"He knows more than he's said."

"Indeed he does. So does our innkeeper. And I think Mr Campbell was going to tell us about the man I saw in the woods before Mr Rose caused that commotion with the broken cup. There are secrets within secrets here."

"And yet they asked us to come."

"I think tomorrow will be interesting."

"I'm afraid," Hammersmith said, "that the boy's parents may be dead, and that everyone here knows it."

"I'm not sure you're right, Sergeant, but if you are, I hope we at least find the boy alive."

"And quickly. It's cold out there."

"Well," Day said. "We shall be of no use to anyone without at least a couple of hours of sleep."

"You go. I won't be able to sleep knowing the boy may be out there in the cold and the dark, feeling abandoned and alone."

"Yes, I'm sure he'll sense your lack of sleep and be comforted by it."

"I didn't—"

"Never mind. Go get whatever sleep you can, and we'll be back at the search bright and early. I promise."

Hammersmith moved toward the stairs, but turned back when Day called his name.

"Mr Hammersmith?"

"Sir?"

"It might be a good idea to lock your bedroom door tonight."

"I always do."

19

———◆◆◆———

The American circled the schoolhouse in the dark, looking for an easy entrance point. The wind was picking up, and snow obscured his sight lines to the village and, in the other direction, the forest. A deep purple hue was visible low in the sky. Dawn was coming. He had followed the men far enough to be sure they had finished for the night and were headed home. There were no tracks or footprints in the snow leading to the schoolhouse, and he concluded that the building wasn't in use.

The door and windows were locked, so the American used the stock of his rifle to break out the large picture window in the back wall, facing the woods. He knocked the remaining chunks of glass out of the frame and pushed his pack and rifle through into the cold dark room. He had two squirrels on a string and he slung them around his neck before climbing through the window. He stood for a moment and let his eyes adjust. He sniffed and identified the overlapping odors of chalk dust and soap and age. The little building contained a single large room with an open door leading to a small storage compartment that had been converted to a crude water closet. Perfect for the American's needs. He didn't imagine that he'd be in Blackhampton for more than another day, but no matter how long his job took to complete, he now had a good base of operations.

He dragged two student desks in front of the broken window and tipped one on end atop the other to keep out some of the wind and snow. He checked the front door and saw there was no way to open it without a key. He'd have to leave the window uncovered when he left this place, but what did he care if a little snow blew in and wet the floor?

There was a framed chalkboard made of black slate near the front of the room, and the American pulled it free from its stand and laid it flat on the floor. He smashed a chair against the edge of the cabinet and broke pieces off of it, laying them on top of the slate. He found a book about talking ducks and tore it apart, wadded the pages, and layered them among the splintered pieces of chair. He had a small waterproof box of matches in his coat pocket, and he used one of them to start a fire on his makeshift slate platform. He had three matches left and decided he would have to replenish his supply before he left Blackhampton. The broken chair burned slowly, and the American moved the desk back from the broken window far enough to allow the smoke an escape route. It wouldn't do to suffocate when he was so close to his goal.

He skinned and dressed the squirrels and set them on the slate by the fire, turning them when the fat began to bubble. When he ate, he noticed that some of the squirrel meat was burnt and some was still raw, but he didn't particularly care as long as he could keep it all down. He had learned long ago to cover his cheek with the palm of his left hand so that food wouldn't fall out of his mouth. It made eating a time-consuming process. When he had finished, he wiped his greasy hands on his trousers and put out the fire. He shoved the back of a chair against the front door of the schoolhouse, under the knob, and bunked down in the far corner of the room.

The sky in the east began to change color, turning for a few minutes the pale grey color of the American's eyes, but he didn't see it. He was asleep.

20

There was no key in the door. The innkeeper had left them vulnerable, with no easy means to lock themselves in. Walter Day checked under his bed and found that the chamber pot with Hammersmith's vomit and the rest of the stew had been removed. A fresh basin had been left in its place. He set the small straw-filled box containing the baby bird on the vanity next to the washbasin. The ball of fluff was asleep, breathing heavily in and out. He imagined its heart beating under the soft feathers. He hoped that the little boy, Oliver, was sleeping somewhere and had made it through another night.

He was dressing for bed when he heard a small noise in the hall outside, a rustle of movement so faint as to go unnoticed if he hadn't been on edge, half listening for it. He turned down the lamp, went to his door, and cracked it open. The flow of shadows among shadows at the end of the hall caught his eye and he closed the door again, pressed his cheek against it, and listened.

He could hear movement outside the next room, Hammersmith's room. There was the faint sound of metal scraping against metal, then soft footsteps approached Day's door. The inspector pulled back and looked around the room for his revolver. The doorknob jiggled and the lock turned over. Day stepped closer and put his ear back against the door and listened as muffled footsteps retreated down the stairs. He tried the doorknob. It turned a quarter of an inch each way, but wouldn't budge farther. He had been locked in his room.

Day crossed to his bed and rummaged inside his open suitcase. He produced a flat black leather pouch and flipped it open to reveal an array of heavy-looking brass keys. He chose one and returned to the locked door, where he crouched and went to work. It took him less than a minute to draw back the lock and open the door.

He stepped into the hall and pulled the door shut behind him, then crept quietly to the stairs and down.

21

Day paused in the shadows of the inn's common room. The twin fires were still blazing, but the lamps had been extinguished and no one was in sight. Bruised early sunlight filtered through the high windows, turning the room purple. From his vantage point on the stairs, Day would have seen anyone leaving the inn by the big front door, which meant that whoever had locked them in their rooms had gone out through the door behind the bar. Day crossed the room silently and poked his head through the door.

He saw a narrow dining room with an oak table and six chairs. A muddy brown tapestry with an embroidered family crest was hung behind the table, which was already set for breakfast. Day crossed to another door on the far side of the room and pushed it open with the tips of his fingers.

The kitchen was small and tidy. A medium-size range dominated most of the far wall, framed by a pair of wooden chairs with straw seats. A faded blue rug had been rolled out on the floor. The oven door was open, and Day could see a roasting pan inside, today's breakfast slowly cooking. Turning his head, Day could see through a narrow doorway into the larder, which was hung with raw meats: rabbits, a suckling pig, and one quarter of a deer. There were no dishes in evidence, and Day assumed that, if the kitchen was here on the ground floor, the scullery must be in the basement. He moved quietly through the room and past the swinging animal carcasses to another open door. A cold breeze wafted through the larder, cooling the meat and leaving a thin coat of snow on the stone floor. He halted again, his back against the outside wall next to the door, and crouched down before looking out.

Outside, a low fence, designed to protect the larder from hungry animals, shielded the inn from the landscape. Day edged forward and gripped the top of the fence, then raised his head to look over it. Calvin Campbell was three feet away from him, looking in the opposite direction. He was squatting by the town well, hidden from the other side of the road by the big stone structure. Day ducked his head back down behind the fence. He was sure it was no coincidence that Campbell was out and about. It was the bird-watcher who had locked the other guests' rooms before going out into the night.

A moment later, he heard footsteps and risked another peek over the fence. A loose formation of village men marched past, bleary-eyed and stooped, miners on their way to the new seam. There seemed to be fewer of them than Day had seen from the carriage the previous evening. Their clothing had been laundered and patched many times, but would never come close to being clean, and some of them wore soft caps pulled down low on their brows. One of them coughed and stumbled and fell to his knees beside the road. Two of the others hurried to him, lifted him under his armpits and, supporting their spasming friend between them, returned to the group. The men walked past the well and the inn's short fence without noticing the inspector or the bird-watcher, both poorly hidden scant feet away from them. They followed the road around a high slag pile and an abandoned pit and then out of sight around the corner of a far building.

As soon as the miners were gone, Calvin Campbell jumped up from his spot behind the old well and hurried down the road in the direction the miners had come from. Day stood and followed from a discreet distance, trusting the light snowfall to keep him partially hidden.

The cobblestones of the town's main road gleamed in the gaslight from streetlamps set every few yards, ice sparkling in the mud between the stones. The buildings along the main road through the center of town were tall and proud and architecturally similar, unlike everything that radiated out from them. Someone had once put thought and effort into planning and building this village, before haphazard growth had laid waste to their good intentions. Beyond the first few yards along the main street, there seemed to be no rhyme or reason remaining. Tudor-style dwellings nestled alongside split-rail cabins and ancient mud-daubed huts. It looked to him as though the place had come together in fits and starts, with no plan, and nothing had ever been torn down to make way for anything better. Next to the blacksmith was the telegraph office, closed and silent at this early hour. Day watched his shadow flow and change and grow as he crossed the road. He was alone and in a strange place and he missed his wife. He missed her terrible cooking. He missed the smell of her hair and the sound of her bare feet in the hall as she approached his bedroom door in the middle of the night. He wondered what she might make of the strange village, like some island far from London, populated by natives who refused to abandon their sinking homes. Or, perhaps, couldn't leave if they wanted to.

But for all that it was doomed, he could still see the appeal of Blackhampton. It was small, but open, the houses and shops and community buildings spread out in a way that London was not. Day had come from Devon, where there was room to move about, and had lived the better part of the past year in London, where there was not. Blackhampton had a bit of the feel of Devon for him. He liked being able to walk without checking for horseshit at every step.

But the air here wasn't filled with the river scent of Devon or the body odors of London. It was burnt and, even filtered through the heavy white snowflakes swirling around his face, it stung his nostrils. The great furnaces filled the sky with smoke, and there was nothing else to breathe. One would, he presumed, eventually become used to it, but after a single night in Blackhampton his throat was as raw as if he'd smoked a pipe the wrong way round. He felt he was choking on ashes. He cleared his throat quietly, aware that any noise would echo through the empty street and alert Calvin Campbell to his presence.

The road curved to the west ahead of them, and Campbell took a furtive look back before following the bend and disappearing from sight. Day stood calmly in the dark doorway of an apothecary and made sure Campbell wasn't doubling back. A spider emerged from a crack in the stones beside Day and he marveled that it was awake and moving about in the bitter cold. Surely it should be hibernating, or whatever it was that spiders did in the winter. The early spring had clearly played havoc with the natural way of things. Day moved away from the wall, reluctant to frighten such a brave soul. From nowhere, a dunnock, grey and brown, flew at the wall and gobbled up the spider, then flew off, past Day, and disappeared against the late winter sky.

Day stepped out of the shadows of the apothecary. He approached the road's curve carefully, in no particular rush. As far as he could tell, there was nowhere for Campbell to go. The village was small and, if he remembered correctly, the road ended just out of town. Even if the bird-watcher broke for the distant trees, Day would be able to see him for quite a distance as he crossed the open fields.

But when he peered around the bend, Campbell was nowhere in sight. Day moved out into the middle of the road and looked in every direction. There was a smattering of smaller stone buildings, a butcher shop, a fish and chips, a farrier, and a handful of cottages and outbuildings. Ahead was the parish church, towering over the homes and businesses nearby. It sat directly on the path, a destination point, whether one intended that or not. Beyond the church, the road ended. There was no dirt path or trail through the tall grasses; it simply stopped. There was nowhere for Campbell to hide except in one of the buildings, and there was no way to tell which one he might be in.

Day stood there for a long time, turning in small circles, surveying the road in both directions. It was possible that Campbell was watching him from a window, but Day didn't care. There was nothing to do but draw Campbell out and question him, or give up and go back to the inn. Day waited for a quarter of an hour, hoping that the giant would leave his hiding place, but nothing happened. The sun began to edge over the tops of the distant trees, and shadows changed, reached and clawed up the sides of the tiny cottages and over the thatched roof of the butcher shop. Birds began to sing.

Day gazed at the church. Mrs Brothwood's note had hinted at mysteries being kept there, and he was tempted to approach, knock on the huge oaken doors and confront whomever he might find. But he wasn't prepared for that. Better to wait until he was better rested and the village, outside of the early-rising miners, had begun to stir.

But he wasn't ready to give up on the disappearing Campbell just yet.

Day backtracked and stopped outside the telegraph office. He pounded on the door until a grumpy old man answered, still rubbing sleep from his eyes with a gnarled fist. Day introduced himself and the man beckoned the inspector inside. The door closed behind him, and silence cloaked Blackhampton once more.

INTERLUDE 1

ANDERSONVILLE PRISON,
CONFEDERATE GEORGIA, 1865

C al? Calvin Campbell. That you, boy?"
Cal didn't look up. He stood still, staring at the louse
wriggling between his fingers. He frowned. The voice
had interrupted his count. He cursed and poked the louse into his
mouth, crunching it between his teeth. He felt a hand on his shoulder and he jerked away, his body tensed for a fight.

"Cal, it's me. It's Joe Poole."

The name stirred shadows in his memory. Joe Poole? Cal still
didn't look up, but he struggled to remember. There had been a kid
in his regiment, a cheerful lad of no more than eighteen or nine-

teen, with curly red hair and an infectious grin and a habit of winking when he talked, letting you in on some private joke, even when the subject was dead serious. Cal shook his head and his long matted hair brushed against his face.

"Joe Poole died at Gettysburg," he said.

"Well, that's news to me, friend. I'm here, same as you, and I ain't dead yet."

Cal finally looked up. Far away, in every direction, were the high wooden walls of the prison. Thousands of men squatted between the walls in the thick mud. Cal could count the ribs of every one of those men. Their faces were sucked tight against their skulls, dead eyes under heavy ridges.

Cal was younger than most of the others, but larger, too, tall and broad-shouldered. Like the rest of them, his beard had grown out. He was one of nearly fourteen thousand British citizens who had enlisted to fight in the American Civil War. He had joined the Union army for the same reason most of his American friends had joined, and he had fought bravely alongside them until he was captured by Confederate soldiers and eventually taken to Andersonville Prison. Everyone here was a soldier, but there was no order.

The remains of Cal's torn and dirty uniform hung loosely on his body, but he counted himself lucky to have clothes at all. Smaller, weaker men routinely had their shirts and trousers stolen and then had to make do with scraps. Joe Poole was still wearing his blue Union jacket. It was soiled and the cuffs were frayed, but it was valuable and Cal knew it would be taken from him. He glared at Joe.

"You made me lose my tally," he said.

"You don't look so good," Joe said. But he winked when he said it, showing that he meant well, that there were no hard feelings.

"Go away."

"Good Lord, Cal, how long you been in here?"

"Sixty thousand. Almost sixty thousand. I lost count just now."

"Sixty thousand what, Cal?"

"Lice. I get them and I count them. Five hundred every day. I stop counting when I get five hundred."

"You pick five hundred lice offa yerself every day?"

"Not today. Lost count today."

"You pick five hundred lice offa yerself every day and you got fifty thousand."

"Sixty. Sixty thousand."

"How many days that make?"

"It hardly matters."

"That's too tough for me to figure. I don't do math."

"It's a lot of days."

"Everybody here have lice?"

"Haven't talked to everyone here yet, so I don't know."

"Cal, ain't you happy to see me?"

"Not especially."

"I thought we was friendly."

"We were. That's why I'm not happy to see you here."

Joe Poole stopped talking. Cal saw something white glistening in his arm hair and grabbed it between his long fingernails. He brought it up and looked at it more closely. It was a maggot, not a louse. It had rained the night before, and all the waste holes the prisoners had made, the holes they'd scraped dirt over, had burst open and boiled over with maggots. Cal didn't count maggots. He only counted lice. He popped it into his mouth and returned to searching himself for lice.

"It don't look so good here, Cal. This place? Seems real bad."

Cal ignored him.

"You got one of those?"

Cal looked up again and saw that Joe was pointing at a shebang. There were hundreds of shebangs spread out between the prison walls, makeshift shelters scrabbled together from pieces of old tents, tattered clothing too far gone to wear, sticks, mud, dried feces, and blankets. For a second he saw the place anew through Joe's eyes and he was horrified. He shook his head and sniffed and plucked another maggot from his arm.

"Cal, don't eat that. Quit eatin' them. It's a bug."

"Bugs are food, too." Cal tried to laugh and choked. He coughed and heaved, his empty stomach cramping. After another moment, his body settled. It took too much energy to vomit.

When he had stopped gagging, he held the maggot up in a mock salute. He stuck out his tongue and placed the maggot on it and drew his tongue slowly back in. He could feel the maggot blindly writhing across his tongue. He closed his lips and crunched down on it, releasing the tiny bit of precious liquid at its center. There was a spark of salt and it was gone.

"Oh, God, Cal, stop doin' that."

"How long have you been here, Joe?"

"I just now got here. Got captured at Chickamauga and moved around a bit, here and there. Thought I was lucky to see a familiar soul here, but it don't seem like it so much now."

Cal noticed that Joe didn't wink at him this time. Cal's stomach turned again, and he knew the sensation didn't come from eating the maggot. He had eaten too many of those now. It didn't bother him the way it had a couple of months ago.

"I'm sorry, Joe."

"Gosh, no, Cal. I'm glad to see a friend."

"I don't think I can be your friend, Joe. Friends are a bad idea here."

"Seems to me like this is the place you need a friend more than anything, Cal. More than anything."

Cal barely heard what Joe said. He turned his head and waved his arm: *Go away*. It was too hard here. There was no room for friends. Cal had made a friend his first day in Andersonville, and the man had died in his arms two weeks later, foaming at the mouth and bleeding from his ears. Cal had carried him to the wagon they brought through to collect the dead, and the man had weighed no more than a child. He had taken the man's blanket before giving him over to be taken to one of the mass graves outside the wall. The blanket was infested, and that was the night that Cal had begun counting lice.

Having a friend could only hurt a man in Andersonville.

"Cal, I don't know what to do." Joe's voice had become small and sad, like an echo. "I'm lookin' at this place and I don't see what there is for me here."

Cal walked away from Joe Poole. There was nothing Joe could do for him except make him care, and caring was a dangerous thing to do in Andersonville. Here it was every man for himself until death.

As far as Cal was concerned, the sooner death came, the better.

"Cal! We got a problem!"

Cal looked up from the work he was doing on their shelter. A sudden squall the night before had ripped a hole in the side of the shebang he shared with Joe Poole. It had been three weeks since Joe had come to Andersonville, and Cal's life had improved immeasurably. He still spent much of his day picking lice off his body and clothing, but he no longer counted them. He had other things to occupy his mind. He and Joe had built the shebang over a shallow hole they dug with their hands near the western perimeter of the stockade. They'd used bits of canvas tent material that they'd bartered for, sewn them over a framework of branches, and spackled it all over with mud. It wasn't waterproof, but it was warmer than sleeping in the open the way Cal had been before Joe came along.

He stepped outside and shielded his eyes. The rain had come and gone, and now the sky was bright and pale, almost white. Joe was running toward him. He estimated that Joe had lost at least twenty pounds in the last three weeks. But without Joe and his eternal optimism, Cal was sure he would have died already.

"What's the problem?" Cal said.

"It's Duane."

"Shite."

Joe made a *come on* motion and Cal followed him at a trot. Running used energy they couldn't afford to waste, but Cal could no longer see the point in being alive in Andersonville if he wasn't there to help his friends.

Duane was one of a handful of new kids they'd taken under their wing. He'd been puny to begin with, and came into the prison without shoes or a hat. He told them he'd been grateful to be captured. His regiment had run out of supplies and had taken to hunting in the woods for squirrels and rabbits. Of course, squirrel and rabbit sounded like gourmet dining after a week at the prison. The only meat they got here was generally already rotting. Cal figured the boy had weighed maybe a hundred and twenty pounds when he'd arrived, and Andersonville certainly hadn't fattened him up. There was a time when Cal would have been able to pick Duane up and sling him over his shoulder like a newborn calf.

He followed Joe until he saw other prisoners running and he joined them, losing sight of his friend in the crush of skin and bone. The crowd had gathered as close to the southern perimeter fence as it could get. It was the section of their little village where criminals were herded. Hundreds of prisoners surrounded a bare spot in the dirt where Duane was facing off against two emaciated men. The men were caked with dirt and their bones pressed against their flesh from inside. Their hair was long and dark and filled with mud and it swung from side to side as they moved. They were so starved that they moved slowly. But everyone was starved and everyone's perceptions had changed. The action seemed quick to Cal. One of the two men had a stick that was sharpened to a point at one end, and Cal wondered, for just a moment, where the man had got a knife to sharpen it. He realized that the man had probably rubbed it against a rock for days on end and at the same time he realized that it didn't matter. The stick was pointed at his friend Duane.

Cal glanced up at the guard tower that jutted out of the perimeter fence above them and to the east. The guard was close enough for Cal to see the color of his eyes: pale grey, almost as colorless as the sky. The guard's rifle rested casually on his shoulder, but Cal knew it was a pose. Grey Eyes was ready to shoot the instant anyone stepped over the dead line onto the eighteen feet of bare earth that was off-limits to prisoners. Crossing the dead line put a man too close to the fence and guards were authorized to shoot, no questions asked. Duane and his attackers were within inches of that line. Cal searched the crowd for Joe and found him near the second of the two attackers, dancing around, out of reach of the homemade spear.

"Bring him back, Joe!" Cal nodded his head toward the guard tower. Joe winked back at him to let him know that he'd heard and understood.

Cal punched the nearest attacker in the ribs and the man staggered backward. Cal's fists lacked the strength they'd had before Andersonville, but the other man's rib cage was a xylophone and there was no padding of fat or muscle to protect him. He could tell the blow had hurt. From the corner of his eye, he saw Duane stumble and fall dangerously close to the dead line. And he saw Joe grab Duane's feet and pull, dragging him slowly away from the line.

The second attacker had wheeled around and was approaching Joe with his spear. Cal reeled toward him, his adrenaline rush fading already and his energy reserves dangerously low. But as weak as he felt, he knew the others were faring the same or worse. He could see that Duane's attackers were running out of steam now that they'd encountered resistance.

But Duane didn't realize that the fight was winding down and he twisted away from Joe, staggering to his feet. He pulled his jacket tight around him and lurched across the dead line.

"My jacket!" he said. "Mine."

The first shot hit Duane in the shoulder and spun him around. He went down on one knee, and for a split second his eyes met Cal's. There was no understanding in them, just an unspoken question. The puzzlement of a loyal dog. The rifle report bounced off the high wooden planks of the fence, and the sound of the second shot was lost in the echo. The top of Duane's head disappeared in a purple spray of brains and gore.

Cal looked up at Grey Eyes. The guard had already slung his rifle back over his shoulder and stood casually watching, leaning on the stock. When he saw Cal, he smirked.

Cal swallowed hard and looked around him. Everyone else—the attackers, the crowd, even Joe—had disappeared, had quietly slunk back to their shebangs and their chess games and their endless grooming rituals. Cal and Grey Eyes and Duane were three lonely points in a triangle.

Cal clenched his fists and looked down at Duane's body. The boy's foot still twitched. The jacket he had tried so hard to keep was drenched with blood and would be stiff and useless within a couple of hours. Cal couldn't even move the body because it was over the dead line and out of reach. There was nothing he could do for Duane.

He turned and walked away, and he could feel those grey eyes watching him with every step he took.

The gates opened and the dead wagon rolled through at ten o'clock. Duane's body had been stripped and he lay naked in the mud.

Cal and Joe had divided his clothing between them. The extra layers would help keep them alive during the deadly cold nights. It was the only good thing that could come from Duane's death. They had tried to wash Duane's blood out of the jacket, but the waste in the river water had only made it worse. They'd buried the jacket instead. In a few days, they hoped to be able to dig it back up and use it to help fortify their shebang. By then, it was possible the smell might fade.

There were only seven dead this morning. Some mornings there were as many as a hundred bodies waiting for the wagon. Cal waited for the others to pile their dead friends on the wagon, then he and Joe each took an arm and a leg and swung Duane onto the hard planks of the wagon bed. It was a struggle. Duane didn't weigh more than a hundred pounds, but it was dead weight, limp and unyielding, and they were weak.

The driver shouted to the horses, and the wagon turned around and rolled back through the gates. Cal and Joe followed after. They had volunteered for wagon duty this morning. It was a coveted job because it got them outside the fence for a few minutes.

Cal walked past Grey Eyes. He could feel the guard watching him. Cal's fists clenched and unclenched, but he kept walking, kept his eyes glued to the ground. And then he was outside the stockade.

He took a deep breath. The air smelled different out here, away from the crush of unwashed bodies, the shallow holes where the men buried their waste, and the stretch of river that leached filth from the surrounding mud. The clean air was almost solid, like something he could eat if his teeth were sharp enough. He gulped it in. For a moment, and only for a moment, he felt like a man again.

The wagon led them to a long shallow trench, and they unloaded the bodies, pulling each dead man onto the ground with a heavy thunk, hefting him between them and swinging him gently. They gave Duane an extra swing, getting him as high in the air as they could manage before letting go. They watched him fly free, his bony arms and legs twisting gracefully before disappearing over the lip of dry earth to land somewhere out of sight atop yesterday's dead. Neither Cal nor Joe looked into that trench. Each of them knew the odds. They'd be down among the dead men themselves one day. Maybe soon enough to keep Duane company.

When it was empty, the wagon rolled away. It would return in a couple of hours with the day's bread rations, stacked where the bodies had been. Cal knew that the wagon wouldn't even be swept out before the bread was piled in.

Grey Eyes gestured with his rifle, and they turned back toward the stockade. Men rarely tried to escape. They were too weak, from hunger, from thirst, from lack of sleep, and from the parasites living under their skin. They were no match for a rifle.

Cal gulped clean air one more time before passing through the gate. He held it in his lungs and listened as the doors swung shut behind him. He looked at Joe and saw something new in the other man's eyes. Watching Duane fly had changed something in Joe. He reached out to touch Joe's shoulder, expecting the ready smile and the wink, some sign to indicate that Joe would be all right, that the prison hadn't broken him. But Joe only shook his head and walked away.

Cal watched him go. He opened his mouth and finally took another breath and let Andersonville fill his lungs.

Cal woke early, but the sun was already peering over the horizon and pale light shone through the flap of the shebang he shared with Joe Poole. Cal had heard something, some noise that had awakened him. He looked over, but the old shirt that Joe used as bedding was wadded and abandoned in the corner. Cal rubbed his eyes and struggled out of the low shebang on his hands and knees. He stood and stretched and groaned and looked around. Few prisoners were moving about yet.

He went behind the shebang and relieved himself, but standing still made him feel anxious.

He couldn't place it. There was a strange smell in the air or a taste at the back of his throat, a tingle somewhere at the base of his brain. Something was wrong. More wrong than the usual wrongness of Andersonville. Without knowing why, he took off at a trot toward the corner of the stockade where Duane had died.

He passed two prisoners who were already playing chess with rocks in the dirt. One of them looked up at him and shook his head, as if he knew what was happening. But Cal understood that he was wasting energy moving so fast. He was a veteran by now of the prison system and should know better than to try to move quickly. That was all the other prisoner had meant with his gesture, but it felt like more than that. Cal didn't slow down.

Until he reached the dead line.

Joe stood there by the low interior fence with his back to Cal. Cal called out Joe's name, but his voice sounded soft and low even to him and he was certain that Joe hadn't heard him. But Joe turned his head and smiled. He had been waiting for Cal. Joe pointed, and Cal looked across the line. Against the wall of the stockade, eighteen feet past the dead line, there was a patch of green against the brown. Cal squinted and the green blur came into focus as a stem with two small leaves that were spread out across the mud. At the top of the stem was a small yellow bud. It was a dandelion. The first growing thing that Cal had seen in five months.

He caught his breath and looked over at Joe, but Joe was already stepping over the low fence, passing the dead line. Cal called out, but the air was caught in his chest and his voice was a whisper.

"Joe."

Joe didn't turn, didn't indicate that he had heard. He walked slowly, confidently, toward the tiny green and yellow plant. The dirt at Joe's feet exploded, and Cal looked up at the guard tower. Grey Eyes leaned against the low railing of the deck, his rifle pointed casually in Joe's direction. Cal reached out, but he couldn't make his voice work, he couldn't call out.

Grey Eyes pulled his trigger again and the leg of Joe's filthy trousers parted at the seam, a puff of linen escaping into the air. At the same time, a pockmark appeared at Joe's feet. He kept moving, seemed not to notice.

Cal reached out to Grey Eyes and the guard noticed him, smiled, and pulled the trigger again. Joe's shoulder exploded in a spray of gristle and bone. He staggered, but kept his feet. Cal looked back at Joe, and a split second of time extended indefinitely as Joe slowly winked. There was no pain; Cal understood that. Joe smiled and there was something new in his eyes, and something gone from them. Cal understood what Joe was telling him: It was all over. Andersonville wasn't there anymore. Joe was free. He was flying.

Joe reached out toward the dandelion, his face a mask of joy, and he couldn't possibly have felt it when Grey Eyes's fourth bullet smashed his skull and pounded a small piece of his brain into the dirt under the dandelion's leaves.

Cal stopped himself, his fingers inches away from the dead line, and he looked up to see that Grey Eyes's rifle was pointed at him. He looked back and watched as Joe's legs buckled and he fell sideways, already gone, his good shoulder taking the impact of all that useless meat.

Cal closed his eyes and all he saw was Joe, that good man, that good friend, the only person who cared whether Cal lived or died.

Joe was winking at him that one last time.

22

━━━◦◦◦━━━

A thin band of clear sky ran across the horizon east of Blackhampton. Above it was smooth grey cloud cover, completely unbroken. The sun rose and was visible for a half an hour from the main road of the village, then passed up behind the clouds and was gone again. Nearly an hour passed before the sky broke and the air filled with billowing pristine white snow, unsullied as yet by the pervasive ash from the mines.

By nine o'clock that morning, the road was invisible. So were the distant trees, the grass, the roofs of Blackhampton's homes and businesses. Workers at the new seam were sent home for the day. Jessica Perkins didn't go to the schoolhouse. She knew that parents would have their children working, shoveling snow from front stoops and rooftops before the weight of it could cause damage or even force their houses straight down into the tunnels below (as had happened to the Baggs family home the previous winter). And so no one discovered that the schoolhouse had been put to other use in the night. The grey-eyed American awoke and rolled up his bedding, cleaned and loaded his rifle, and headed out into the storm to find breakfast. At the inn, Inspector Day made a halfhearted attempt to wake his sergeant, but finally decided to let him sleep. Instead he went in search of something to feed his always-hungry baby bird. At the northernmost edge of the village, right outside the depot, young Freddy Higgins shivered in his carriage and listened for the warning bell from the train, which he hoped was still on schedule. He had brought heavy blankets with him, but could not seem to get warm. Constable Grimes passed the giant furnaces and headed out toward the woods, hoping to be there and back before the men from Scotland Yard woke up. Bennett Rose fed the inn's twin fireplaces. He checked the various charms and wards he had hung around the ground floor doors and windows, and he closed his eyes in silent prayer for the visitors from London. Upstairs, Calvin Campbell lay on his bed and dreamed about his lover's absent smile, and wondered if that smile would ever return to her face. Down in the deepest old tunnels beneath Blackhampton, a man paced back and forth, staring at an unmarked grave scraped out of the rock and dirt and wondering how things had gone so wrong. He had no idea there was a storm up above, but he had just decided to quit the tunnels and see if there was news in the village.

The storm blew on, howling through the village like a curse, and more than one person shuddered, recalling the children's rhyme, the horrible singsong warning about Rawhead and Bloody Bones.

23

When Hammersmith awoke later that morning, he assumed it was still sunrise. His bedroom was dark and still. He sat up and spent a few minutes coughing so hard that his ribs hurt and his throat burned. When he had stopped, he rummaged through his suitcase for tooth powder and hurriedly readied himself, brushing his teeth and rinsing himself in the basin. He wiped his face with a clean towel and felt a sharp spike of pain. When he looked at the towel, there were streaks of fresh half-clotted blood. The gash in his cheek hadn't healed.

There was a knock at his door.

"One moment, please!" he shouted.

He was still in his underpants and vest. He made a quick check of his suitcase and realized that he had forgotten to bring a change of clothing. He cursed himself under his breath. He would have to hope that the previous day's clothes weren't too worse for the wear. But his jacket and trousers weren't in the wardrobe where he'd left them just a few hours before. His shirt hung there by itself. There was no iron in the room, and he'd never used one anyway, so he patted the wrinkles in his shirt with a damp hand, licked his thumb, and rubbed the worst of the dirt and blood stains. He put the shirt on and opened the door a crack, keeping his bare legs out of sight. Day was standing in the hall holding a wooden hanger up so that Hammersmith could see his own jacket and trousers.

"I took the liberty," Day said. "You were dead to the world when I checked on you earlier."

"Come in." Hammersmith looked both ways down the hall and opened the door wider so that Day could enter the room, then he shut the door quickly and took the hanger from Day.

Hammersmith's trousers had been brushed and pressed. The jacket was spotless.

"My father is a valet," Day said.

"I didn't know that."

"It's not something I generally mention. But I've learned a thing or two from him. There was nothing I could do about your shirt."

Hammersmith pulled the trousers on and tucked in his shirt. "Thank you," he said. "Did you grow up on an estate, then?"

"I did," Day said. "But it was not all one might wish."

"That seems to be the way of all childhood."

"Perhaps. Are you quite all right? I could hear you coughing from my room."

"I'm perfectly fine."

"Well, at least you've caught up to your sleep," Day said.

"Strange," Hammersmith said. "I don't usually sleep much at all."

"And I usually sleep more than I did. It's this place, I think."

"How is your little bird?"

"Mr Rose was kind enough to provide warm milk and bread. The bird's asleep now."

"Let's hope Rose didn't drug its milk. He seems to . . ." Hammersmith paused and turned his back to Day while he let out another long shuddering series of wet coughs. When he had caught his breath, he gave Day a sheepish smile. "My apologies."

"Are you sure you're all right?"

"Just the wet air in those woods, I imagine," Hammersmith said. "We should get moving."

"I don't suppose you've got another shirt you could wear? That one's beyond repair."

"I forgot to pack a change of clothing," Hammersmith said.

"Forgot? How could you . . . ? Never mind. At least wash your face. We do represent London for these people."

"But I did wash my face. Does it look bad?"

"You're straight out of a penny dreadful."

"Well, there's little I can do about it."

"You mystify me, Mr Hammersmith," Day said.

"Blackhampton mystifies me."

"Yes, that, too."

"There are too many agendas at play here."

"It does seem that way," Day said. "But Dr Kingsley will arrive sometime today and he's not keen on wasting time. We've got the dress you found last night and the eyeball that the little girl found."

"Hopefully the doctor can tell us something more about one or the other."

"Or both, preferably. Meanwhile, I don't feel as though we've made much headway in those woods."

"I really don't see how we can unless we've got a hundred men, marching abreast."

"Neither do I. But I'm curious about the man I saw last night. What's his role in all this? The hideous wound across your face reminds me of him."

Hammersmith touched his cheek again and winced.

Day chuckled. "We must try to determine who that is out there," he said. "That's my suspect at the moment, though I'm not completely certain a crime's been committed."

"I think the innkeeper knows something," Hammersmith said. "Why else would he try to drug us?"

"I think Calvin Campbell knows something, too. He locked us in our rooms last night."

Hammersmith raised an eyebrow. "He did what?"

"He locked us both in our rooms. I let myself out and followed him."

"You let yourself out?"

"Yes. I brought my keys. The special keys."

"Did he see you?"

"No. I imagine he thought we were both sound asleep and would never know. He came back round and unlocked the doors just after dawn."

"I certainly wouldn't have known. Where did he go? When you followed him?"

"I'm afraid he disappeared."

"He knew you were there."

"I don't think so. He tiptoed down the stairs, very quiet, very nervous. And he did come back and unlock our doors. Why do that if he knew I was already out?"

"Should we question him directly?"

"I think we'd better."

"It seems I missed a great deal while I slept," Hammersmith said. "You should have come and got me."

"I tried, but you looked a bit rough."

"We have a lot to do."

"You snore, by the way."

Hammersmith frowned, but said nothing.

Day chuckled. "To work, then. I'd like to find out which tunnels are no longer in use and see about putting together a crew of men to take a look down there."

"Why haven't they done that already?"

"I wondered that, too. In fact, they hardly seem to have looked for the missing family at all. Constable Grimes is the only man here who seems to care."

"Apparently half the village is sick, after all."

"True."

"But we also have an innkeeper who drugged us, presumably to keep us from going into the woods. Is it possible he didn't want the dress found?"

"Perhaps."

"And we have the mysterious Mr Campbell, who locked us in our rooms for the night."

"We have a lot of questions to ask."

"A tour of the village would help, too." Hammersmith grimaced.

"There seems to be an endless number of places three people might hide. Or be hidden. The woods, still, of course. Then there are the tunnels, as you said, every house in this town, even the well."

"The schoolhouse doesn't seem to be in use."

"Worth taking a look inside."

"And I want to get a look inside that church. When I was out and about, I didn't see a rectory here."

"Ah, yes, the note from Mrs Brothwood. It's the only clue we've got. And not much of one. We need more clues. We need to narrow down the field before we run out of time here. It's hardly likely, but if we can solve this today, we may be able to get you back to your wife by tomorrow sometime."

"I still fear she'll have the baby before I can return."

Hammersmith softly coughed. He wiped his mouth and tapped his head. "I have an idea."

"Does it involve getting out of this stuffy room?"

"You read my mind."

"After you, Mr Hammersmith."

Hammersmith tugged his forelock and preceded Inspector Day to the staircase.

24

They could hear the distant chattering of voices as they came down the stairs, and when they reached the bottom step, the inn's front door swung open and Freddy Higgins limped inside, followed closely by a cloud of swirling snowflakes. He turned and pushed the door shut against the wind. He seemed smaller and more pale than he had on the previous evening, but Day had never seen the boy off his carriage.

"There they are," Freddy said. "You almost missed 'em. Train'll be leaving soon and the weather's comin' on thicker. Better get 'em to the depot, quick as I can, gentlemen."

"Missed who?" Day said. "What train?"

"The London to Manchester. You nearly slep' through, you did." Freddy turned his head and coughed into the crook of his elbow.

Day gave Hammersmith an exasperated look and turned to the empty common room, as if looking for an answer there. The lamps had been lit and the place was warm and cozy. The chattering of voices was slightly louder now, and Hammersmith walked toward the door at the far end of the room. Just as he reached it, the door opened and Claire Day stepped through. Without a word, she rushed to her husband and hugged him. Hammersmith looked away at the panes of colored glass in the wall above the bar.

"How long have you been here?" Day said.

"Not long at all," Claire said. "And yet we must be off already. I've decided to visit my sister for a bit and let you work."

"You should have come upstairs."

"Well, I would have if you'd slept any longer. I almost didn't get a chance to see you."

"But I wasn't asleep. I was pressing clothes."

"Mr Rose said you didn't get in until the sun was up."

"Very nearly. But apparently I can't sleep when you're so far from me. Didn't he tell you I was up and about?"

"He said you went back up."

"Let me have a look at you."

"I look the same as I did yesterday and the day before. Absolutely enormous."

"Nonsense."

"Well, come on. We have to get back before the train leaves again, and the others are dying to see you." She turned to Hammersmith. "You, too, Nevil."

"Lovely to see you, Mrs Day."

"They're in the dining room." She took Day's hand and led him through the door at the back of the room, and Hammersmith followed them.

"There they are," Bennett Rose said. He was clearing breakfast plates from the big oaken table. "Caught up on your beauty sleep, have you, Mr Hammersmith?"

Day ignored him and held the door open for Hammersmith, who didn't appear to have heard the innkeeper. Claire pulled out a chair and sat down with a sigh. Day swept his eyes over the other four people at the table.

"Dr Kingsley," he said. "You're here, too? We weren't expecting you until later in the day."

"Early train," Kingsley said. "I'd like to get back tonight, if at all possible."

The doctor pushed his chair back and stood. He was a small man, lean and wiry, with a wild shock of prematurely grey hair. There was always something about his manner that suggested he was only ever there for a few short moments and everyone should make the best of it before his next appointment. There was a huge man sitting next to him who looked nervous about being there. Day nodded at him.

"Henry," he said. "Good to see you."

"Hello, sir," Henry said.

Henry Mayhew was Dr Kingsley's assistant, a simple, good-natured man who had been living on the street until Inspector Day found work for him with the doctor.

"And you've brought your daughter, too," Day said. He shook the doctor's hand and glanced at the young girl sitting next to him. "Good morning, Fiona." Fiona was fifteen years old with long blond hair, a sharp fox's face, and wide eyes that seemed to see everything at once. She paid not the slightest attention to Day, but stood up and hurried around the end of the table, making a beeline for Hammersmith.

"Oh, my," she said. "What's happened to your face?"

She reached out toward Hammersmith's face, but pulled her hand back at the last minute, as if she might be burned by him.

"I'm fine," Hammersmith said. He glanced at Day, shrugged, and covered his cheek with his palm. "Is it really as bad as all that?"

"Father," Fiona said. "Do something."

Kingsley rubbed the side of his nose and reached for the satchel on the floor at his feet. He came around the table and nudged his daughter out of the way. He peered up at the wound on Hammersmith's cheek and clucked his tongue.

"It's not deep. Just needs to be cleaned." The doctor rummaged in his bag and found a vial of alcohol and a laundered rag. "You were right about his clothes, though, Fiona."

"My clothes?" Hammersmith said.

"She insisted we stop in at your flat. We talked to your landlady there, Mrs Flanders, and she sent along a fresh shirt for you."

"How could you possibly have known that I'd forgotten to bring a change of clothing?"

"You tend not to look after yourself," Fiona said. "You're always too busy looking after others."

Hammersmith sucked in his breath as the alcohol-damp rag touched his cheek. Day smiled and looked away. He pulled out a chair and sat down between his wife and the schoolteacher.

"Good morning, Miss Jessica," he said.

Jessica tore her eyes away from Hammersmith for just a moment before looking back at him while she talked to Day. "And good morning to you, Inspector. I trust you're well rested."

"Surprisingly so," he said. "Are there no classes today?"

"The weather."

"It does seem a bit worse out there. But surely the snow will taper off soon. It's a bit late in the season for a bad storm, isn't it?"

"Yes, it really is," she said. "But by the end of the day we're sure to be completely snowed in. At least that's what some of the villagers are saying. They've even shut the seam down."

"How could they possibly know what the weather will do?"

"Mr Rose says a dead black stork was found in the center of town this morning. Means a bad storm's on its way."

"I never saw—" Day said.

"Tut," Kingsley said. He pulled the rag back from Hammersmith's face and pursed his lips. "What rot."

"I'm sorry?" Bennett Rose said. The innkeeper had been quietly busy in a corner of the room, polishing flatware, but now he turned and fixed Kingsley with a steely gaze. "I'll ask you to be respectful while you're in my place."

"I don't understand." Kingsley stood holding the rag, a look of genuine confusion creasing his face. Day could smell the sharp tang of alcohol from halfway across the room.

"Mr Rose takes a bit of getting used to," Hammersmith said.

"Our customs are important to us," Rose said. "Sometimes the customs of a place is what binds people together. It's not somethin' to jest about."

"I assure you, there was no jest intended."

"Well, then."

"Your superstitions have no basis in fact or reason. They mean nothing and should not come into consideration when discussing any provable thing," Kingsley said. "But I meant no jest."

"Well, you're . . . you . . ." The innkeeper's face gradually assumed the color of his name, a deep pink hue blossoming from somewhere beneath his collar and moving rapidly across his fleshy face. He sputtered, but was unable to form a complete sentence. He pointed a thick finger at Kingsley, turned on his heel, and stalked out of the room.

Kingsley blinked hard and scratched his nose with the same hand that held the rag. He gasped at the concentrated odor of the alcohol and dropped the rag back into his satchel. "I'm sure I don't know what came over him," he said.

"The people here are quite keen on their beliefs, Doctor," Jessica said. "I have found that superstitions are often to blame when people intuit information from their surroundings. That doesn't make the information wrong."

Kingsley smiled. "Then please tender my apologies. You are a most perceptive young woman. Meanwhile, I've made your face as presentable as possible, Mr Hammersmith."

"Thank you. If you don't mind, I think I'll change my shirt."

Hammersmith took the clean white shirt from Fiona and went to the stairs and up. When he had ascended out of view, they all heard him cough once, loudly. There was a moment of silence, and then the echoes of a fresh coughing fit bounced down the stairwell at them. Day rose halfway from his chair, alarmed that Hammersmith might fall back down the stairs, but the coughing sounds retreated down the upstairs hallway and were shut off by the quiet click of a bedroom door closing.

"He must have been saving that up the entire time you were working on him, Doctor," Claire said.

"I'm glad he didn't let it go in my face."

"He sounds dreadful," Fiona said. "Has he caught cold here?"

"I'm afraid so," Day said.

"You must take care of him, Father."

"A cold will pass without any help from me," Kingsley said. "But he must rest."

"There's not much chance of getting Nevil to rest," Day said.

"No," Fiona said. "He's very dedicated."

"There are a lot of people here who've come down sick," Miss Jessica said. "It's possible he's got what they have."

"Surely not," Day said. "We've been here one night."

"What's the village sick with?" Kingsley said.

"I'm sure I don't know."

"It would be odd for him to have caught it so quickly, but I ought to talk with your doctor as soon as possible."

"I could take you."

"Actually, it would be helpful if you could first arrange a visit with the Price children," Day said. "The remaining Price children, that is. They trust you."

"But didn't the sergeant talk to them last evening?"

"All but one."

"Oh, you mean Virginia," Jessica said. "The youngest of them. But surely she's not important."

"She may have seen something useful," Day said. "Children often place importance on different things than we do."

"If you think it might be worthwhile, I would be happy to take you to her," Jessica said. "But we should hurry. This storm is only going to get worse."

Day opened his mouth to speak, but closed it again when he heard the sound of footsteps on the stairs. Hammersmith appeared on the landing, looking considerably more dignified in a fresh shirt. He was carrying a small fabric-wrapped bundle tucked under his arm. His face was pale and he was sweating, beads of dew glistening on his upper lip and across his brow. Kingsley crossed the room and laid the back of his hand against the sergeant's damp forehead.

"Fiona, bring me a thermometer," he said.

Hammersmith waved him away. "I'm fine."

"You're not fine."

Fiona rummaged through the satchel and produced a mercury thermometer, which she handed to her father. But Hammersmith clamped his lips shut. Day suppressed a chuckle as he watched Kingsley try to forcibly insert the thermometer past Hammersmith's gritted teeth. Kingsley gave up and handed the thin tube of glass back to Fiona.

"There are other places I could insert this, you know," he said.

But Fiona was already putting the thermometer back in the bag, so it was an empty threat. Hammersmith risked opening his mouth.

"I'm just a bit worn out from spending a night in the woods," he said. "Nothing more."

Kingsley clucked his tongue. "Nonsense. You must rest. I order you back to bed."

Hammersmith shook his head, and Kingsley scowled at him. Day had been right: The sergeant would never voluntarily neglect his duty. If he was conscious and capable of walking, he would work.

"I'm afraid Sergeant Hammersmith is too valuable to me, Doctor," Day said. "There's only the two of us, and we must solve this case before we return to London tomorrow."

Hammersmith gave Day a grateful look. Day smiled back at him. Better to give Hammersmith a task that wasn't strenuous than to fight him and allow him to go off on his own. Besides, stubbornness wasn't the worst trait for a policeman.

"Doctor, I brought these down for you to see," Hammersmith said. He held out the bundle and laid it on the edge of the table. Day recognized the fabric. It was the runner from under the washbasin on his vanity. Hammersmith carefully rolled the cloth out and caught the bloody dress and the small box in his other hand.

"Evidence?" Kingsley said.

"We think so."

Kingsley opened the box and stared at the shriveled eyeball inside. He nodded and closed the box, set it on the table, and picked up the dress. He unfolded it on his palm, the sleeves and the hem hanging down off the ends of his fingers.

"Blood."

"It is, isn't it?"

"It does look like it. I'll have to test it."

"Did you bring the proper equipment?" Day said.

Kingsley made a face at him.

"Yes, of course you did," Day said. The doctor was always prepared.

"I'll need a few hours. It's mostly a matter of observing chemical reactions, but I'll want to be sure."

"Good," Day said. "While you're doing that, we'll need to find

witnesses. An entire family doesn't disappear without someone seeing something. Nevil, I need you to accompany Miss Jessica and
question Virginia Price."

"But surely I—"

"It's vital that we discover anything she might know."

Hammersmith nodded glumly. "I'll leave now," he said.

"But you haven't eaten yet," Fiona said.

"I'm not hungry."

Kingsley cleared his throat. "I know it's no use to protest. But I
strongly advise against any activity. One never knows about these
provincial maladies. If something settles in your lungs . . ."

Hammersmith shook his head and waved a weak hand at the
room, encompassing all of the people, as well as a fireplace and a
low-hanging chandelier. "I tell you I'm fine. There's nothing to be
concerned about. Please, let's stop discussing me as if I weren't capable of managing my own affairs."

Fiona gave him a pitying look, but said nothing. Day knew
what she was thinking. Hammersmith was capable of a great many
things, but managing his own affairs was not one of them.

"You're anxious to work and we've interrupted," Claire said. "I
thought perhaps you had already solved the case and you'd be glad
to see us if we stopped in."

"We are glad to see you," Day said. "And though we haven't
solved the case yet, we can see you to the depot."

"We'll leave immediately," Claire said.

Day saw a flush of humiliation on her cheeks, and an inexpress-
ible sadness took root in him. It had been six months since a murderer had paid Claire a visit while Day was out of the house working
his very first case for the Murder Squad. The killer hadn't harmed

her, had meant the visit as a threat to the inspector, a warning to abandon the investigation. That man was behind bars now, but he had shown the Days just how easy it would be to hurt them. Claire was a strong woman, but Day understood why she was uncomfortable being left at home alone, pregnant and vulnerable.

"We can keep the train waiting for another few minutes, I think," Day said.

Hammersmith grimaced, clearly anxious to get started, but he nodded. Neither of the policemen would feel at ease until the ladies were safely away, but neither of them wanted to see them go.

"It's settled then," Day said. "Sergeant, later this morning you'll get an accounting from Virginia Price. I'm going to pay a call on the vicar and his wife. We'll meet here directly after and arrange to explore the mines. I only wish we had more men, but perhaps by then Constable Grimes will have found some warm bodies. I don't want to be out there fumbling about in the dark again."

"Speaking of fumbling about blind," Hammersmith said, "where is Mr Grimes this morning?"

25

Constable Harry Grimes had lived and worked in Blackhampton his entire life. Unlike most of the men in the village, who carried on their legacies down in the mines, his
father had been a policeman, and Harry had followed in his footsteps. He knew every square inch of the village and the names of
all the people who lived there. He knew their secrets and he kept
them. He knew about the charms in Bennett Rose's attic and he
knew about the priest hole in Mr Brothwood's church. There was
no part of Blackhampton that he didn't know intimately. But he
had not spent a lot of time in the woods, and so now he was having trouble finding the spot he had visited the previous night with
the policeman from London.

He had hoped to make a quick trip out, just to take another look
at the place where they'd found the bloody dress, and to be back by

breakfast. He had not slept well and had awoken with a sour taste in his mouth and the vestiges of a nightmare circling his consciousness. He had pulled on his trousers and hurried out the door, consumed by a single thought: If a bloody dress had been found just off the path in the woods, that very bend in the path might yield more clues if he returned in the daylight.

Assuming he could find the spot again.

He tromped along, swiping at the low-hanging branches over the path and muttering under his breath as the hems of his trousers brushed against the bracken, growing more waterlogged with every step. He had neglected to change into boots, and his finest black horsehide shoes were no doubt ruined. He stepped on a sharp stone and felt it through the sole of his right shoe. He stopped and leaned against a tree to take the weight off his right foot. He looked around him, trying to get his bearings. He knew that he and Hammersmith could not have penetrated too far into the woods in the dark. It occurred to him that he might have already passed the place where the dress was found. He frowned and bent his foot so he could see the bottom of his shoe, to see if the rock had made a hole in the leather. Glancing down, he saw broken branches and a long smooth smear across the ice by the side of the path.

He had found the right spot!

If he hadn't stopped, he would have missed it, would have walked right past. He sent up a silent prayer, thanking whomever the patron saint of sharp stones might be. He pushed himself off the tree trunk and moved off the path, carefully examining the ground, forcing the stiff wiry branches of low-growing bushes aside. There was a shallow slope on the western side of the path, and he put his foot down too hard on a patch of ice, slipped and fell, and slid downhill on his bottom. He grabbed a fistful of thin spring grass and stopped himself, felt the cold through the seat of his trousers.

Hammersmith had spotted the white dress somewhere nearby. It was a slim hope that there might be more clues out here, but if there was anything at all to be found, Grimes wanted to be the one to bring it out of the woods. He wanted to show the men from Scotland Yard that Blackhampton was not so backward and inconsequential as they no doubt thought it was. And, moreover, that Grimes himself was a good policeman, every bit their equal. It was foolish pride, he knew, but good work was often the direct result of pride.

He stood and brushed snow off his trousers and looked around. The bushes Hammersmith had crawled under weren't as impassable as they had seemed to be in the dark. In fact, just two feet to the right was a second, narrower trail that wound around the roots of the nearby trees and skirted the thorny shrubbery. He made his way over to it and followed it around, digging in his heels so as not to fall again. He stopped again a few feet farther along, where he judged the dress had been found. There were indentations in the mud, possibly made by Hammersmith's elbows and knees. Low to the ground, a bit of pale lace was caught on a thorny twig. Grimes carefully pulled it off and stuck it in his pocket, mildly disappointed that there wasn't more to find. Still, it was something.

He looked up through the branches, trying hopelessly to judge the time by the position of the invisible sun in the smooth grey sky. Were Day and Hammersmith awake yet? Was breakfast finished? The London police might be doing anything by now. Possibly questioning the villagers, narrowing down the options for further searching. That's what Grimes would do in their place. He should be with them when they talked to his people.

He turned, headed back up the trail, and saw a flash of lavender in the trees above. He squinted. A pale purple ribbon was looped around a limb between him and the path ahead. He reached for it, but it was just out of reach.

This was a clue. Or it might be. Better than a scrap of lace, at least.

Excited, he braced a foot against the base of the trunk above the tree's roots and lunged upward. His fingers brushed against the silky fabric. He jumped again. And again. But the tip of the ribbon darted away from him, anchored by the tree at its other end, dancing in the low steady breeze out of the north.

He wrapped his arms around the trunk and attempted to shimmy up it like he'd done on every tree in the village common when he was a child. He was bigger now, though, and older, his arms and legs less flexible. He grunted and inched his way higher a bit at a time. He didn't try to hurry. He didn't want to loosen the ribbon only to watch it flutter away on the breeze. He made his methodical way upward, bracing himself carefully with his back against the tree behind him, making sure he was stable before reaching out and untangling the ribbon from the branch. It came loose easily and he smiled, held it up to the light, and admired the way the sun shone through the thin material. There was a cluster of minute black dots along one edge of the ribbon. Blood? This was a good clue indeed. Inspector Day would be most impressed.

He looked down and began the short slide back to the ground. He heard a shrill whistling sound from somewhere nearby, but before he could raise his head to look for the source of the noise, a hole the size of a sixpence coin materialized above his left eye. Almost at the same instant, another, larger, hole appeared below his right ear and a .45 caliber bullet deposited a thimbleful of his brains in the bark of the tree beside him. He grunted once before dying.

Constable Grimes's body tumbled four feet down the side of the tree and landed in a heap under the thorny bushes beside the trail. His dark blue uniform rendered him nearly invisible in the icy darkness of the thicket.

His lifeless fingers opened and the lavender ribbon floated away, curling in the breeze. It snagged for just a second on a thorn, but twisted loose. It drifted up through the trees and out of the woods and across the long barren fields toward the village.

26

———

Nine hundred yards away, the American lowered his Whitworth rifle.

The policeman was Calvin Campbell's friend and that was the only reason he had died. The American had seen them together the night before and had decided to make the game more interesting by killing Campbell's friends first. It seemed somehow fitting, given their history.

From his vantage point high up in a tree, he had tracked the policeman's clumsy movements through the woods. The American had taken his time unsnapping his gun bag and quietly pulling out the rifle, all the while watching the policeman move closer. He had pulled out the Whitworth and flipped up the sight, carefully loaded the rifle with one of the unique hexagonal bullets the model was known for. The shape of the bullet was slim and elegant, and when it rocketed through the air, it whistled, giving a split-second warning to anyone within range. The American *liked it that his rifle whistled. It made the game seem a little more fair somehow. He had rested the rifle's thirty-three-inch barrel in a fork of the tree. There was a slight breeze, cold and from the north. He had adjusted for the wind and waited for the policeman to walk into range.*

Then the policeman had climbed up a tree and made the job even easier.

Now the American flipped the sight back down and stowed the rifle back in his bag, snapped it shut, and slung it over his shoulder. He climbed easily back to the ground and made his way up the path, back toward the abandoned schoolhouse on the edge of the village.

Without realizing he was doing it, the American began to whistle through his teeth as he walked along.

27

H ow are you?" Claire said. "Really?"

"Happy to see you," Day said.

The door to his room was open, and Day sat on the wooden chair next to it. Claire reclined on the bed. Her feet hurt, and Kingsley had advised her to lie down. Fiona Kingsley paced nervously in the hallway, just out of sight, but not out of earshot. She took her responsibilities as governess and watchdog seriously. Day longed for even a few minutes completely alone with his wife, but he was content enough to take what he could get.

"I shouldn't have come," Claire said. "I couldn't stop myself from getting on the train, but feel silly about it now. I'm keeping you from your work."

"I'm still happy to see you."

Claire smiled.

"Is he behaving himself?" Day said. He regarded Claire's swollen belly with a mixture of suspicion and anticipation.

"He?"

"I assume that's a son."

"Is that so?"

"What else could it be?"

"Oh, I don't know. It seems to me there might be another possibility, but it escapes me."

"You may want to consult with Dr Kingsley about that. You have some strange ideas."

"You know, now I'm going to make sure this is a little girl."

Day grinned at her and looked down at his folded hands, beyond them at the toes of his shiny shoes. He genuinely didn't care whether the baby was a boy or a girl. The possibilities were equally terrifying.

Claire put a hand on her husband's chest, reading his mood, but misunderstanding its cause. "You'll find that lost little boy," she said. "And his parents. I know you will."

Day tried a smile. "I appreciate your faith, but I'm not so sure."

"I am. I'm certain they're somewhere warm and safe, waiting to be found."

"I hope you're right."

"Oh," Claire said. "I made something for you." She maneuvered through the pregnant woman version of jumping out of bed: swinging her feet around and placing them solidly on the floor, jacking herself upright, and pushing off the wall behind her. Day stood and took her elbow, helped her to her feet. He was amazed by how ready she was to bring another Day into the world. At any moment, their tiny family would be increased by half again.

Or, according to the sobering statistics that Kingsley had privately shared with him, there was a very good chance that Claire, or the baby, or both, would die in childbirth and Day would become a family of one. He shuddered and smiled at his wife and blinked hard, forcing the thought to disappear. Only it didn't completely go away. It never did. It had lived with him for six months.

Claire crossed the room, heavy and graceless and, Day thought, breathtakingly beautiful. She fetched her bag from the floor of the wardrobe where he had placed it and rummaged through it.

"Aha!" she said. She unraveled from the top of the bag what appeared to be a long skein of the winter sky, grey and bristling. She took the ashen coil and looped it around his neck. He immediately began to itch and resisted the urge to scratch himself. "It's a muffler," she said. "I made it for you myself. Do you like it?"

He gripped the end of it and hauled it up to his face. It was really nothing more than a tube of some low-grade yarn, rough and charmless. Claire was still learning to be a homemaker after a lifetime of privilege, and Day was overwhelmed that she had tried so hard to make something for him, even something as wretched as this shapeless grey thing that was now making his neck itch so badly that it burned.

He wrapped his arms as tightly around her as he dared, as tightly as her belly would allow him, and spoke into her hair, smelling of lavender and apples, sweat and Blackhampton ashes. "I love it so much."

The baby bird, invisible in its box on the vanity, woke up and chirped, and a deep voice floated in from the hallway: "I hear a bird."

Day let go of Claire and took a step back. He looked at the door, but didn't see the owner of the voice.

"Henry?" Day said.

Henry Mayhew peered into the room, a floating head, the rest of him out of sight behind the doorjamb. "The doctor sent me, only I didn't want to bother you."

"It's all right, Henry. Come in."

The bashful giant shuffled into the room. "The boy with the broken leg said the next train's coming and the doctor says you have to get on it and go to Manchester, Mrs Claire."

"Broken leg?" Claire said. "I don't think Freddy's leg is broken, Henry. I think he was born that way."

Day stole an anxious look at Claire's middle, as if he might be able to see inside and make sure their unborn baby was whole and healthy. "How much time do we have, Henry?"

"No time, Mr Day."

"Then we'd best get you on your way, my dear," Day said.

The bird peeped again, and Henry went to the vanity and stared down into the straw-filled box. "It's little," he said.

"It's a baby," Day said. "I found him in the woods last night and I haven't decided what to do with him yet. He's an agreeable chap, but he demands a lot of me."

"You should show him to Dr Kingsley right away," Henry said. "He could help."

"You're probably right. I haven't had a chance."

"Do you want me to do it?"

"If you'd like."

Henry nodded, taking the new responsibility seriously. He lifted the box and whispered an answering chirp at the little bird.

"Actually, Henry," Day said, "if it wouldn't be too much to ask, could you watch him for me?"

"Oh, not me, sir. I'm not good at things."

"I think that's a marvelous idea," Claire said.

"I'm quite busy here," Day said. "You'd be doing me a tremendous favor."

"I'll try." Henry looked frightened. "Is he hungry maybe?"

"Oh, Henry, he's always hungry."

"I'll get him food."

"He likes bread crumbs soaked in warm milk."

Henry's frightened expression was replaced by one of sheer panic, and Day laughed despite himself.

"I believe Mr Rose has a good supply of those things."

"Oh, good," Henry said. "Because I don't have them."

"Go ask him. We'll be right down."

Henry nodded and rushed out of the room. They listened to him clattering along the hall and down the stairs. Day picked up Claire's bag, and his smile wavered as he motioned her toward the open door. She touched his cheek as she passed him. Fiona was still waiting in the hall and took Claire's elbow to help her down the stairs. Day took another look at his room, now lifeless and empty.

He blew out the lantern and followed his wife and never returned to that room.

28

◦◦◦

Kingsley gazed out across the fields at the hazy trees on the horizon. He thought he could hear something echoing across the ice. A low whistle. He strained to pinpoint it, but the breeze picked up and the sound dissipated, blown away like another errant snowflake.

"Father?"

Kingsley looked at Fiona and smiled. "Thought I heard something," he said.

"I could stay and help you here. Mrs Day will be fine with her sister."

Kingsley smiled again and glanced around at the others on the platform. Inspector Day was huddled with his wife, both of them whispering. Kingsley had seen many men afraid to touch their pregnant wives for fear they might break them, but the Days stayed in constant physical contact, reaching out to touch each other gently on their arms, their faces, their hair. The wind carried snatches of their conversation to Kingsley.

"It'll only be a week or two," Claire said.

"Two?"

"Never mind that. I'll be back in London before the baby can come."

"But I'll be back in London tomorrow."

"The storm might keep you."

"What will I do while you're in Manchester?"

The wind changed direction and their conversation was lost.

Across from them, Hammersmith sat on a long bench next to Henry Mayhew, the doctor's assistant. From Kingsley's vantage point, it looked like Henry was propping the sergeant up.

"I don't know Mrs Day's sister or her abilities," Kingsley said. "I need you to watch over her."

"Yes, but—"

"I'll have Henry here to help me."

Fiona frowned and looked away, toward the bench and Hammersmith. Kingsley's smile turned sad and he shook his head. He knew why she wanted to stay. The girl was growing up entirely too fast. He would have to keep a close eye on his youngest daughter in the future.

Jessica Perkins, the village schoolteacher, stood on the periphery of the group. She carried Claire's bag, but Kingsley didn't fully understand why she had come along. There was something about her that impressed him. Perhaps she simply needed something to do. She looked up at him and raised her eyebrows in a question. He thought for a moment before calling her over. As Jessica approached,

Fiona took a step back and fidgeted with the pad of paper she always carried. She stared at her feet and didn't acknowledge the schoolteacher.

"Dr Kingsley," Jessica said.

"Miss Perkins, I have something of a favor to ask of you, while we wait for the weather to do . . . what it is that weather does. You're accompanying Sergeant Hammersmith to see the children, correct? The siblings of the missing boy?"

"I believe I am."

From the corner of his eye, Kingsley saw Fiona bristle. He ignored her. "I was wondering if you would attempt an experiment for me."

"An experiment? Nothing dangerous, I hope."

"Not at all," Kingsley said. "At least, I don't think it ought to be."

He was interrupted by the distant whistle of the approaching train. *That,* he thought, *must be why I heard whistling earlier.* He had only a few moments left in which to say good-bye to Fiona, and so he filled Jessica in on his plan as quickly as he could, trusting that she understood what he wanted to achieve.

29

They both looked up when they heard the train's whistle.

"All I have to do is hop onto the train as it pulls away and I could go with you," Day said.

"Lovely as that sounds, there are people here who are depending on you," Claire said. "You can't abandon them."

"But I could."

"But you won't."

Day sighed and shook his head. "You're not telling me the things I want to hear," he said.

"True. I'm a terrible wife."

"You're no such thing."

"You know, as easy as it would be for you to jump on the train and come with me, it might be even easier if I were to not get on the train in the first place. I could get a room at the inn here."

Day looked up at the sky. He almost reached out to put a hand on his wife's pregnant belly, but there were too many other people nearby. "No," he said. "If Mr Rose is correct, there's worse weather coming. You might be trapped here, and with the baby on its way . . ."

"I would be trapped here with my doctor." Claire rolled her eyes in Kingsley's direction. The doctor was at the far end of the platform, deep in discussion with the village's schoolteacher.

"Also," Day said, "and this is no small thing, there's something very wrong going on here in Blackhampton. I wouldn't be at all surprised if murder's been done. Can't have you near that."

"As opposed to Manchester, you mean? Or London? That crime-free utopia?"

"I don't even know what that word means. You've been reading too much."

"What else do I have to do with my time?"

"Think about me."

"I do that while I'm turning the pages of my books. For seconds at a time."

Day chuckled.

"I wish you'd let me stay," Claire said.

Day opened his mouth, but Claire put her hand up before he could speak. "I understand," she said, "and I shan't argue further." She looked past him at the bench on the depot wall. "But I do think Nevil ought to go to London on the first train back. He looks a fright."

Day turned and glanced at Hammersmith. "He's as stubborn as they come. Even if I ordered him, he wouldn't go."

"Is there anything we can do for him?"

"The best we can do for him is to solve this case."

Hammersmith saw them looking and smiled, but he looked tired and anxious. As they watched, he raised his hand and absently wiped his nose. A moment later, blood gushed forth with astonishing force, running down over the front of his overcoat. He seemed astonished and sat there, letting his nose bleed. Day leapt away from Claire, reaching for his handkerchief as he moved toward Hammersmith, but Kingsley beat him to the bench. The doctor laid Hammersmith on his back and produced a rag from his satchel. He pressed the cloth to Hammersmith's nose and held it there.

"I'b fide," Hammersmith said.

"You're fine?" Kingsley said. "That seems to be your motto, Mr Hammersmith. And yet you are rarely fine. We must strengthen your grasp of the language so that you can more accurately communicate your state of being."

"Jus' a dosebleed."

"Doctor," Day said, "could this nosebleed have to do with the cold he's caught?"

"In my experience, a cold doesn't produce nosebleeds. But dry winter air certainly can. This weather isn't helping him."

"Perhaps you should return to London," Day said. "I can carry on here. I have Constable Grimes to help."

"An' where is he?" Hammersmith said.

"I suspect he's around somewhere, probably trying to prove he can do the job as well as we can. He'll turn up."

"I'll be here whed he does."

"You won't do me much good if you collapse in your tracks, you know."

"Neber happed."

"Knowing you, it never will."

Day felt a light tap on his shoulder and turned. Claire had come up behind him. She smiled. "Here," she said. "This may come in handy." She put her handkerchief in his hand. It was an old thing from before their wedding, and it had a monogram of her maiden name stitched in one corner: *CC*. Day made a mental note to buy her a new set of handkerchiefs.

"It will at least remind you of me," Claire said.

"I hardly need a reminder. And I'll be back home tomorrow evening. Missing you."

Day smiled at her, but he was worried. He worried about his wife and he worried that he'd never get to the bottom of Blackhampton's mysteries. It seemed an impossible task and not something he could finish by the following day's train. Hammersmith was right. Day would need his sergeant if he was going to make it home. He needed all the help he could get.

30

The Price house was a boxy two-story dwelling butted up against the back of another row of railroad cars that had been converted into homes. One of the cars had sunken into an abandoned coal pit, half out of sight below ground, the other half sticking straight up into the air as if it had been caught in the act of diving down an unseen tunnel. The Price house was also sinking, but more slowly. The ground floor was partially underground and the front door had been modified to accommodate the steady descent. The doorway had been lengthened as far as it could possibly go, and the upper edge had been recapped. The door itself had been removed and reinstalled two feet higher than it had originally been. A narrow landing had been built just inside the front door, with a series of shallow steps leading down into the small parlor.

When the Prices' housekeeper answered the bell, Jessica Perkins noticed that the door scraped against the ceiling. There was a shallow groove there in the shape of a crescent moon and a faint black smudge from years of contact with the top of the door. She had been to the house many times, escorting her students home, but now she was trying to see the place through Sergeant Hammersmith's eyes, trying to imagine what he saw when he looked at Blackhampton.

Raising the doorway had only partially solved the problem of the sinking house. On the inside, the home seemed perfectly normal, but Jessica estimated that the top of the doorjamb was still well short of six feet high. Sergeant Hammersmith had to duck his head to enter the house and he stumbled on the inside landing. Jessica caught his elbow before he fell, and he smiled gratefully at her. She looked away to hide the sudden heat she felt creeping across her cheeks.

The housekeeper let them in and showed them to a set of faded but comfortable chairs, then left them so she could fetch the children. Hammersmith settled into his chair with a visible sigh, leaned back, and closed his eyes. Jessica saw that his hands were shaking, vibrating against the seat cushion.

The parlor was all that Jessica could see of the house. All that she had ever seen of the house. It was modestly furnished, but pleasant. Cheaply framed floral prints adorned the walls, which were painted a cheery yellow. The furniture was solidly constructed and simple. Built, she guessed, by a local carpenter at least a century before.

When the housekeeper returned, she was trailed by the three children. First came Anna, perhaps half a foot shorter than Jessica and ten years younger. She scowled at each of them in turn, her gaze lingering on Hammersmith perhaps a moment too long. Then came Virginia, a little girl wearing a yellow dress that matched the parlor's walls, a purple ribbon in her hair. She was only five years old, too young for school. Jessica hardly knew her. Following the two girls was Peter. He had straight sand-colored hair and an open intelligent expression. He nodded a greeting at his teacher and leaned against the wall next to the doorway, his arms folded across his chest.

"Is he all right?" The housekeeper pointed at Hammersmith.

"He's dying," Anna said. "There was an omen."

"He's not dying," Jessica said. "He's sick, is all, just like half the village."

"I'm not dying." Hammersmith stood, his hands folded in front of him, and smiled at the three children. With a bow, the housekeeper faded into the shadows of the hallway. Jessica could see nothing of her except her starched white collar and the toes of her white shoes.

"Good morning," Hammersmith said. "Some of you know me already. Hello, Anna. Hello, Peter. And hello, Virginia. We haven't met yet. My name is Sergeant Hammersmith. You may call me Nevil, if you'd like. I'm visiting you from London and I'd like to talk for a bit, if you wouldn't mind terribly."

Jessica could see that he wasn't comfortable talking to children. From the look that passed between Peter and Anna, they could see it, too. She decided she might have to take over the conversation if it began to turn.

Anna curtseyed, but said nothing. And, like her sister, Virginia curtseyed. She gave Hammersmith a big smile and bobbed her head, her blond curls bouncing against her apple cheeks. "I am very pleased to meet you, sir," she said. Jessica covered her mouth and stifled a laugh. There was something entirely too studied about the little girl's mannerisms. Jessica had only met the youngest Price girl a handful of times, but here and now, she seemed like a miniature adult.

Hammersmith inclined his head toward her. "I'm happy to meet you, young lady. I'd like to talk to you about your family." Clearly exhausted by the effort of standing, he sat back down and closed his eyes. Jessica popped up and felt his forehead. It was a furnace. She imagined his brain was cooking inside his skull.

She put her lips next to his ear and whispered, "Perhaps we should return another time."

Hammersmith waved a weak hand at her. "This is fine," he said. "I only need a moment."

Jessica decided to minimize Hammersmith's effort. She turned to the little girl. "Virginia, do you know how long your brother's been missing?"

"Weeks, I think."

"No, a few days, at most."

"Oh, well, it seems like weeks, doesn't it?"

"Did you see your brother on the day that he went missing?"

"But if I don't know what day he went missing, how do I know whether I saw him?"

Jessica saw Peter shift in the doorway. There was a sheen of sweat on his upper lip that gleamed in the low light.

Hammersmith opened his eyes. "What were your parents doing the last time you saw them, Virginia?" he said.

"My father was kissing me on my forehead. He told me 'Good night, my sweet princess,' because he always calls me his princess."

Anna looked away, and Jessica thought she heard a faint snort of derision from the older Price daughter.

"And your mother?" Hammersmith said. "Did your mother kiss you good night as well?"

The light went out of Virginia's eyes and her expression hardened. The tendons stood out against the thin pale flesh of her throat, and her tiny hands balled up into fists. "My mother went away to the city a long time ago, sir," she said.

"My apologies. I meant your stepmother, Hester. Did she kiss you good night?"

"Hester does not kiss me."

"I see."

"Hester will not be staying with us for very much longer."

"What do you mean?"

"My father was lonely when my mother went away. Hester is only keeping him company for a short while. He told me so himself."

"He did?"

"I never lie. Lying is for bad children and scoundrels."

"I wonder," Jessica said. "Would it be possible to get a glass of water?"

The housekeeper stepped out of the shadows. Jessica was reminded that Hester, the second Mrs Price, had once been a member of this same household staff. "Of course. I should have offered right away," the housekeeper said. "It's just that things have been a frightful mess."

"Were you here the night the Prices went away?" Hammersmith said.

"Oh, no, sir. I'd gone ahead home. I ain't a stay-in housekeeper. I've got a place up the road."

"Did we pass it on the way in? Which is yours?"

"It's one of the old rail cars, sir. The green one."

"Oh, I didn't know that," Jessica said. "That one's quite pretty, I think."

The housekeeper almost smiled and looked down at her toes. "Thank you much, ma'am. Green's always been my favorite color."

"Mine, too."

"Thank you. I'll be gettin' your water now. One for the mister, too?"

"Yes, please. And for the children, too, would you?" Jessica said. "I imagine they're thirsty."

She watched the two older children, Peter and Anna. Both of them suddenly snapped to attention. They had been sulking, bored, while she and the housekeeper had talked about the green railroad car. Now they were bristling with nervous energy.

"No," Peter said. "I mean, thank you, but we're not thirsty."

"Not at all," Anna said.

"I'm a little bit thirsty," Virginia said.

"Then have some milk," Anna said.

"Okay," Virginia said. "I will have some milk. Thank you, Sister."

"I'll be right back," the housekeeper said.

"I'll help you," Jessica said. "You have a lot to carry and you appear to be alone here."

The housekeeper led the way down a narrow back hall. She turned and gave Jessica a grateful smile. "Thank you, ma'am. There was never much of a staff to begin, but now none of 'em come round no more 'cept me. Their aunt's supposed to be comin' next week to take the children, but she couldn't get away before and there's no one else to watch after 'em. They got nobody left, ma'am, and I couldn't leave 'em all alone up here, could I?"

"You're a good person."

The housekeeper beamed and hurried away down the hall. Eventually it opened into a small anteroom filled with pots and pans on hooks above a sideboard. Through another door was the kitchen, slightly bigger. On a long butcher block against the far wall, a pitcher of milk and a pitcher of water sat side by side. The housekeeper found three chipped glasses in a cupboard under the butcher block and poured water into two of the glasses. She filled the third glass with milk and reached for a silver tray in the same cupboard.

"Oh, I don't think we need that, do we?" Jessica said. "We each have two hands."

The housekeeper smiled again and nodded. Jessica quickly picked up the two water glasses, leaving the milk glass for the housekeeper, and led the way back through the two doorways and down the dark hall. She quickened her pace, trying to get well ahead of the housekeeper, and managed to make it back to the parlor first. She handed one of the water glasses to Virginia Price.

"Here you are," she said. "A fresh glass of water."

Virginia had just opened her mouth to speak when Peter rushed forward and grabbed the glass from her. "No," he said. His voice was loud and shrill. "I mean, she asked for milk, not water, didn't she?"

"Of course she did," Jessica said. "My mistake."

She took the water glass from him and stepped aside while the housekeeper handed the little girl her milk. Jessica turned and started to walk toward Hammersmith, who held his hand out for a glass. She put her left foot in front of her right and let it drag, tripping herself. She went down in a heap. Miraculously, one of the glasses landed on its bottom on the floor. Water splashed up and out, but the glass remained half-full. The other glass spun away and rested on its side against the baseboard across the room, a trail of water curled behind it in decreasing arcs. Jessica had planned her fall and tried to land gently, but there was a loud popping sound from somewhere in the vicinity of her hip and a flash of yellow behind her eyes. She found herself rolling about on the floor, sopping up the spilled water with her favorite dress. There was no graceful way to recover, and she was mortified when she discovered that she was being lifted up, firm hands beneath her arms, and she turned to see Hammersmith.

"Are you quite all right?" he said.

Jessica shook her head, unable to talk just yet. She had done the right thing, she was sure of it, but she had done it in the wrong manner and injured herself. She tested her weight on her right leg and it held her. It seemed she hadn't done any permanent damage.

She snuck another peek at Hammersmith and saw that he was concerned. He was standing just on the other side of her, uncomfortable and useless. It embarrassed her to see how pale, sweating, and disheveled he was, and yet he was the one worried about her.

She took a deep shuddering breath and was surprised to find that the entire world seemed to shudder with her. She glanced at the upright water glass at her feet and saw that the liquid inside was vibrating. There was a screeching, rending noise that came from everywhere at once and echoed in her ears. The housekeeper grabbed little Virginia around the waist and pulled her to the side of the room, pinning her against the wall. The two older Price children moved to the wall nearest them and braced themselves. Jessica reached out toward Hammersmith, who seemed confused. They stood in the middle of the room as the house bucked and shook and seemed ready to come to pieces around them.

31

Inspector Day stopped at the telegraph office. He inquired within and found that there was a message waiting for him. The message was surprisingly long, and it took him some time to read it all. He read it again, folded the paper and slipped it into his breast pocket, then continued on his way.

He suddenly had a lot to think about and so he took his time. The sky was still a uniform grey, no sun, and snow was falling faster, decreasing visibility to just a few feet ahead of him. But the cold breeze had died down and he left his overcoat open, enjoying the fresh air. The path wound along slightly uphill around slag heaps and old covered coal pits. His feet slipped from under him and he caught himself before falling. He slid forward, one foot, then another, making slow but steady progress. The town revealed itself to him a bit at a time through the snow. It looked much different in the grey daylight than it had in the predawn night, remote and ominous and unnaturally empty.

He came around the familiar bend in the path and was struck anew by the beauty of the church. It was an immense building, constructed entirely of river rock and giant rough-hewn timber. There was no pretension on display; everything about it seemed functional, but a great deal of thought had gone into its structure and its preservation. Small iron-rimmed stained-glass windows ringed the high walls, and the shingled roof gave way to a clerestory that, in turn, gave way to a tall bell tower with a spire atop. The rock walls were stained with ash, and the building had obviously settled and sunk over time, its foundation cracked and repaired, but it had been kept up marvelously, the windows sparkling, the metalwork gleaming. The snow and fog wrapped it like a blanket, and the isolation he had felt walking through the rest of the village was different here, cozy and welcoming.

There was a wide porch that swept across the entire width of the front wall, simple stone steps and a rock-capped rail. On the topmost stair, the giant bird-watcher Calvin Campbell sat waiting. He rose and took a step down toward Day.

"How odd," Day said. "I was only just reading about you."

"Were you?" Campbell said.

"There's much you haven't seen fit to share with us."

"I'm not the sort to share."

"I think you ought to try anyway."

"I will, if you insist, but first there's something I'd like to show you, if you've a moment," Campbell said.

"What's that?" Day said.

"Follow me."

Campbell walked toward the woods beyond the church and turned. He waited to see if the inspector would follow. Day hesitated. To follow this strange man into the frozen woods seemed like suicide, particularly given what he now knew about the supposed ornithologist. But detective work was about finding things, learning things, and Day had the bug. If there was something out there, he wanted to know it, *needed* to know it. Curiosity had killed the cat, but the cat had clearly been a detective. In the end, he'd really had no choice.

But Day wasn't stupid. He reached into his jacket pocket and pulled out his Colt Navy. He showed it to Campbell and raised his eyebrows. Campbell nodded, message received. Day would go along, but Campbell had better watch his step. Without a word spoken, Campbell turned and walked past the tree line. Day followed along, the gun down at his side, held loose but ready.

"Ow bist!"

Day turned, his gun coming up without any conscious direction from him. A young man was racing toward them. The first thin trees, outliers of the woods, were between them, and visibility was low, but Day lowered his gun. As he drew near, the young man's features came into focus and Day recognized Dr Denby. The doctor appeared to be out of breath and stopped a few feet away from Day. He put his hands on his knees and breathed hard. Day glanced back and saw that Campbell had stopped and was patiently waiting farther back in the trees.

Denby held up a finger, then he coughed. He turned his head to the side and coughed again, a deep barking sound that came from somewhere deep inside and didn't make it all the way out. His whole body spasmed, and Day thought he could see a fine red mist spray from the doctor's lips. There was a long moment of silence, and Denby took a rattling breath and stood up straight. He wiped his mouth on his sleeve and came toward Day with his hand out. Day moved the gun to his left hand and shook the offered hand.

"Sorry. Saw you from the window," Denby said. "Terribly sorry about all that."

"Are you quite all right?"

Denby grinned sheepishly and pushed his hair back from his eyes. "Hazard of being a doctor, I suppose. The humors are always out of balance. But never fear, I recover quickly."

"I certainly hope so."

The doctor looked over at Campbell, who was still waiting. "Mr Campbell. Good to see you, sir."

Campbell nodded, but said nothing.

"I heard you've brought in another doctor," Denby said. "Someone from London?"

"We did."

"I hope I didn't give the wrong impression last night. I'm completely at your disposal, you know, whatever you should find. Of course, I do hope the Prices are safe and well, but I'm available should the worst come to pass."

"Thank you. We mean no offense. We'd arranged for Dr Kingsley to join us here before we ever arrived ourselves. It was no reflection on you or your abilities. Perhaps the two of you could work together. You know the people here, after all."

"Oh, absolutely. Very wise of you, actually, bringing him along. My hands are rather full. We've lost another two people in the night to this illness."

"Lost them?"

"They were older. It's unfortunate, but their bodies couldn't withstand treatment as well as some of my younger patients."

"What treatment is that? I don't . . ." Day was interrupted by a shuffling noise. He turned and nearly bumped into Calvin Campbell, who was standing directly behind him.

"Dr Denby," Campbell said. "You might be useful."

"Sorry?" The doctor appeared to be nervous, and Day understood why. Campbell was intimidating. Quiet and commanding and subtly dangerous. Like the military man Day now knew him to be.

"I was going to show the inspector something I found out here, and you might be able to say something about it if you come along."

"Say something about what?"

"Come."

Campbell turned and walked away into the dappled shadows, leaving no time for argument or refusal. Denby shrugged his shoulders at Day and meekly followed along. Day breathed deeply through his nose. He took his flask out, uncorked it, and took a sip. The heavy brown liquid warmed his chest. He looked around at the trees and then up at the featureless sky. He already missed his wife. And he was reasonably certain he was getting nowhere with the current case. He worried that he would never make it home to her.

He recorked the flask, stuck it in his pocket, and plunged into the woods close behind the doctor and the surly giant.

32

Hammersmith felt like a stranger in his own body. Like someone small and tired inside someone larger, looking out through the larger person's eyes at a place he'd never been and didn't understand. Across the room, a framed drawing, pen and ink, fell off the wall and the glass smashed. A cabinet walked itself sideways and toppled forward, narrowly missing Jessica Perkins. The chandelier above Hammersmith swayed back and forth, slowly, then faster until it began to twirl in ever-widening circles. The rug under his feet bunched and crept about the floor, only anchored by his own feet.

But he didn't fall.

In fact, Hammersmith couldn't feel that anything unusual was happening to the house. He could see the evidence of some seismic shift all around him, but he couldn't feel it. He stood rock-steady, or so he thought, as everything around him went utterly mad.

The Price children all sank immediately backward against the walls and slid to the ground, covering their heads with their forearms. The housekeeper disappeared somewhere back in the shadows of the hallway behind her. Jessica pushed Hammersmith away from the center of the room, and he fell backward against the sofa. Jessica rolled across the ground and fetched up against the tips of his shoes as the chandelier came loose from the ceiling and crashed to the floor where Hammersmith had been standing only seconds before. Teardrop-shaped crystals smashed against the rug, came loose from their wire fasteners, and propelled themselves outward in every direction. One of them hit Hammersmith in the knee. He thought it was beautiful the way it caught the light and reflected it back in a spiral.

And then everything stopped moving.

The Price children stood back up, all at once, as if this were part of the normal course of daily events. The housekeeper reemerged from the back hall with a broom and began sweeping up glass. Jessica picked herself up and brushed off her skirt. She tested her leg, put weight on it and winced. She smiled at Hammersmith as if embarrassed, then quickly looked away.

"Are you quite all right?" Hammersmith said. He still felt like a prisoner in someone else's body, and his voice came to his ears like a distant echo.

"Yes, thank you," Jessica said. "This sort of thing does happen."

"What sort of thing was it?"

"The house sank."

"It sank?"

"Yes, I'd judge that was at least an inch or two."

"It sank into the ground?"

"Into the tunnels beneath us."

"You should really stop building houses atop tunnels."

"Some houses weren't built atop tunnels," Jessica said. "I'd guess the tunnels were dug under this house after it was put up. The buildings here and the mines have grown together. They're intertwined. There's a relationship in a village that depends on the people, but goes beyond us."

"Couldn't the tunnels have been dug around the houses?"

"The tunnels follow the seam. Coal is king here."

"Good lord."

"Are you all right?"

"Yes, thank you. I think you saved my life just then."

"They shouldn't have a chandelier in here anyway."

"You know, I didn't feel the tremor at all."

"Perhaps it's because you've been shaking so badly," Jessica said. "You were shaking just as much as the house was."

All at once, Hammersmith was no longer a stranger looking out through his own eyes. His body came back to him and he could feel the bitter cold in his limbs and across his chest; he could feel himself shaking so hard that he was driving his own body deeper into the cushions of the sofa, every muscle tensing so that it hurt.

"What's happening?" he said.

"You're sick," Jessica said.

"I can't be as sick as all that."

"But you are. You can't help it."

"I can't?"

"No. You must have drunk the water here."

"What does the water have to do with anything?"

"I think it's in the water."

"What's in the water?"

"I don't know, but we've got to get you to your doctor right away. He's the one who guessed."

The last thing Hammersmith felt before he blacked out was Jessica grabbing him under the arms and hoisting him up. He tried to move his legs, tried to help her, but then he was gone.

33

The woods on this side of the village were more lush. The trees were farther away from the furnaces and, therefore, not as blackened. Fewer dead trunks, more new growth. Thick ash hadn't fallen this far out, season after season, obscuring the ground cover, killing the green. The snowfall was irregular, soft drifting flakes giving way to occasional showers of ice and snow as the leaf canopy bent under the accumulation and let it all go in a sudden cascade of freezing white.

Day moved along quickly, already acclimated to walking in the forest. He followed their faint trail and caught up to the others within a few minutes. Calvin Campbell was moving easily through the trees and brush, obviously used to the terrain, and just as obviously moving slowly so that the others could keep up. Dr Denby was having the most trouble. He stopped every few yards to catch his breath, and Day worried about the possibility of another coughing spell.

"How far is it?" Day said. He had to shout because Campbell was several yards ahead, barely visible through the tangle of branches.

Campbell stopped and turned, waiting for Day and Denby to catch up. "Not far," he said. "Not long ago, this would have seemed much closer to the back of the church. Where I'm taking you. The undergrowth would have been brittle and the leaves wouldn't have grown in yet on all these trees." He pointed up at the tops of the trees, but kept his eyes on Day. Deep shadows emphasized the cruel lines in the giant's face. "Someone would have needed to come this far in to be sure nobody would see them from the church's belfry."

Day turned and looked back the way they'd come. It was hard to be sure, but he thought he might still be able to see the high grey stone walls of the church through the trees. But then he might have been looking at a small slice of the heavy sky.

"See who?" he said. "Who are you talking about?"

"I don't know," Campbell said. "Come, we're almost there."

Campbell turned and crashed away deeper into the woods. Day and Denby hurried after him. Day listened to the wilderness around him, on alert for some sort of attack. He still didn't understand Campbell's motives. But the only thing he could hear was Denby's heavy breathing behind him. Campbell had left him behind in the woods the night before, and it was entirely possible that it was a habit with the bird-watcher. Then Day swept a springy branch out of the way and found Campbell just ahead of him, squatting down over something in a natural clearing in the forest.

He came up behind Campbell and could see the giant's muscles ripple and tense, uncomfortable with his back to anyone, but he didn't move away. Day took a step closer and saw something bulky, something pink and grey and soft, lying near the outer edge of the clearing.

Day reared back and bumped into Denby. The doctor craned his neck to see past Campbell, and Day saw the color drain from his face when he realized what he was looking at. The process of recognition took the doctor a few seconds longer than it had the inspector, but Denby was used to treating burns and scrapes and broken arms and fevers. Day was used to murder scenes and all that they entailed.

The mass of flesh that had been pushed up under some low-hanging branches was once a small pig. That much was clear from the shape of the remaining ragged ear that Day could see when he turned back for a second look. But the pig had been changed by the carpet of maggots that lay frozen in place across its skin and in its many gaping wounds. There was no blood. Not anymore. Animals had been at the body, tearing open the pig's belly and carrying away most of the juicy internal organs. The brief early spring had helped the denizens of the woods break the pig's corpse down into its various component parts, but the return to winter had interrupted that process. Still, its hindquarters had been burrowed into, and there were various exit points higher on the corpse where those burrowing creatures had come back up for sunlight and air.

Campbell broke a low branch off a nearby tree. It was thick with new green leaves. He used it as a brush, swiping at the pig's corpse, scraping off the layer of crunchy white maggots until more of the pig's skin was visible. He used his free hand to wave the doctor over. "What do you think?" he said.

Denby leaned over the body and then squatted to get a closer look. "Dead a week, at least," he said.

"I thought maybe we could heal it," Campbell said. His sarcasm was lost on the doctor. "Anything else you can tell us?"

Denby looked stricken. "What exactly would you like to know?"

"I'd like to know what killed it," Campbell said. "Is that something you can tell from looking at it?"

"A knife. It was killed with a knife or some other small sharp object. A miner's wedge, perhaps?"

"A lot of wounds there."

"Someone timid did this. None of those wounds is deep. A lot of shallow work done."

"Why would the pig sit still for that?" Day said.

"Bound by the feet. Ligature marks, front and back. The two front feet tied together and the same with the two back feet."

"Trussed up?" Campbell said.

"No, not pulled up on a trestle or a branch, the way it might be if someone were hunting."

"Then what?"

"Just tied."

"Pig won't sit still for a thing like that."

"Well, a wild hog wouldn't. But pigs are smart. If this one belonged to someone, it might wait, might trust its owner until it was too late to fight back."

"Anything else?"

"I don't know what you . . ." Dr Denby doubled over with no warning and began to vomit, each spasm taking an apparent toll on his frail body. Pale brown liquid splashed into the snow. After a minute or two, he fell over on his side and, before either Day or

Campbell could get to him, he hit his head on a log. He lay there, bleeding heavily from a scalp wound that looked, to Day's untrained eye, to be fairly minor. Day looked about for something to staunch the wound, grabbed up an end of the muffler Claire had made him, and thought better of it. He didn't want blood on it. Instead, he found Claire's handkerchief in his breast pocket and squatted over the doctor, pressing the clean cloth against his head and staunching the flow of blood. Denby's breathing was wet and labored, but steady. Day leaned against the log and looked up at Campbell. The inspector and the bird-watcher watched each other for a long moment. Tension crackled through the clearing.

"What are you doing in Blackhampton?" Day said.

"Helping you find Oliver Price."

"I told you. I've read about you."

"You don't know me. You don't know my life."

"I didn't say I did. I said I've read about you. I received a telegram from Scotland Yard this morning. I know you killed a man."

"I've killed a lot of men."

"You killed someone in London ten years ago. Over a woman."

"I did my time."

"Who was she?"

"Someone I loved. And still love."

"So you killed for her?"

"I don't allow anyone to threaten the people I care about."

"Did she wait for you, at least? The woman you went to prison for?"

Campbell was silent.

"I'll ask again," Day said. "Why are you in Blackhampton? Are you running from something? Hiding from something?"

"I've done nothing wrong. Unless you're going to arrest me—"

"I'd prefer it if you just talked to me."

"I could talk. But I think we ought to do something about this." Campbell gestured at the heap of Denby lying next to the dead log in the forest clearing. "That's a lot of blood."

Day agreed. He peeled Claire's handkerchief back and looked at the wound. It had stopped bleeding. Denby's skin was pale, and there was a trickle of blood running from a corner of his mouth. Day tossed the handkerchief into the brush (another excuse to buy her something with the proper monogram) and opened Denby's jacket. He undid the top few buttons of the doctor's shirt to make his breathing easier. As the shirt came open, Day gasped. He looked up at Campbell and saw that his eyes had grown large, his lips pressed tightly together. Day unbuttoned the rest of Denby's shirt and stood up. He stepped back, side by side with Campbell. He heard the bird-watcher draw in his breath.

Denby's entire torso, everything that had been covered by his shirt, was a writhing mass of dark wet shapes. Leeches writhed over the doctor's flesh, their fat bodies pulsing and bloated, filled with blood.

34

Kingsley had commandeered the inn's dining room over the strenuous objections of Bennett Rose, who had stalked off into the common room and had not been seen since. Kingsley covered the oak tabletop with a fresh linen bedsheet, and his assistant, Henry Mayhew, fetched in his microscope, slides, and a small crate full of tools and chemicals. A portion of the sheet was pulled away from one corner of the table, and a small burner was filled and set on a plate. Henry lit the burner and adjusted its tiny flame.

Kingsley spread the tiny floral dress across the opposite corner of the table and examined it under his lens, checking each of the dark stains for telltale signs of dirt clumps or paint buildup.

"First," Kingsley said, "shall we see if this is blood?"

"It looks like blood to me, sir," Henry said.

"And to me. But let's be certain."

He dabbed at the middle of the largest stain with a dampened cotton swab and rolled the swab across a glass slide. He rummaged in his satchel until he found a small vial of clear liquid, labeled *Acetic Acid Chloride*. He unstoppered the vial and the air above it began to smoke. Quickly, Kingsley filled a dropper and restoppered the acetyl chloride, then added a single drop of the liquid to the slide. Holding the slide in a pair of tongs, he carefully heated the mixture, then moved the slide over to his microscope. He set it on the platen and clamped it down, then angled the small mirror underneath to catch the room's lamplight and deflect it up through the slide. He bent over the lens and drew in a sharp breath. He stood and beckoned to his assistant.

"Look, Henry. Right in there."

Henry hunched down and looked through the leather eyepiece. He stood and shook his head, showed Kingsley a puzzled expression. "I don't see anything. I'm sorry."

"Crystals, Henry. Crystals are already forming on that slide. Take another look."

Henry sighed and looked again. He straightened and took a step back and smiled at the doctor, but said nothing.

"You still don't see them?" Kingsley said.

"I don't know what a crystal looks like, sir."

"That's okay, Henry. I suppose you can take my word for it. The presence of crystals means that we have found blood."

"Where?"

"On the slide. There's blood on the slide."

Henry's eyes grew wide and he gasped. "It must've come from that dress."

Kingsley chuckled. "I think you're right. Shall we see what else we can determine by looking at the dress?"

"I can't see anything except a mess, sir."

"Hmm. I see a mess, too. But there may be more to that mess than we at first suppose." Kingsley walked the six feet to the other end of the table and gestured at the dress. "You aren't familiar with Lacassagne's patterns of blood."

"Sir?" Henry said.

"There are shapes here."

"I don't wanna see no more blood, sir, crystals or no."

Kingsley smiled at the simple giant. "You don't have to look, Henry. I'm used to talking to myself in the laboratory. Or to Fiona, if she's around. I know we haven't quite got used to each other, but if you'll only let me talk aloud, you don't really have to listen to what I say."

"I will listen, sir. Only I still won't look, if it's all right."

"As I said. No looking. If I catch you looking . . ." Kingsley wagged a finger at Henry, who grinned.

"No looking, sir. Won't do it."

"Good man." Kingsley picked up his lens and peered at the dress. "So, what I see here are splashes and what I would call spurts."

"Spurts?"

"Just listen, Henry. If these stains are blood, then this dress was not worn by the victim. Whomever, or whatever, this blood belonged to was facing the person who was wearing the dress. Blood left a body, some body, and moved outward along what appear to have been several different trajectories, each of them making a mark on this dress."

"Who was it, sir? Who was the bleeder?"

"I don't even know that it was a person, Henry. It might have been livestock."

"A horse, sir?"

"Perhaps. But if so, not a terribly large horse. Not even a pony. Look at this."

"Please no, sir."

"I mean to say, *looking* at this, the blood exited some body and landed in a sort of a wave upon this one. It tapers in a specific way. The heart was pumping full force here." Kingsley pointed at a spot high on the front of the dress.

Henry continued looking away.

"But then here," Kingsley said, "it has become weak and isn't pumping so hard anymore." He pointed to a different spot, lower on the dress. "If we are to assume that the person wearing this dress was present as the wounds happened upon the other body, then we can see that the heart pumping this initial spurt was not so large as all that, was it?"

Henry shook his head. He looked a bit green, and Kingsley set down his lens. He patted Henry on the back in a reassuring way.

"So," Kingsley said, "a smallish creature of some sort was repeatedly injured. Blood exited its body and landed on this dress through, I would imagine, more than three apertures in the flesh of the injured body. There are droplets here, and here, indicating that either this dress or the injured body was moved as it bled out. Perhaps turned as the extent of injuries was fully realized by the person inflicting them. Or possibly to get a better angle, if someone was working to bleed out a lamb or small pig."

"I like bacon."

"Of course you do. So do I."

"I don't like it when people's hurt, though."

"People or pigs, we all hurt."

"But we don't eat people, sir."

"Well." Kingsley frowned at the dress. "Most of us don't."

35

Day and Campbell spent a few frenzied minutes plucking leeches from Dr Denby's torso and throwing them at the icy dirt. When they had finished, the doctor's pale flesh was dotted everywhere with angry red rings. Day buttoned Denby's shirt while Campbell rose and began grinding the squirming leeches under his heels. Blood oozed out into the patches of snow, white laced with pink, the forest floor like marble.

Denby stirred and his eyes half opened. "Brothwood," he said. "Needs me." He struggled to rise, but sank back against Day. "More will die, Inspector."

"What do you mean, more?" Day said. "Is the Price family dead?"

But Denby had lapsed back into unconsciousness. Day looked up at Campbell, who towered above him, staring off in the direction of the village.

"Who's dead?" Day said. "Do you know?"

Campbell shook his head. "He's a doctor, not a murderer. He's talking about the sickness, I'm sure. It's spreading through the village more quickly every day."

"Has he smothered everyone in these blasted creatures, then?" Day gestured at the leeches all round him. Campbell had destroyed most of them, but those that remained had stopped moving, frozen or hibernating.

"I don't know," Campbell said.

"It's entirely possible our missing family is in someone's house, isn't it? They could have gone visiting and collapsed."

"No."

"It's possible."

"I've checked every house."

"You've visited everyone?"

"I'm a bird-watcher, remember? I can travel about the village with field glasses and nobody thinks anything of it."

"You've been peering through windows?"

"I have."

"For the sport of it?"

"For the boy."

"Why do you want so badly to find that boy?"

"Why do you?"

"It's my job."

"Is that all? It's only your job?"

"Of course not. But I know why I'm here. I don't know why *you* are. I don't even know who you are. Not really."

"I thought you did know that. You have a telegram, don't you?"

Day laid Denby's head gently on the ground and stood so that he could face Campbell. "I know that you spent time in prison for killing a man in West Bromwich," he said.

"I did, yes."

"And now you are here in Blackhampton, and I want to know why."

"I have to be somewhere."

"You were released?"

"I was a prisoner for ten years. I've paid the price for my crime and I'm a free man."

"What's your connection to the missing boy?"

"We should get back to the village."

"You're not telling me anything, and I've let you go on keeping secrets long enough. You've been out in these woods, you found this pig or you killed it yourself, you know things about these people, and yet you're a stranger here."

Campbell drew in a sharp breath, and his gaze focused on Day. He hesitated for a long moment, as if weighing the words he wanted to use. Finally, he spoke. "I have no secrets," he said. "But it would be easier for me to show you than to tell you."

"Show me what? You've shown me your dead pig. Is there more?"

"I think there is. It's hard for me to know."

"Then show me."

Campbell nodded. He stooped and lifted Dr Denby as if he weighed nothing and led the way back to the path out of the woods. Neither of them spoke as they walked under the trees and through the brush. To Day, the path seemed shorter going back than it had been on the way to see the dead pig. The densest part of the woods fell behind them quickly, and the brush thinned out as the high grey walls of the church came into view. They had never gone very far from the village. Day was a reasonably fit man, but he struggled to keep up with Campbell, who was far older. Before long, the trees gave way to a narrow dirt path that widened out and led directly to the back of the church. Campbell led the way around the side of the massive building and up the wide stone steps to the entrance. He stopped there and turned, the limp Dr Denby draped over his forearms like an old bathrobe.

"Whatever you see," Campbell said, "whatever you think, you must continue the search for Oliver Price. That must remain your only goal here."

"What do you mean?" Day said. He was slightly out of breath and he could feel a sheen of sweat on his forehead despite the cold wind.

"You'll know in a minute," Campbell said, "but first promise me that you'll keep looking for the boy."

"Of course I will."

"Good." Campbell turned and shouldered the tall oak doors open and was swallowed by the solid shadows of the parish church. His voice came again from somewhere nearby, but completely disconnected from the world of white snow and bright grey daylight: "Come."

Day found his flask and took a long swallow, then put it away in his pocket and followed the bird-watcher into the darkness. His eyes gradually adjusted to the gloom of the foyer, but he could hear voices from deeper in the building, a burbling river of human noise, moaning and singing and occasional cries of pain. Campbell waited for Day to acclimate before pushing through the inner doors and leading the way into the sanctuary.

Directly ahead was an aisle that ran down the center of the

sanctuary to a raised altar. There were three steps down from the foyer to the sanctuary, and Campbell pointed them out to Day, cautioning him against tripping. To Day's right, pews filled half the room, row upon row of them, far more seating than the small village needed. But the pews were stacked too closely together for anyone to sit, almost on top of one another. Day realized that the pews had been removed from the left side of the room and piled between the remaining pews on the right. The empty half of the sanctuary had then been filled with makeshift beds. Dozens of people lay in cots or on blankets on the floor. Most were unconscious, sweating and moaning in their sleep. Some lay awake but delirious, calling out to absent loved ones or crying for help. Older children from the village, those who weren't already ill, moved between the rows, pressing wet cloths to the foreheads of their friends and relatives, spooning room-temperature broth into their mouths, and whisking away chamber pots, filled to the brim with vomit and worse. The enormous room was thick with the mingled odors of human bodies and excrement and incense.

"What's happening here?" Day said.

"This began before you arrived. People fell ill and didn't recover."

"Here in the church?"

"Dr Denby was unable to visit everyone in their homes. There were too many. The vicar was kind enough to offer up the space, and some of the men helped move the pews."

"And now Denby's sick, too."

"It does seem that way."

Brothwood chose that moment to approach them. He had been out of sight, somewhere among the sea of bodies. He had a small rug rolled up under his arm. Behind him, a pretty woman stared at Day with something like panic in her eyes. She was not young, and her face was lined with sorrow and pain, but her beauty was unmistakable, even in that place. She looked at Campbell, then away, and put a hand up as if to shield herself from their gaze. She dropped the damp rag she was holding and then walked quickly away, toward the altar. Day tried to watch where she went, but the vicar distracted him. Brothwood smiled a greeting at Day, but there was sadness and guilt in his manner. He touched Dr Denby on the arm, then led Calvin Campbell to a section of floor that was not yet occupied by the sick and unrolled the rug he was carrying. Campbell laid the doctor down on it and stepped back.

"Mr Brothwood," Day said, "why didn't you mention this to me last night?"

"What bearing does it have on your mission here?"

"The missing family might be in a house somewhere here, sick and in need of help. Not out in the woods or down in the tunnels. Our thinking may have run in entirely the wrong directions."

"I told you," Campbell said. "I've looked in every house in this village."

"And Dr Denby and I have been inside nearly all of them ourselves," Brothwood said. "Virtually no house is untouched by this plague." He shook his head at the ground and made a small motion for Day to follow him. Campbell nodded and then walked away from them in the direction of the altar, the direction the woman had gone.

Brothwood took Day by the elbow and turned him the other way, toward the foyer, but Day pulled away and pointed at the altar. Campbell was already gone. "What's back there?" Day said.

"Beyond the pulpit?"

"Yes."

"My rooms. Mine and Mrs Brothwood's, of course."

"Why would Mr Campbell go to your rooms?"

"Did he?"

"And who was that woman helping you when we came in?"

"Woman?"

"There was someone helping you minister to the sick. A woman. Where did she go?"

"I'm not sure who you're talking about. Many of the village women have volunteered to help, taking shifts here."

"Who is helping today? Right now?"

"I'm not absolutely sure. There's no requirement, you know; nobody organizing things. This all came on so quickly."

"How long ago?"

"Three or four days, perhaps. It's spread so fast. We weren't prepared. But, Inspector, this has nothing to do with your search for the boy. You mustn't let this, all of this illness, distract you from your duty."

"Everyone seems to be concerned with my duty. If you're all so worried about the missing family, why haven't you gone out searching yourselves?"

Brothwood wordlessly gestured at the room full of stinking, writhing bodies, their cries echoing off the high beams of the vaulted ceiling. The implication was clear enough: There weren't enough people left standing to conduct a search.

"Where is Mrs Brothwood?" Day said. "I'd like to speak to her, if I may."

The vicar turned and walked away, and Day followed him. Brothwood led him to the far end of the room, where an old woman lay on a straw-filled mattress against the stone wall. Her hair was long and white and tangled with dry sweat. She lay slowly writhing, her gnarled hands clenched in agony, her mouth half-open in a rictus of pain. It took Day a long moment to recognize the vicar's wife.

"It set in last evening," Brothwood said. "Soon after we returned from the inn."

"God," Day said. "What's happening here?"

"The Devil, I fear."

"I don't—"

"Someone did something dreadful to those people. To the boy, Oliver Price. Rawhead has come to live here, been welcomed by these evil deeds. That's why we need you. You and your friend Hammersmith. You're untouched by this. You can make it right."

"You don't need policemen, you need doctors."

Brothwood sucked in a deep breath and pointed in the direction of Denby's limp body, somewhere on the floor behind them. "Our doctor. And not even a cot left for him."

Day watched a dust mote dance through a beam of dim blue light. "How fortunate, then, that I've brought the best doctor in England for you." He motioned to a boy who was perhaps ten or twelve years old. The boy wrung a damp cloth out in a shallow bowl of water and laid it on an older boy's forehead, then stood and approached the inspector. "Go to the inn, boy," Day said. "Find Dr Kingsley and a man named Henry and bring them here immediately."

"Sir, my brother . . ."

"If there's any hope for your brother, you'll find it at the inn. Now, go."

The boy nodded and, with one quick look back at his unconscious older brother, hurried away, through the foyer and out of sight.

36

This presents a problem," Kingsley said. He held the shriveled eyeball up to the light and turned to Henry. "It's a real eyeball, of that I have no doubt. But I have no way of knowing whether it's a human eye or not."

"It should be in someone's head if it is," Henry said.

"Yes, that's where I prefer to keep my own eyes."

"Me, too."

Kingsley turned away before Henry could see him smile. The gentle giant had brought a touch of innocence and unaffected humor to the laboratory, something Kingsley hadn't known he needed or wanted there. It was much appreciated.

"So," he said, "the eyeball may not be particularly useful as evidence. But the bloodstained dress is another matter entirely."

He was interrupted by a commotion from the inn's great room.

Kingsley laid the eyeball back in its wooden box and led the way through the wide door out of the dining room. Bennett Rose was standing in the middle of the common room, holding his daughter Hilde in his arms. Her splinted leg stuck straight out like a flagpole.

"Here now," Kingsley said, "what's this then?"

"She won't wake up," Rose said. "She's not breathing."

For all the man's boorishness, Kingsley felt for Rose. He understood all too well the fear that went hand in hand with being a parent.

"Lay her down there," Kingsley said.

Rose put Hilde down on the hearth and smoothed her hair.

"How long has she been like this?" Kingsley knelt over the girl's body and put his ear to her mouth. He sat up and motioned at Henry. "Light my pipe, will you, Henry?"

"Your pipe, sir?"

"Yes, and be quick about it." He turned to Rose. "Well, man? How long since she last took a breath?"

"I don't know. She was like this when I found her. In her room."

"She's still warm," Kingsley said. "Pardon me, Mr Rose. This may appear indelicate of me, but I'll ask you to trust me. Perhaps look the other way, if it bothers you."

He cracked his knuckles, applied his long thin fingers to Hilde's abdomen, and began massaging the muscles through the coarse material of her dress, moving his hands in an upward motion toward her throat, then back down to begin again.

"Here now," Rose said. "What're you doin' that for?"

"For only a slim chance, I'm afraid. The girl's choking."

Kingsley continued kneading the girl's belly and chest, while her father stood watching, suspicious and hopeful.

"Henry," Kingsley said, "have you got my pipe lit?" He sat back on his heels.

"Yes, sir," Henry said. "But it makes my stomach feel bad."

"You're not used to the smoke, is all. Hand it over, please."

Henry placed the pipe in Kingsley's outstretched hand and ran out of the room. A moment later, they could hear him retching in the kitchen. Kingsley sniffed and dragged on his pipe, aware that Bennett Rose was fidgeting on the periphery of his vision. The doctor moved into position over Hilde's smooth, still face. He bent down and blew a mouthful of smoke past her lips, careful not to touch her with his own mouth. He did it again and then stopped, puffing on the pipe and waiting.

"You and your London ways," Rose said. Kingsley could see that the man was working himself up, preparing to blame the doctor for the death of his daughter. "Givin' her a smoke when she's already gone."

"Perhaps not gone yet," Kingsley said.

And at that moment, Hilde began to cough, hacking up great glistening dollops of mucus. She sputtered and choked, ratcheting forward with each gulp of air, bringing up gob after gob, all over herself and the hearth. Then she settled back down into a deep sleep, breathing regularly, her chest rising and falling in a comforting and utterly normal way.

"You did it," Rose said. He spoke quietly and ran his hand over Hilde's forehead, but he didn't look directly at the doctor, perhaps ashamed by his premature readiness to blame Kingsley for his daughter's death.

"A buildup of mucus. We needed to break it up and get her to expel it. Nothing really."

But Kingsley was secretly relieved. And secretly worried. The odds had been against him, and he had no way of knowing how long the girl had gone without oxygen. If she woke up, she might still be changed forever, a simpleton or worse. He shook his head and stood up, shouted in the direction of the kitchen door. "Henry, would you be so kind as to carry this young lady to a room upstairs?"

"I can do it," Rose said.

Before Kingsley could answer, the front door opened and three people stumbled in out of the blowing snow. The schoolteacher, Jessica Perkins, was supporting Sergeant Hammersmith, who appeared to be semiconscious. Behind them trailed a young boy Kingsley hadn't seen before. With a quick backward look at Hilde to make sure she was still breathing, the doctor rushed to them. He took Hammersmith's other arm and led the three of them to the fire. Jessica and Hammersmith collapsed in separate chairs.

"Sir?" the boy said. "Would you be Dr Kingsley? Or Henry?"

"In a minute, lad," Kingsley said. The boy nodded and squatted at the hearth. He held out his hands and rubbed them together as close to the fire as he could get. He glanced at the sleeping form of the girl there, but didn't appear curious. His overcoat was threadbare at the elbows and hadn't been buttoned. Kingsley was astonished by how poorly the people here took care of themselves. He turned his attention to Jessica. "What's happened?" he said. He loosened Hammersmith's collar and shouted over his shoulder to Rose. "Bring water."

"No," Jessica said. "You were right. It must somehow be the water. I did what you asked and practically forced well water on the children. The older two wouldn't drink it and they prevented the little one, Virginia, from drinking."

"Mr Rose, please ignore my request for water," Kingsley said. "Perhaps a glass of beer, instead."

Rose retreated to the kitchen.

"And this child?" Kingsley pointed to the boy on the hearth. "Who is he?"

The boy looked up at him and grinned. "I'm Baggs, sir. Nicky Baggs."

"My pleasure, young Mr Baggs."

"We ran into him right outside," Jessica said. "He was coming in at the same time."

"Then we'll get to him in a minute," Kingsley said. "You won't mind waiting, lad?"

"No, sir. But not more than a minute, please, sir."

"Good man," Kingsley said. He turned to Jessica. "So Mr Hammersmith has been drinking the water here, hasn't he?"

"I believe so."

"And the children are drinking something else?"

"Milk and ginger beer."

"Exclusively?"

"It appears so."

"And you? Have you been drinking the water?"

"I can't remember. I have a cistern I draw from at the schoolhouse. I don't know the last time I drank anything else."

"But there's a central well?" Kingsley said. "A source for most of the people in the village?"

"Yes, of course."

Rose returned and held a glass of clear amber beer out to the doctor. Kingsley took it from him, looked at the unconscious form of Sergeant Hammersmith, and took a swallow of the beer himself.

He wiped his mouth with the back of his hand and set the glass down on the hearth near the boy.

"Mr Rose," Kingsley said. "Do you get the inn's water from the village well?"

Rose nodded.

"We must get word to everyone not to drink any water from that well until we know more," Kingsley said. "I may be able to test it. Meantime, we should all be drinking beer and milk."

"Too late," Rose said. His voice was barely audible. "Sickness has got 'em already."

"Got who?"

"All of 'em. Mrs Rose among 'em."

"Your wife is sick?"

"Everybody's sick. Little Hilde, too, now. She was the last in my family besides me."

"It may not be too late. Which room is Mr Hammersmith's? We'll need to lay him down."

"Sir?" the boy said. "Is it all right if I tell you now? It's only that I'd like to get back to my brother."

"What is it, lad?"

"The policeman from London says to tell you—if you're the doctor, that is—he says to tell you that you're to come to the church right away."

"Please go back and tell him that I haven't time. I have sick people here who need my attention."

"But there's only two here, sir."

"Yes, son. Two sick people."

"It's only that there's lots and lots of them at the church, and now they're without a doctor."

"Lots of what?"

"The sick, sir. Must be maybe a hundred."

Kingsley rocked back on his heels and pushed a hand through his wild hair. An instant later, he was shrugging his overcoat on. He hurried through the door to the dining room and began shoving his tools into his satchel. He hollered back in the direction of the great room as he packed. "Henry, can you carry that girl as far as the church? We'll care for her there. Miss Perkins and I can handle Hammersmith between us."

He shut the satchel, latched it, and took a quick look around the room. He had everything. He ran back into the great room and found Jessica buttoning the boy's overcoat for him. Henry stood at the front door, holding Hilde in the crook of one arm.

Hammersmith stood beside him. "I only needed to sit down a moment. I'm feeling quite a bit better now." He smiled and reached for the doorknob and nearly fell down. "Farther away than I thought it was," he said.

Henry put his free arm around Hammersmith's shoulders. "I have him, sir. I've got them both. You just lead the way."

Kingsley smiled. At least there was something he could count on. "Come on, then," he said. "Let's see what we can do to help these poor people."

37

D o I understand correctly?" Day said. "This was once Blackhampton's inn?"

"Oh, yes," Brothwood said. "It only became the parish church many centuries after it was built."

The inspector and the vicar were standing in the foyer, just inside the door, with the sea of sick villagers spread out before them across the sanctuary. Day positioned himself so that he could see the main doors of the church, his back to the rows of makeshift beds. He hoped to see Dr Kingsley come running in at any moment. But he had Mrs Brothwood's note in his pocket, the note that indicated her husband was hiding something. Day watched the vicar's eyes.

"So the inn where I'm staying . . . ?" Day said.

"Is relatively new, yes. Built well within the past century," Brothwood said.

"Why would one turn an inn into a church?"

"Why, I suppose it had something to do with the beauty of the architecture and, of course, the size of the place. One needs a decent-size building to house a place of worship."

"Even in a village as small as this?"

"Most particularly in a village this size. Everyone here comes to church on a Sunday, and the place must accommodate them all. We don't have the luxury of multiple houses of worship."

"Where did guests sleep? When this was an inn, I mean."

"Oh, all of this was quite different, as I understand it. Of course, I wasn't here at the time."

"Of course."

"The rooms down here were all torn out and the altar was brought in. The pews were built locally, I believe. A carpenter who lived here at the time."

"That must have been a lot of work for a local carpenter."

"Yes, it must have been."

"And so you live in the back of this place, rather than in a proper vicarage?"

"It's somewhat unusual, but not unheard of."

"Wouldn't the architecture of an inn, particularly an inn built many centuries ago, have features that a proper parish church would not?"

"I'm sure I don't know what you mean."

Day smiled. "Of course. Merely thinking out loud, Mr Brothwood. Do you mind if I look around the place?"

"Please do. I have sick people I should tend to."

"I won't keep you."

Brothwood hurried away. He stopped halfway down the aisle

and looked back, then turned and moved off down a row of bedrolls spread out on the hardwood floor. Day glanced around the foyer and took a last longing look at the front doors before stepping down into the sanctuary. He frowned at the three steps that separated the room from the foyer door and kicked at them. They seemed solid enough.

He followed along in Brothwood's general direction, but avoided looking at the sick people on the floor. He kept his back to them and his eyes on the floorboards and the timbers in the ceiling. He walked down the center aisle and took a moment to genuflect at the great gold cross over the altar before examining the apse. The altar itself was simple and sturdy, constructed of solid wood, perhaps by the same carpenter who had long ago built the pews. The top of the altar was a flat slab of river rock, polished and shining. There were candles at either end, and Day moved each of them to assure himself that they weren't secretly levers that would move the altar. When nothing happened, he felt mildly foolish and looked surreptitiously about to see if he was being watched. He imagined Brothwood must be somewhere nearby, paying close attention to him, but he couldn't see the vicar anywhere.

There was a large hollow ball on a chain hanging beside the altar, and Day sniffed it. The scent of incense was nearly overpowering. Here in the apse, the incense masked the odors of vomit and excrement. Perhaps Brothwood stole odd moments for himself up here away from the stink of illness.

There was an unlatched door on the wall near the south side of the pulpit, and Day used the toe of his boot to push it open, keeping his head back. Nobody came barreling through, and so he moved cautiously into a small room that was dimly lit by candles in the four corners. The walls were bare plaster broken by evenly spaced wide timbers, stained dark. There was a bed against the far side of the room and a compact wardrobe next to it. A fireplace was built into the adjacent wall near the foot of the bed, its embers long since burnt out, the chimney cold. Opposite the fireplace was Mrs Broth-wood's writing desk. Day recognized the stationery stacked to one side, next to a quill pen that still rested in the inkwell. It was a cheerless place, and Day wondered at the fact that there were no feminine touches. It didn't seem as if Mrs Brothwood had made many contributions to her living quarters.

Day circled the room once, stomping on the floorboards as he went. Mrs Brothwood's note had said that someone was under the floor, but the floor sounded solid to Day. He was certain he was on the right track, though. He went to the door and closed it, then moved to his right, tapping on each of the regularly spaced timbers set into the plaster and lathing. He put his hands as high over his head as he could and rapped his knuckles against the wood, work-ing his way down, listening for irregularities and feeling for loose boards. He did this again and again, one timber after another, until his knuckles were sore and swollen. He pulled the bed and the wardrobe out from the wall and examined the space behind them, then pushed them back again. When he got to the fireplace, he felt around the outside of it and across the mantel, then began prodding the stones in the surround. Halfway across the top of the fireplace, just under the mantel, a round stone moved. The stone looked like it had been handled more than the rest of the fireplace had been. It was dark with the oils from many hands, and it had been worn smooth. He sucked in his breath and took hold of it. It twisted under his hand, and he wiped his palm on the leg of his trousers to get a better grip.

"Excuse me, Inspector."

Day jumped and turned quickly away from the fireplace. The vicar was standing in the open door. Day hadn't heard the door open and he wondered how long Brothwood had been standing there.

How much of Day's search had the vicar seen?

"Yes, Mr Brothwood." Day's voice was breathy and too loud. He could feel his heart beating hard in his throat.

"Dr Kingsley is here, Inspector. He's asking for you in the sanctuary."

"Is he, now?"

"Your sergeant is with him."

"Very good. I'll, um . . . I'll go right now and have a word with them."

Day gestured for Brothwood to lead the way. Day took one last look at the fireplace and followed the vicar out of the little room.

He was now certain there was someone or something concealed under the hearth. He had suspected there was a priest hole here and now he felt he knew where the secret entrance was. He would be very glad to get Hammersmith's help in uncovering the Brothwoods' secret hiding place and finally beginning to unravel the many mysteries of the little village.

38

You don't look any better, Nevil," Day said. "Sorry to say."

"I've had a bit of a rest," Hammersmith said.

"You might call it that," Jessica said. "He's been dead to the world."

"He's very ill," Kingsley said.

"Bring him over here," Day said. He led the way to the abandoned side of the sanctuary, where the pews were stacked nearly on top of one another. Hammersmith sidled between two of them and sat heavily. He gave Day a wan smile. "Just for a moment," he said. "I'm a little dizzy, is all."

"How sick is he?" Day said.

"He's been drinking the water here," Kingsley said. "Have you?"

"I'd have to think," Day said. "But I'm not fond of water. I believe I've stuck with beer since we arrived."

"Sensible of you."

"So whatever he's got . . ."

"I believe it may be typhoid. Or something very like typhoid."

All thoughts of secret hiding places in the village church left Day's mind. He frowned, suddenly worried about his sergeant. Hammersmith was capable of withstanding a great many things, but this was alarming. "Typhoid?" he said. "Is that fatal?"

"Not necessarily. He needs rest. He's got a fever."

"And he got typhoid from the water here?"

"I believe so," Kingsley said. He nodded at Jessica. "Miss Perkins here was kind enough to undertake a little experiment on the Price children for me."

Day took a step back. "You experimented on children?"

"Quite harmless," Kingsley said.

"What did you do to them?"

"I wouldn't harm my students, Inspector," Jessica said. "I merely offered them a glass of water."

"But you said there's typhoid in the water," Day said.

"Yes," Kingsley said. "That's my working hypothesis."

"What if they'd drunk it?" Day said.

"They didn't drink it," Kingsley said. "That's *why* I think there's typhoid in the water."

"But how would they know that it was in the water?"

"That's a very good question."

"How does typhoid get into water?"

"Another good question. Much like cholera, it depends on tainted sewage entering the water supply. Dr Snow proved that beyond question some thirty years ago."

Day turned to Jessica. "How might the water supply here become tainted?"

"It can't be," Jessica said. "Everybody knows to keep our waste far from the water we drink. We're not savages here, Inspector."

"And yet . . ." Day waved his hand in the direction of the moaning hordes at the other end of the sanctuary.

"I tell you it can't have happened," Jessica said.

"Is there another way? Can typhoid work some other way than that, Doctor?"

"Well," Kingsley said, "I suppose it needn't be waste itself. If, for instance, an infected person had lost consciousness, perhaps fallen into the well . . . It's possible, but surely someone would have noticed a thing like that."

"I think someone did," Day said. "Constable Grimes sent to Scotland Yard because there are three missing people in this village. Three missing people and any one of them might have been sick, any one of them might have taken a tumble into that well."

He stood there for a brief moment, staring at Kingsley as the implications sank in. Then, without a word, he spun on his heel and ran from the sanctuary, took all three steps into the foyer at once, and banged through the heavy front doors. He was gone before anyone else could react.

39

<hr/>

Day hit the road running. He took the main street away from the church and the deep woods behind it and raced headlong toward the center of the village. The wind was blowing much stronger than when he'd entered the church, and the snow drove straight at him, a billowing white curtain. He was still wearing his overcoat, but he'd left his hat behind, and his ears were numb within seconds. His feet slipped on the icy cobblestones and he adjusted his pace, twisting his boots slightly with each hurried step to gain better traction. His feet sank deep in the snow and his boots filled, soaking his socks, freezing his ankles.

He misjudged the bend in the road and stopped short, his nose inches from the front of the apothecary. He turned and fished his gloves out of his pocket, decided from memory where the road curved, and set out again, going more slowly now, pulling on his gloves as he went.

It was much like swimming, he thought. Swimming in some arctic current.

It took him nearly half an hour to reach the well at the center of town. He couldn't see the inn, but he knew it was only a few yards away from him. The same journey, going the other way, from the inn to the church, had taken him perhaps ten or fifteen minutes earlier that morning, before the sun had risen and brought the storm with it.

He stood at the mouth of the well, close enough to tumble into it. It was made of the same grey stone as the older buildings in Blackhampton, stacked and mortared into place. Day judged the surrounding wall to be roughly three feet high, a sloped cover over the top that allowed most of the current snowfall to slide off and pile at the base of the well in an ever-widening wedge.

He took a deep breath and uncorked his flask.

"You're not going down there, sir."

Day turned, his mouth full, brandy fumes stinging his throat and nostrils. He swallowed and caught his breath before he spoke. "How on earth did you keep up with me, Nevil? You're ill."

"Not so ill as all that, sir," Hammersmith said.

"I thought I was moving awfully fast."

"I did think I'd lost you for a bit there, but then you materialized out of the snow before me. Your dark overcoat was easy enough to follow."

"Ah, you must have caught up at the bend in the road. You've got a better sense of direction than I have."

"You can't have thought I'd let you go out alone in this."

"I didn't think at all. Just wanted to get here."

"You weren't planning to go down that well, were you?"

"I believe I was."

"It's not necessary."

"It probably is. There's a body down there, I'm sure of it. Maybe three bodies."

"They'll keep."

"The baby might be down there."

"Little Oliver."

"Yes, little Oliver."

"Still, let the storm pass."

"And there's a church full of sick people. We need to find out what they've got so Kingsley can go about curing them."

Hammersmith nodded. "I'll do it, then." He peeled off his coat and let it drop in the snow.

"Don't be a fool, Sergeant. You're so weak, you can barely stand."

"I told you. I just needed a rest, and now I've had it."

"After running through that storm? Look at you. You're weaving where you stand. You can barely stay upright in this wind."

"You're not ramrod straight yourself, sir. It's a strong wind."

"And you don't like tunnels, Nevil. Enclosed spaces."

"Nobody likes tunnels."

"Someone must. A village full of miners."

"Where are they when we need them?"

"Sick."

"Where's Constable Grimes? This is his village. He should do this."

"I haven't seen him yet today and I don't want to wait," Day said.

"I'm going in, and I'll brook no more argument. Besides, I need you up here to make sure I get back."

Hammersmith stared at him for a long moment without speaking.

"It's an order," Day said. "You're staying here. Now put your coat back on."

There was another silence, and then Hammersmith reached for his overcoat. "You'll stay in constant contact with me as you go," he said. "You'll shout out to me the entire time."

"I'll be glad to."

Hammersmith shrugged his coat on and buttoned it. He stepped closer, and they both stood at the lip of the well, their knees touching the stone wall. Day was on guard, mildly worried that Hammersmith might try to jump in. His sergeant was often too impulsive for his own good. But much of Hammersmith's energy seemed to have drained from him, blown away by the bitter wind. They peered down into the well, but there was nothing to see. Nothing but inky blackness.

"How deep do you think it is?" Day said.

"Deep," Hammersmith said. "Judging by the water levels round here, I'd say maybe two hundred feet. Maybe more."

"That's deep enough."

"There may be nothing down there to find, sir."

"I pray that there isn't. But we have to find out," Day said. He sighed. "Here, hold my flask for me, Nevil. I'd better get going before I lose my nerve."

40

Freddy Higgins sat slumped in his seat, unconscious, rocked to and fro by the sway of his carriage as the horses raced down the only real road in Blackhampton. They chuffed and clopped through the snow, their steamy breath trailing behind them, streamers in the dim gaslight that lit the silver-grey afternoon.

The horses knew the village. One of them was four years old and had grown up here, been raised by Freddy from birth. The other had come from Wolverhampton, sold to the blacksmith in return for services rendered, and had been on loan to Freddy for more than a year. The younger of the two tended to pull ahead and then adjust for the gait of the older horse. They made the turn in the road easily, even though neither of them could see it buried in the snow, and pulled up short at the church, nowhere else to go. The younger one whinnied and bucked, and the carriage shook on its axles.

A moment later, the vicar Brothwood appeared at the double doors, hugging himself against the cold. He took one look at the motionless boy in the driver's seat of the carriage and turned around, disappeared into the darkness of the foyer. Long seconds ticked past, and then Dr Kingsley emerged, summoned by the vicar. Behind him, Henry Mayhew lumbered into view. Kingsley hopped down the wide snowy steps of the church and checked Freddy's pulse. He turned and pointed, and Henry came to him, taking the steps all at once. The giant lifted the sick boy from the carriage and turned and carried him into the church.

Kingsley lingered. He frowned at the carriage and at the horses, unsure about what to do with them. But his concern was for the human beings moaning inside, and he could hear them even through the blowing wind, and so he left the horses there stamping in the cold and went back inside to tend to young Freddy.

41

The well's roof protected a simple pulley system with a thick rope that extended down into the dark. Hammersmith reached out and grabbed the rope. He bent a loop in its length and tied a bowline knot, then yanked it up snugly against the pulley assembly. He stepped back and cupped his hands, blew on them, and rubbed them together.

"That should hold," he said.

"Do you want my gloves?" Day said.

"You'll need them."

Day looked at the rough length of rope and nodded. "I suppose I will," he said.

He brushed snow from the stone ledge and sat down, gathered the ends of his overcoat around his legs, and swung around so that he was looking into the well. There was nothing to see. The curved irregular wall extended down a few feet and then faded to black. It was impossible to gauge how deep it was.

"Give me a stone."

Hammersmith looked around him. The landscape was smooth and white. He shuffled away to where he imagined the side of the road to be and reached his bare fingers under the thick blanket of snow. Watching him, Day winced in sympathy. Why didn't the sergeant own a pair of gloves?

It took Hammersmith a bit of searching, but he finally fished a small stone from under the snow cover and brought it to Day at the well. Hammersmith's fingers were bright pink and dripping wet. He handed over the rock and then jammed his hands into his pockets to warm them.

Day dropped the rock into the well. It fell out of sight, and they both listened. They heard it clatter once, twice, a third time, stone on stone. Then a soft distant sound that might have been a splash.

"Well," Day said, "I suppose that tells us this thing isn't deceptively shallow."

"I had hopes," Hammersmith said.

Day smiled. "No point in waiting longer, I suppose." He looped the rope around his right hand and tested his weight, then pushed off from the lip of the well and swung out so that his feet rested against the far side. The well was wide enough to accommodate him easily, but still felt constricting. The back of Day's overcoat scraped against the far side as he lowered himself. He kept his knees bent and walked himself down, the rope held tight in his left hand. He let out a bit of slack at a time, running it up through the loop in his other hand. He worked his way downward, inch by inch, the rope burning the palms of his hands through his gloves and squeezing his fingers tight together. The light faded so gradually that he didn't notice when the darkness closed around him completely. He simply worked at lowering himself into the ground and put all thoughts of the miles and miles of earth around him out of his head. The stone walls inside the well were jagged. River rocks had been fitted together around the shaft centuries earlier, but there had been no care taken to keep them smooth or regular. The wall wasn't meant to be seen or touched, only to keep the well from falling in on itself. Day found ledges and niches for his boots, which made the journey easier, but he took care not to get his toes caught.

He didn't want to end his career in a Black Country well.

He stopped after what seemed an eternity and braced his back against the wall behind him, his legs locked and his feet flat against the stones across from him. He didn't release his grip on the rope, but he let it go slack. His arms ached and his legs were sore. He could no longer see anything of himself; his own body was invisible to him in the darkness. He looked up and held his left hand above him, and the silhouette of the tip of his thumb completely blocked the pale grey circle that was the opening of the well. He still had no way of knowing how deep the well was or how much farther he had to go to reach the bottom of it. He looked down and around and up again, but there was nothing to see except that circle of light far away.

"Hammersmith! Nevil!" Day's voice echoed and bounced around him, frightening in its starkness. He could hear panic rising in it.

The sergeant's voice floated down to him, amplified by the well, so that he might have been dangling on another rope next to Day. Or even waiting for him somewhere down below. "I'm here."

"Thank God!"

"I haven't left. But I haven't been able to see you in quite some time."

"You're looking?"

"I am, but it's no use."

"I can't see you looking."

"Do you see my head at the top of this thing?"

"No."

"I'm here," Hammersmith said again.

"I must be deep if you blend in with the daylight up there."

"Do you want to come back up?"

"No," Day said. He wasn't sure he could climb back up if he tried. His arms hurt and his chest felt tight. He had assumed that Hammersmith would help get him back to the surface by pulling on the rope, but now he wasn't sure Hammersmith would be strong enough to do the job. Perhaps if the well weren't so deep and the sergeant weren't so sick. Still, there was no point in stopping. They would figure out a way to get Day back up when he was all the way down.

He slid his back against the wall and let more slack go through the loop, lowering himself again.

"Keep talking, Nevil," he said.

"What do you want me to say?"

"Anything, man, just give me something to concentrate on aside from this hole in the ground."

"I'll do my best." There was a long period of silence, and Day thought that the sergeant had misunderstood him. He didn't want to have to ask Hammersmith to talk again. It would make him seem weak and frightened. Then: "Sorry," Hammersmith said. "We've been joined by others up here. People from the village."

Day was overwhelmed with relief at hearing Hammersmith's voice. He grinned and spoke to the tiny circle of light far above him. "There are still people in the village?"

"Apparently not everyone is sick."

"How many up there?"

"Three," Hammersmith said. "Two strong men, both of them miners, and a woman. They heard us out here. Curious about what we're doing."

"Did you tell them?"

"A bit of it. Not much to tell yet."

"Not much to do yet, either, but don't let them leave." Day took a deep breath and blew it back out through his mouth. Now there were people who might be able to help Hammersmith pull him back up. A lucky break. He took another deep breath and noticed a change in the air. He could smell something. Water? Decay? Something organic at any rate, something aside from cold stone and his own sweat.

"I might be reaching the bottom of this thing, Sergeant," he said. His voice moved around him, back and forth against the stones, loud and hollow and eager-sounding. "It feels warmer down here."

"What's that, sir?"

"Just wait."

He opened his hands a fraction and moved faster down the well until he felt his palms burning through his gloves. He tried to clamp down on the rope, but he was falling too quickly. He pushed his feet out and caught the opposite wall, but slipped and fell farther, his head now below his feet, traveling upside down toward the bottom of the well. He panicked and lost his grip with his left hand, grabbed at the stones beside him. There was no purchase to be found there, and he plummeted faster. The vertical tunnel vibrated with a deep roaring noise, and some small part of him realized that he was shouting.

There was no one to help him.

It was the realization that he was utterly alone in the dark well that brought him back to his senses. The rope was still looped around his right hand, zipping out below and above him. He kicked out his feet again and pushed against the wall and tucked his chin against his chest and slammed his back into the stones behind him. At the same time, he clenched his right fist and found the rope with his left hand, wrapped it around his forearm, around his elbow, back around his hand another time. His descent slowed and then suddenly halted, yanking his arm up and out. There was a jolt and a flash of pain in his shoulder, and Day gritted his teeth, braced himself sideways against the walls of the tunnel. He concentrated on catching his breath. One in, one out, one in, one out. He could hear his heart beating. And he could hear Hammersmith's voice, small and tinny, from somewhere far above him, no longer amplified, too distant to have been audible above his own howling.

"Sir? Sir, are you all right?"

"I'm here, Nevil!" He had to shout to send his voice hurtling upward toward that pale little spot that represented the sky.

"What happened?"

"I decided to take the express route to the bottom!"

"Can't hear you well, sir! I'm coming down there!"

"No, Nevil! Stay where you are!"

"You're okay?"

"I'm fine, I think! Fell and hurt my shoulder, but I'm okay!"

"Is it broken?"

"I don't . . . Wait a moment!"

He repositioned himself, made sure he was wedged solidly, feet against one side, back against the other, and let go of the rope. Immediately, his hand felt cold and his shoulder began to throb painfully. He tested it, moved it in small circles, back and forth. Agonizing pain, but nothing broken, so far as he could tell.

"It will heal, Nevil! I'm going on!"

"Carefully, sir!"

Of course, carefully. "Yes, thank you, Nevil!"

Day looped the rope around his left hand now, letting his tender right shoulder hang loose and naturally at his side, and walked himself slowly downward, scraping the back of his overcoat against the stones behind him. He was breathing hard again and grunting, and the sound was unsettling, but he was his only company. He could hear Hammersmith talking up above, but he couldn't make out the words.

A moment later, the seat of his trousers began to feel cold, and he gradually realized that he was wet. The thought crossed his mind that he had lost control of his bodily functions, but then the wetness spread out across his thighs and up his spine, and he realized that he had backed into a cold pool. He adjusted his grip on the rope and eased his legs down and splashed into the well water. He kicked his legs and windmilled his aching arm and let out a huge whoop of triumph. The thought crossed his mind that he was now trapped at the bottom of a well in the middle of nowhere, and he smiled to think that, despite his circumstances, he had never been so happy to be alive.

"Sir!"

"I'm all right, Nevil! I've reached the bottom!"

"Is it iced over?"

"Not at all! It's still warmer than it is up there, but the water's cold!"

"Hurry! You can't stay there!"

"Are you sure? I'd love to stay!"

"What's that, sir?"

"Nothing, Sergeant! A little humor!"

He paddled around in the narrow space, taking care not to lose track of the rope. He bumped into something hard and felt its contours with his free right hand. It was the bucket. He used it to brace himself, which freed up his left hand. He kicked in a small circle, running his hands over the walls. The stones here were smooth and damp, polished by centuries of water. There was a thick organic odor wafting up from the water, like a warm stagnant soup. The bucket thunked into something, and Day turned toward it and reached out. His gloved hand brushed against a handful of moss and he spidered his fingers, feeling outward until he realized that the handful was too delicate to be moss. He groped at the object and felt a soft curve, a small bony ridge. The moss was hair, and there were pliable swellings under it. Day realized he was holding his breath, praying that he had found an animal of some sort, a squirrel or a badger that had taken a tumble into the well. But as his fingers continued to explore, he knew what he had found and his heart sank.

"Nevil!"

"I'm here, sir!"

"I think I've found him, Nevil!" Day said.

He turned the object over in the water, dead and limp and yielding.

Yes.

"I've found Oliver Price!" he said.

INTERLUDE 2

———◦◦◦◦———

ANDERSONVILLE PRISON,
CONFEDERATE GEORGIA, 1865

T he dead wagon rolled out through the high gates of the Andersonville stockade. Calvin Campbell was in the bed of
the wagon, jostled about along with four other prisoners.
Cal was the only one of them still breathing. Shallow breaths
through his mouth because the dead men had begun to ripen in the
hot Georgia sun. One of the men had open sores on his arms and his
throat, and Cal watched maggots writhe in and out of the wounds,
slimed pink with blood over their pearly whiteness. He gagged and
closed his eyes, concentrated on keeping his gorge down.

After what seemed to Cal like most of the day, but couldn't have been more than twenty minutes or so, the wagon stopped and the bodies were pulled out, one at a time. He listened to them thunk into the ground like so much meat. The man next to him, the maggot farm, was second to last out of the wagon. Some of the larvae were left behind, wriggling blindly on the bare planks. They would burn to a crisp in the sun and be buried under the day's bread rations before long.

Cal felt a hand close over his ankle, and then he was being dragged the length of the wagon's bed. He braced himself for impact with the ground, but another hand grabbed his other ankle, and then someone had his wrists and he was being hoisted through the air. He risked opening an eye and looked up. One of the men carrying him was Richard Devine, a friendly fellow who had taken Cal's shebang and his tattered clothing in trade for helping him hide in the wagon that morning. Devine saw him looking and gave him a slight curt nod. Cal glanced at the second man, but didn't know him. A friend of Devine's, he supposed. They carried him to the trench, the same trench where Joe and Duane rested, and they heaved him up and through the air. He felt himself start to tense and forced his naked body to go limp. His arms and legs flopped and he clenched his jaw despite himself, anticipating the coming impact. His shoulder hit the side of the trench and he bounced away, landed solidly atop a mound of skin and bone and mud. He was glad the trench was nearly full and he wasn't one of the first to be thrown in a grave. A new trench would be much deeper, and the fall might actually kill him. His shoulder felt bruised, but nothing seemed to be broken.

He laid still and listened, and after a few minutes he heard the wagon roll away. Far in the distance, he could hear soldiers laughing and birds calling. He heard a cricket chirping somewhere close by. He realized he was holding his breath and he let it out all at once. He had made it. He was outside the walls and he hadn't been discovered.

He took a fresh breath and immediately vomited into his beard. He felt the warm liquid run across his chest and down his arm.

The trench was full of a week's worth of dead bodies. Hundreds of them. And he would have to wait here among them until dark. At least ten hours. Once the sun went down, he would need to climb out of this hole and make it to the river without being seen. He tried to vomit again, but there was nothing left in his stomach. He hoped he would get used to the stench, but it seemed unlikely. The air was so thick he could see it, like a poisonous fog that crept across the top of the trench, thick wet tendrils, searching him out. Cal took another shallow breath through his mouth and passed out.

Grey Eyes dropped his cigar and ground it under his boot heel. He listened to the night: the river burbling below him, crickets chirping nearby, and a bat squeaking somewhere in the woods ten yards away from him. He squinted at the dark tree line and then up at the moon. It was a sliver, barely enough to light the way down to the water.

He rested the barrel of his rifle against a river birch and unbuttoned the fly of his standard-issue grey uniform trousers. A moment later he felt the release of pressure in his bladder and he sighed.

Four feet to his left the water erupted, and Grey Eyes turned as something huge, a dark shape against the darker sky, moved toward him up the riverbank. He let go of himself, letting urine stream down his leg as he reached for his rifle, but the shape was on him too fast and he felt rough hands grab him and spin him off balance. The other man—it was clearly a man—pulled Grey Eyes backward toward him, one hand against the guard's forehead, pinning the back of his head against the other man's chest. Grey Eyes reached across his body for the knife on his belt, but the other man already had it.

Dry lips rasped against Grey Eyes's ear, and a low voice whispered, "This is for Joe Poole, you cold-eyed bastard."

Before Grey Eyes could call out, he felt the tip of the knife puncture the thin flesh of his right cheek. He felt warm liquid flow down his jaw and he grabbed for the other man's arm as the knife was dragged across his face. There was a split second of resistance and a slight pop and his lower lip fell free and slapped against his chin. There was a flash of blinding pain and Grey Eyes saw bright pinpricks of light. The other man let go of him, and Grey Eyes sank to his knees and toppled forward into the river with a splash. He heard footsteps in the grass, someone running for the tree line, and he wondered whether his attacker had kept his knife. It had been a gift from his father when Grey Eyes had joined the Confederate Army two years ago. It occurred to him that he might never see his father again. Darkness washed over him and he began to sink into it, but then he felt cold river water flowing over and through the wound in his cheek and the pain abated enough that he regained his senses. He rose slowly, fighting the pull of the current, and crawled up onto the bank. The pain in his cheek returned, but he used the pain to help him focus. A prisoner had escaped, had meant to slit his throat, but had missed. Had the knife gone in two or three inches lower, Grey Eyes knew he would be dead.

He moved forward, one hand held out in front of him, until he found the river birch. His rifle was still there. The other man hadn't seen it in the dark. Grey Eyes smiled and nearly passed out from the pain. He would have to remember not to smile again until his cheek healed. He rose to his *feet, dripping river water and blood, picked up his rifle, and walked to the tree line.*

He paused there and looked back at Andersonville. Once he stepped into the trees, Grey Eyes knew that he would be counted AWOL. The army didn't have the men to pursue him, but it went against his grain to abandon his post. It was a matter of honor. His father hadn't raised a quitter. That was one more thing his unseen attacker would have to answer for when Grey Eyes found him.

The thing to do would be to go back to camp and raise the alarm, muster a force to search the woods. But that would take time, and the man in the dark might get away.

Grey Eyes shouldered his rifle and slipped quietly into the woods. He would find that other man, even if it took him the rest of the night.

Hell, even if it took the rest of his life.

West Bromwich, The Midlands, 1871

The girl could not have been older than seventeen, and so Cal tried to ignore her. But she had come to the pub every night for the past week, and every night he had been there, too, at the same table in the corner, nursing his whiskey. It was evident that he had caught her eye because she had passed by his table several times every evening, and each time she passed, she lingered a bit longer in front of him, swirled her skirts a bit higher, and batted her long lashes in his direction. He supposed he stood out as a stranger in the village, something new and perhaps even exotic, and he felt certain it was time to move on. She was a pretty girl, but he preferred to keep to himself. She was too young for him and likely to want something lasting, besides.

Cal Campbell had not stayed in the same place for longer than a month in the last six years. He had struck out north from Andersonville, begging and borrowing food and clothing, stealing when he had to, and had booked passage on a British supply freighter as a deckhand.

He had landed in Liverpool and made his way to Maidenkirk, staying long enough to assure his family that he was alive and reasonably well. His father had given him a purse containing two hundred pounds and suggested that Cal move on. He understood. He was practically an American now, an embarrassment to his father.

At the train depot in Dumfries he had seen a man from a distance. The man's teeth had been visible through his cheek, and there was something familiar about him. He wanted to get close enough to see that man's eyes, to see the color of them, and when he realized that he expected them to be grey, he knew he had been followed.

Grey Eyes, the terrible guard from Andersonville, was alive. He was alive and he had followed Cal all the way from America.

Cal had hopped the first train going south and had changed trains three times that first day. He had been careful not to leave a trail and had watched behind him at every station. Grey Eyes was conspicuous and Cal didn't think the guard could surprise him, but if he had followed him this far he would not easily give up. Still, Cal could lead him on a merry chase.

By the time Cal arrived in West Bromwich, he had lost track of the number of cities he'd lived in. The Black Country village was just another stop in the peripatetic life he now led. He planned to stay there for a week, perhaps two, then move on again. He wouldn't stay anywhere long enough to give the grey-eyed American a chance to find him.

But the girl was interesting.

On the third night the girl made a play for his attention, he smiled at her. He hadn't meant to. He couldn't help himself. He immediately stood and left the pub, but he returned the next night.

And the next night.

Tonight he pretended not to notice the girl, but he saw her smile, trying to catch his attention, and he knew she was the only reason he was still in that village. He thought of Joe Poole and his friend's ready smile and finally he began to understand that he was lonely. He had worked so hard to avoid human connections, to avoid anything that might make him weak or vulnerable, that he had neglected the small part of himself that still craved the company of others.

He knew he should move on, leave West Bromwich and never look back.

Instead, he stood and went to the girl and bowed.

"My name," he said, "is Calvin."

"It's good to meet you, Calvin," she said. "My name is Hester."

42

What did he say?" Campbell said. "I can't hear him."

"He said he's found the boy," Hammersmith said.

"Oliver? He's found Oliver down there?" The Scotsman looked stricken. He was panting, still out of breath after emerging from the midst of the blizzard just seconds earlier. There was a small gathering of men around the well. The blizzard had caused the seam to be shut down for the day, and some of the miners and their families had come out to see why one of the strangers was shouting down into the village well. Word had apparently spread, despite the storm, and the throng was growing. Hammersmith had said very little to any of them, but as more people were drawn to the spectacle, the first arrivals filled them in on the situation. Aside from these short murmured conversations, the villagers had been silent, riveted to the sound of Day's distant voice. Hammersmith saw one of the miners reach out to pat Campbell on the back, as if comforting him.

"He's mistaken," Campbell said. "He must be. It's dark down there. He doesn't know what he's found."

"I hope you're right," Hammersmith said. Several of the other men mumbled in agreement. Nobody wanted Oliver Price to be at the bottom of the well. "Quiet," Hammersmith said. "He's talking."

The crowd went silent and Hammersmith leaned far over the well's lip, listening. He felt Campbell take hold of the back of his overcoat, steadying him, and Hammersmith grabbed the posts on either side of the well as insurance in case the bird-watcher intended to push him in.

"I didn't hear you!" Hammersmith turned his head so that his right ear was out of the wind and concentrated on Day's answering voice. The inspector sounded so far away that he might have been in the next village over. Hammersmith felt Campbell shift his weight behind him.

"Did he say anything more?" Campbell said. "What's he saying?"

"He can't climb back up," Hammersmith said. "He's hurt his shoulder and can't carry the boy back up here."

"Tell him to sit on the bucket and loop the rope around his waist. We'll pull him up," Campbell said.

"That's not very steady. If he falls off the bucket, the rope could slip upward and strangle him," Hammersmith said.

Campbell shook his head. He seemed impatient, less interested in Day's safety than in what he'd found down there. "Then tell him to make a noose, a big loop of some kind, and get it up under his arms."

"Sir!" Hammersmith bellowed into the darkness. "Tie the rope around you! Somehow! Do it so that you're comfortable and so it will bear your weight!"

Hammersmith waited. He straightened up and looked around him. There were perhaps twenty villagers around the well now. Most of them men, but there were three women. Hammersmith guessed that their children had all been left safe and warm inside their homes. Everyone looked grim and anxious. And cold. Campbell was shivering. He was the only person there who wasn't wearing a coat or a hat, or even a jacket. He must have come out in a hurry.

Hammersmith heard a faint echo and leaned back over the top of the well. He listened for a moment and then grabbed the rope and began to pull at the knot. He shouted over his shoulder, "He's ready! Let's pull him up!"

Campbell stepped forward and gently moved Hammersmith back out of the way, then took the length of rope from him. The other villagers stayed where they were, watching the giant Scotsman. Campbell loosened the bowline knot that Hammersmith had tied earlier and pulled the rope through the wooden pulley block until it was taut. Then he hauled the line up, hand over hand, more quickly than any three men could have moved together, the muscles in his massive arms and shoulders rippling with the effort. Hammersmith could hear the rope zinging through the pulley and could see steam from the friction rising in the cold air. It had taken Inspector Day a half an hour to get to the bottom of the well, with gravity on his side. It took Campbell five minutes to bring him back up.

Day was dripping wet, the back of his overcoat in tatters and his gloves hanging torn and useless from his wrists. Calvin Campbell took one look at what Day was holding in his arms and turned and disappeared into the storm. Hammersmith heard his muffled footsteps in the snow, running fast back toward the church. Hammersmith briefly considered following him, but instead he went to Day and helped his inspector back to solid ground where two village women were ready with a blanket for him.

Nobody looked at Oliver Price and nobody spoke a word, but the third woman of the group took the tiny body from Day and carried it away into the storm.

43

⟶⟨◇◇◇⟩⟵

The storm gave the American time to think. He had checked his snares after killing the policeman and found a badger, caught in the wee hours, still alive and snarling. Its meat was oily and dense, but it filled the American's belly well enough. He had to finish chewing each bite and swallow before both hands were free to tear another piece from the badger's carcass. He chewed with one hand pressed over the gap in his face, and while he chewed, he thought.

One of the men from London had seen the American in the woods. The American could have killed him then, but Campbell had been nearby, and so had the village constable and the other Londoner. The odds had been against the American. He liked to kill at a distance, liked to use the rifle. He was good with it. Fighting and killing in close quarters was more difficult and—although he would never admit this, even to himself—the American was afraid. Ever since Campbell had cut away part of his face, the American had avoided people, kept himself at a distance. It was better that way.

But the man from London had seen him. He had probably told Campbell. Which meant that Campbell was either holed away somewhere, waiting out the storm, hiding from the American, or he was already leaving the village, running again. Campbell had never stood his ground, never sought the American out, and there was no reason to think he would decide to do so now.

Campbell had spent the better part of the last decade in another prison where the American couldn't get at him. Campbell seemed to have an affinity for prisons. So the American had waited. He was good at waiting, but he didn't want to wait any longer. There was trouble in this Black Country village and Campbell was mixed up in it somehow. The American needed to end this soon, before Campbell disappeared again.

If Campbell was waiting out the storm, he would be leaving as soon as he could get away. Unless he was leaving now, using the storm as cover. Away from the village, he could go in any direction and lose himself in a big city or in the isolated countryside. Tracking him was a laborious process, and the American didn't want to have to start over. So, whatever Campbell had decided to do, the American felt he only had one logical course of action open to him. The train was the fastest way out of the village, and so Campbell would eventually show up at the depot.

The American gathered his things and packed his bag. He cut two thick badger steaks off the animal's body, wrapped them in pages torn from another book he'd found in the schoolhouse, and stuffed the bundle in the bottom of his gun bag. He cleaned the Whitworth and loaded it and slung it over his shoulder, picked up his bags, and crawled out the window, leaving the fire he'd built there to die out by itself.

The sun was invisible, far above the grey clouds, so the American took a moment to orient himself, using the tree line as a marker. Then he set out, trudging through the deep snow toward the train depot.

He would wait there, and Calvin Campbell would eventually come to him.

44

Henry Mayhew staggered past carrying a long wooden pew. Kingsley estimated the pew weighed perhaps three hundred pounds and he wondered, not for the first time, about the strength of his simpleminded assistant. Henry was of no use when it came to performing even the most straightforward of chemical experiments or basic autopsy procedures, but Kingsley had no regrets about hiring him. Henry was loyal and strong and kind, and he made Kingsley smile, which was a rare enough thing.

Putting the pews back in place was the first thing Kingsley had decided to do after taking a look at the rows of hacking, crying, moaning villagers in the sanctuary. More than half of his new patients were on the floor, some of them lying directly on the cold floorboards. That wouldn't do. Obviously someone, probably the vicar Brothwood, had determined that more bodies would fit in one side of the sanctuary if all the pews were moved to the other side. And Kingsley imagined that the decision had been motivated by a desire to preserve the antique pews. Otherwise, the situation made no sense. And so Kingsley had ignored the vicar's stammered objections and he had put Henry to work restoring the sanctuary's original layout.

It had been slow work. A few patients had been carefully moved to the center aisle and a pew had been positioned in their place. They had been moved back, two patients per pew, feet to feet, their heads at the outer ends, and another row of patients had been moved to the center aisle. More villagers were being moved to the aisle than were being taken back because they took up more room on the pews than they did on the floor, but as pews were moved across from the east side of the sanctuary, space had begun to open up there. Henry, with the help of a few of the healthier volunteers, was ferrying them all the way across the aisle and gradually filling the entire room with sick people.

It looked like a battlefield.

Kingsley had tried to turn the altar into a makeshift worktop, but the vicar had put his foot down and so he had moved the podium down to the middle of the aisle and emptied his satchel on it. He had sent two boys to the apothecary with a few quid and a list of ingredients to bring back. Basically, he'd told the boys to empty the apothecary out. And he was sure there still wouldn't be enough to work with. There had to be more than a hundred seriously ill people to take care of, and Kingsley had yet to see a well-stocked village apothecary. Still, he would assess the situation when the boys returned and begin treatment as soon as he possibly could.

Meanwhile, he and Henry were doing what they could to make the villagers more comfortable.

He helped Henry transfer a thin young woman onto a pew, then stopped by little Hilde Rose's pew to check on her. She was awake, her eyes open and staring at the timbers of the ceiling. She turned her head when he approached.

"I feel all right now," she said. "May I go home?"

Kingsley smiled. "Let's have you rest a bit longer, okay?"

"If you say I must."

"I do say so. I have something for you, though." He reached into his pocket and brought out the tiny box that held the eyeball. "I was told this is yours."

"My eye!" She took the box from him and opened it, peeked inside and closed it again, and held it tight to her chest. "Thank you for returning it. It's such an odd little thing, don't you think?"

"I suppose it must seem so to you."

"You're finished looking at it?"

"I am."

"And was it helpful to you? Do you know who it belongs to?"

"As far as I'm concerned, it belongs to you."

"But it started out in someone's face. We should try to discover who that might have been, shouldn't we?"

"I'm reasonably certain it started out in a pig's face, my dear. I don't think this is a human eyeball, though I can't be sure." Kingsley almost laughed at Hilde's look of disappointment. "It's better that nobody lost an eye, though, isn't it?"

"Yes," Hilde said. "I suppose it is. Oh, of course it is. I'm sorry. It's only that it would be so much more special if it were from a person, wouldn't it? I mean, if the person weren't hurt too terribly."

Kingsley opened his mouth to respond, but before he could speak, the front doors banged open. Calvin Campbell rushed through the foyer and down the central aisle without bothering to shut the doors behind him. He took no notice of anything or anyone, but ran, slipping and sliding in his wet boots, straight to the apse and through the door to the vicar's cramped quarters. Brothwood hurried after him.

Kingsley patted Hilde on her head and stood. He looked for Henry and saw his giant assistant rushing up the aisle toward the foyer. Henry bounded up the three steps and closed the door against the blowing wind and snow. He turned to Kingsley with a puzzled look on his face, but the doctor shook his head and shrugged.

A moment later, someone shrieked. It was a woman's voice, and it came from the small room that Campbell and the vicar had just entered. The voice sank in pitch and became a low wailing sound, longer and louder than the combined moaning of the villagers in the sanctuary. It wasn't recognizably human, there were no words, but it was undeniably the most mournful sound Kingsley had ever heard.

Someone's life had just been ruined.

He and Henry stood, side by side, their eyes riveted to the door. It slowly opened and the vicar reappeared. He went directly to the altar and knelt before the cross. Then Calvin Campbell emerged from the back room, his arms around a woman who could barely walk. Kingsley was good at sizing people up by sight: age, weight, social class, obvious maladies and defects. But this woman's face was distorted by crushing grief, and it was impossible to tell whether she was thirty years old or fifty. She staggered along beside Campbell, who was half carrying her, her long blond hair like a veil, a rough blanket draped over her shoulders.

The two of them walked past Kingsley and Henry without looking up or acknowledging their presence. They went beyond the last of the pews and turned and walked through the foyer. Campbell opened the main doors and led the woman out.

Henry watched after them until they had been swallowed by the storm, then closed the doors again and returned to Kingsley's side.

"Who was she?" he said.

Kingsley glanced to the front of the church where Brothwood still knelt in prayer. "We'll find out eventually," he said.

Henry nodded and crossed the aisle and picked up another pew. There was still work to do.

45

The man in the tunnels had walked slowly south from the unmarked grave and continued for half a mile. He was weak and tired. No sleep and little food in days, so he sat for a bit with his back to the wall. He knew the old seams and pits like the back of his hand. He had spent many lonely nights traversing every passage. He had visited the grave often, each time wondering whether he would finally feel remorse or shame, and each time he had felt nothing at all. He knew that he was an evil man, but knowing it didn't make him feel anything, either.

There was a second grave that had been dug next to the first, an open empty hole, waiting for the man, but he hadn't found the strength yet to lie down in it.

He was far from the active seam, but there were still ways in and out, and he easily found the egress he wanted. When he felt rested, he climbed twenty wooden rungs that were sunk deep into the earth on both sides of the shaft. Nobody used those rungs anymore, but at one time this had been a heavily trafficked shaft and dozens of men had traveled up and down them every day. The ladder here was permanent and would probably outlast everybody in the village. It would last until the tunnel eventually collapsed in on itself.

The rungs were dusted with snow, each rung piled higher than the one below it, but he was still mildly surprised to find himself in the midst of a storm when he poked his head up out of the shaft. He had been in the tunnels for days and had anticipated bright spring sunshine up above.

He hauled himself up onto level ground and adjusted the pack on his back. He squinted into the snow. Ahead was the village well. Beyond it, he knew, was the inn. He was a few paces from the main road. His home was nearby, and he assumed his remaining children were waiting there for him. It was even possible his wife was waiting there, too, but he considered it far more likely that she was already in West Bromwich or Scotland or somewhere even farther away. Maybe she had taken the children with her. The man wouldn't have blamed her for that.

The parish church wasn't far. Beyond that, nothing but wilderness. He judged it was late morning, perhaps early afternoon, but the smooth grey sky gave him no clues. It wasn't nighttime, and that was the only thing he could tell for certain. Constable Grimes might be anywhere in Blackhampton, but he was most likely to be somewhere along the road between the well and the church. That was where the tiny jail, the tiny post office, and all the other tiny businesses were located. The man had just got his bearings and decided on a course of action when he heard a woman crying. The noise was soft, but distinct, muffled by the falling snow and distorted by the wind. The man took a step back away from the road, and a moment later, two shadowy figures staggered past, moving purposefully along the road. They were looking down at their feet and walked right by the man without seeing him.

He was close enough to recognize the woman as his wife. And she was crying. And he was reasonably certain he knew why.

She was not in West Bromwich or Scotland. She had stayed. There was only one reason for her to do that. And there was only one reason she might now be crying, so many days after she had left him.

They were headed in the opposite direction from the one he'd already decided to go in. They were walking toward the inn. He let the couple get a few yards ahead of him and then he stepped onto the road, its cobblestones buried deep under ice and snow, and followed in their rapidly filling tracks.

46

<hr/>

Day and Hammersmith trudged through the snow, half supporting each other, snowdrifts up past their ankles, swirling under the legs of their trousers, and whipping about their calves. Day was nearly frozen solid, his shredded coat and gloves useless, sopping wet. Hammersmith was sicker than he had let on, barely conscious. Blackhampton had not been kind to its London visitors.

They followed in the general direction in which the village woman had taken the baby's body, hoping to find shelter wherever they were going. Then the inn loomed up out of the storm, no more than twenty feet in front of them, the enormous ancient tree sheltering it from the wind like a cliff, and Hammersmith closed his eyes and walked blindly toward it, pulling Day along. Someone opened the door when they got there and someone else ushered them to one of the blazing fires and settled them in big comfortable armchairs by the hearth. Their coats and boots were removed and thick blankets wrapped around them and hot mugs of boiled broth shoved in their hands and, when Hammersmith opened his eyes again, Bennett Rose was standing in front of him with a glass of beer. He set the beer on a little table beside the chair and nodded gravely at the sergeant and disappeared in the direction of the dining room.

Hammersmith sipped at his broth. He didn't care whether it was drugged. Warmth spread through his chest and radiated outward through his arms and into his fingers, down through his groin and legs and toes. He gulped the rest of the broth and set the mug on the little table and took up the beer and drank that, too. For a brief moment, he thought he might vomit it all back up, but it stayed down and he began to feel like a human being again. He glanced over at Day and saw that the same process of transformation had begun to occur in the inspector. He closed his eyes again.

He woke to the sound of the inn's door opening and slamming shut again. He sat upright and looked over the back of the chair and saw Calvin Campbell step across the threshold into the great room. Campbell was escorting, practically carrying, a woman who might have been lovely had her face not been screwed up in a rictus of grief.

Bennett Rose emerged from the back and went to them and took the woman by the hand. He led Campbell and the woman up the stairs.

Hammersmith stood and saw that Day was awake, too. Hammersmith was nearly dry and felt marginally better than he had all day. He left his blanket on the chair and followed Day to the stairs, and the two of them went up. There was a gathering of villagers outside a room down the hall from Day's, and the crowd parted for Day and Hammersmith to pass through. Calvin Campbell was standing just inside the door. He glanced at the policemen, but said nothing. The woman who had come with him was sitting on the edge of the bed, staring down at something there.

Hammersmith crossed the room, looked over the woman's shoulder, and saw Oliver Price's body. The woman was smoothing the baby's wispy hair back from his pale forehead, absently repeating the same motion again and again. Hammersmith shuddered and looked away. Day gripped his arm and moved past him, put a hand on the woman's shoulder, and waited until she looked up at him.

"Mrs Price?" Day said. "Hester, I'm very sorry for your loss."

The woman blinked and a single tear escaped, ran down her face, and dropped from her chin onto the back of Day's hand.

Day stepped away from her and nodded to Campbell before leaving the room. Hammersmith followed him. Bennett Rose stepped out into the hallway after them and shut the door behind him. They went quietly to the stairs and down before Hammersmith finally spoke. "Shouldn't we question her?" he said.

"When she's had some time," Day said. "I have a feeling whatever's happened here has reached its conclusion, and not in the way Hester Price hoped it would. She doesn't have anywhere to go now."

"Do you think she killed her child?"

"No," Rose said. Hammersmith was surprised to hear him speak. "No woman would end her own child."

"No," Day said. "I agree, but not for that reason." He and

Hammersmith had both seen crimes against children. They were aware that mothers were as capable of evil acts as anyone else. "I think the only thing keeping her here was the hope that Oliver was still alive."

Day crossed to the hearth and took a seat. Hammersmith reluctantly followed. Bennett Rose fetched mugs of beer and sat with them. He seemed to need something to do, and he seemed to want company.

After a time, Rose cleared his throat to get their attention. "I woulda made tea, but I don't know about the water."

"Yes," Day said. "Beer might be safer at the moment."

"I did somethin' last night," Rose said.

"You drugged us last night," Hammersmith said.

Rose nodded and looked at his feet and mumbled something incoherent.

"I'm sorry?" Day said. "I can't hear you."

Rose looked back up at him. "It was the wrong thing to do, but I meant no harm by it. Just wanted to keep you somewheres Rawhead wouldn't take you."

"That's foolishness," Hammersmith said. "You might have killed us if you'd got the dosage wrong."

Rose's expression was pure misery. "I know it."

"I'm afraid there will be consequences, Mr Rose," Day said.

"All I'd ask is you remember why I did it. That I was tryin' to help. A good night's sleep's all I wanted for you."

"We'll try to keep that in mind."

Rose nodded again and slumped back in his chair. Hammersmith would have liked to be able to talk freely with Inspector Day, but even if Rose left the room, there was nothing to talk about. Not really. They had discovered two of the three missing Prices. The case was nearly finished and all the little mysteries of Blackhampton were resolving themselves. Sitting and waiting made him feel restless. All they needed to do was find Sutton Price and they could go home.

As if on cue, the inn's front door opened and a man lurched across the threshold. He was disheveled and wore a week's worth of beard. His eyes were wide and wild, and they settled on the two policemen before the man had come even three steps into the room.

"Who are you?" the man said.

Day stood up and adjusted his jacket. "More properly," he said, "who are you, sir?"

"That's Sutton Price," Rose said. He jumped to his feet and pointed at the scruffy man, an outlet for the innkeeper's guilt and nervous energy. "Where were you? Where were you when your son was dying?"

Sutton Price ignored the question. He pointed at the back door next to the bar. "Is my wife through there or upstairs?"

"She's upstairs," Day said.

Bennett Rose scowled and turned and walked away from them, disappearing into the dining room. The door swung shut behind him.

"Is she with him?" Sutton Price said.

"Who do you mean?" Day said.

"You know who I mean." Price dropped his pack on the floor and rooted through it. He came up with a revolver, but he didn't point it at the policemen. Instead, he moved toward the stairs. Day's Colt Navy was in his hand instantly, pointed at Price's center mass.

"Please put your weapon down, Mr Price."

"I can't do that." Price's voice was even and measured and reasonable.

"What do you have planned, sir?"

"I'm going to kill him and take my family back."

"I can't let you kill anyone."

"I understand," Price said. In one fluid motion, he swung the revolver up and pulled the trigger. There was a roar of exploding gunpowder and a piece of the mantel splintered away behind Day. Before Day could return fire, there was a corresponding blast from the back of the room and Price's pack burst open, scattering its contents over the floor of the great room. Bennett Rose strode through the dining room door, a rifle held at his waist, pointed at Price.

"I meant to miss you with that shot, Sutton," Rose said. "But I won't miss again, trust me on it."

Price's revolver wavered, suddenly presented with three possible targets. Hammersmith used that split second of indecision to launch himself across the room. He rammed into Price, knocking him on his back, the revolver spinning away across the floor. Day walked calmly to Rose and pushed the end of the rifle's barrel down toward the floor.

"Thank you, Mr Rose," Day said. "That's quite enough shooting for one day."

"I've ruined my own floor," Rose said.

"With good cause."

There was a clatter of footsteps on the stairs, and Calvin Campbell appeared on the landing.

"What's happened?" he said. Then he saw Hammersmith helping Sutton Price to his feet and his face went pale. "Keep him away from her," he said.

Price roared back at him. "She's mine!" Hammersmith had to restrain him, pulling his arms up behind his back. It wasn't easy to do given that the sergeant still felt weak and sick to his stomach.

"You're a monster!" Campbell said. "You killed your own child!"

The fury went out of Sutton Price, and he sagged against Hammersmith. "He's really gone, then?"

"You know he is," Campbell said. "You've not only killed your boy, but Hester, too. She'll never recover from this."

"I didn't do it." Price's voice was soft now, barely audible in the huge front room of the inn, drowned out by the sound of the crackling fires on both sides. "I've spent the week looking for him, hoping he was somehow alive."

Campbell looked down at his feet. He was still blocking the landing, as if to keep Price from running past and up. When he spoke, his voice was as soft as Price's, but there was steel in it and everyone clearly heard him. "Then you're a fool. Even if that's the truth, you've done everything wrong."

"I want to see him. At least let me see my own son."

Hammersmith looked over Price's sagging shoulder at Day, who nodded.

"Keep a hand on him, Sergeant."

"Is it wise to let him upstairs?"

"We can't keep a man from his own child." Day turned to Bennett Rose. "If you wouldn't mind keeping your rifle near to hand."

"I'll keep my eye on Price," Rose said. He seemed grateful for the chance to do something, to make amends for drugging them.

"Let's take him upstairs, then. Just for a moment. Let the man have his grief."

They made a strange parade up the stairs of the inn. Calvin

Campbell led the way. Next came Sutton Price, Hammersmith right behind him with a hand gripping his elbow. After them came Bennett Rose, his rifle held casually at his side, but loaded and ready. Day followed behind them all, watching everyone involved, trying to fathom the connections between them.

Campbell entered the small room that held Oliver Price's body. Hester Price hadn't moved from the side of the bed. Her fingers still absently traced the contours of her son's face. Campbell went to her and put a hand on her shoulder, and she reached up and laid her hand over the top of his.

Sutton Price entered the room silently and went and stood beside his wife on the other side. There was a long moment, and then an anguished shriek boiled up from somewhere inside him. He threw himself across the tiny body on the bed. Hester finally noticed him, and her reaction was immediate. She lunged at him, beating her fists against his back, screaming at him.

"You did this! You did this to him!"

Price didn't even seem to notice her. Hammersmith and Day stepped in and took her arms and pried her away from her husband. Calvin Campbell stood useless at the side of the bed, seemingly unable to decide what to do.

The blast of a rifle round into the ceiling ended the drama. The shot echoed back and forth and around the room, and plaster sifted down like snow over everyone. The sound had the effect of calming Hester Price, and she went limp in Day's and Hammersmith's arms. Hammersmith looked at Rose and saw that he was once more pointing his rifle at Sutton Price.

Rose looked back at Hammersmith. "She's right," he said. "It's clear now, isn't it? He must've killed his own child."

"I thought you believed in a monster," Day said. "Something called Rawhead."

"But there's no arguin' with the evidence."

"What evidence?" Hammersmith said.

"Just look at him."

Hammersmith looked at Sutton Price, but saw nothing he hadn't seen already.

"Not him," Rose said. "Look at the boy."

Hammersmith looked past the father at the son's body. Thick black liquid bubbled up from little Oliver's mouth and ran down his cheek, soaking into the pillow beneath his head.

There was no doubt that the boy was dead.

And yet he had begun to bleed.

47

You're not very clever, are you?" Virginia Price said.

Henry Mayhew looked up at her and wiped his forehead. He was staying busy, helping the volunteers at the church in whatever little ways he could, moving heavy pews across the sanctuary and bringing buckets of snow inside to melt by the fire, providing fresh water for the villagers. All of it was hard labor, but he was proud and happy to be of use. Now Henry had found a pew that was stuck tight to the floor beneath it and he was down on his knees, working to free it.

He smiled at Virginia. "What did you say?"

"My name is Virginia. What's yours?"

"Henry."

"Hello, Henry. I'm pleased to make your acquaintance. I said that you're not very clever."

"No. I'm not." He bent and continued to pry at the underside of the pew, but he could still hear the little girl behind him. He stopped again, but didn't look back at her.

"I'm very clever, Henry," Virginia said. "My father tells me so."

"It's good to be clever."

"But you wouldn't know about that."

"No."

"Then why does the doctor keep you if you're so dull?"

"I'm strong. And he's nice."

"He doesn't seem nice to me. He seems grumpy."

"He's grumpy and nice."

"You can't be both. You must choose one or the other."

"He's much more clever than anybody else, so I think he knows how to be different things at the same time."

Virginia laughed, the tinkle of chimes in an empty space. "You make no sense at all, Henry. I like you."

"Thank you." Henry scowled at the floor. The girl had made him self-conscious, and he could feel his face flushing with humiliation. "There are other children here," he said. "You could play with them if you wanted to."

"But I don't want to. They bore me terribly. You're much more interesting; very like a child, but huge. Huger than a normal adult, I think."

"I'm big."

"Do you know any games we might play? You probably don't, if I have to guess, but I could teach you some."

"No, thank you." He got his fingertips under the edge of the pew and yanked upward. It didn't budge, but the fingernail of his left index finger tore and he gasped with the pain. He turned his head, but couldn't see Virginia. He could still feel her presence behind him, though, could hear her breathing. He checked his finger and saw a tiny bubble of blood forming along the side of the torn nail. He stuck it in his mouth and sucked on it. It was salty and metallic. "You should go play with someone else," he said, talking around the finger in his mouth. "I don't want to play any games."

The girl laughed again. "You said that once already, you numpty."

Henry nodded. She was right. He had repeated himself.

"Do you live in London?" the girl said.

"Yes."

"Do you live with the doctor? Are you his son? That would explain why he keeps you around."

"No. I have my own home."

"You can take care of yourself?"

"Yes. My home is very small. The inspector made it for me out of a lamppost."

"Oh, he did not. You're fibbing."

"I'm not fibbing. He really did."

In fact, Inspector Day had found Henry Mayhew living on the street and had given him the key to a small jail cell that was hidden within the wall at Trafalgar Square, nestled just under a lamp. Henry had moved into the spartan space, and there was just barely enough room in it for him to lie down. He owned almost nothing. Day had changed Henry's life forever with that one small act of kindness, and now Henry tried to follow his example by donating his time and wages to help others. There were many people still living on the streets of London, too many to count, people who didn't have the luxury of a clean dry lamppost home in the square.

"You're a liar," Virginia said. "A liar and a half-wit. I really do like you very much."

Henry shrugged. The pain in his finger had passed. He tugged on the pew again, and this time it came loose with a loud ripping noise. He pulled it loose and tried to stand with it, but his right foot wouldn't come out from under him and he fell forward, slamming his head against the side of the pew. He lurched sideways and rolled onto the floor, his head throbbing, sudden tears in his eyes. He wiped his face with the back of his hand and looked at his feet. His bootlaces were tied together. The little girl was doubled over, laughing. Henry sniffed. It seemed to him that the girl's laughter wasn't a happy sound. He pressed the palm of his hand against his temple until the throbbing sensation subsided enough to be tolerable, then bent and began untangling his laces.

"You should have seen yourself," the girl said when she had caught her breath. "You looked funny."

"You tied my feet together. That wasn't nice."

"Well, of course it wasn't. It was a prank. Pranks aren't meant to be nice."

"I don't like pranks."

"You're not clever enough to think of any or you would like them."

"I don't think I would."

"Have you ever seen a pig bleed?" the girl said.

Henry ignored her. He left his boots untied and stood.

"I have. Seen a pig bleed, I mean," Virginia said. "Its eyes get very big when it gets cut. They bulge out. It's quite funny. That's what you looked like when you fell down."

Henry said nothing. He stooped and lifted the pew, turned and moved across the aisle. The girl skipped ahead of him and put out her tiny foot to trip him, but he was ready for more pranks and stepped easily over her leg, moved her gently out of the way with his elbow. The girl backed up and pouted at him.

"You're no fun at all, you know."

Henry ignored her. He carried the pew across the sanctuary and set it down. He looked carefully around for the girl and saw her running down the aisle toward two other children. She had lost interest in him. He breathed a big sigh of relief. There were more pews that needed to be moved, but he decided to sit, to rest for a minute and relace his boots.

When he was ready to get back to work, he checked to see where the cruel little girl was. He didn't want any more pranks.

It seemed to him that it was better to be nice than to be clever.

48

Day didn't understand how it was possible for a dead body to bleed, and he didn't stop to ponder it. His Colt Navy had cleared his jacket and was aimed at Bennett Rose before the innkeeper could move his own weapon. Sutton Price stood numb by the bed, staring at his son. There was no immediate danger from that side of the room. First things first.

"Give me your rifle, Mr Rose," Day said.

"I have to shoot him, Inspector," Rose said. "I have to. He killed his own boy."

Calvin Campbell had been standing, dazed, next to Hester Price, but now he took a step toward Sutton, his massive fist raised above the miner's head. Hammersmith grabbed Campbell's fist and appeared to be trying to force it to one side, but Campbell didn't budge. Even so, Day trusted his sergeant to handle that situation for at least the next few seconds. The rifle was still the biggest threat in the room.

"We don't know that he did anything yet," Day said.

"We do. The boy's bleedin'. Show a murderer his victim, bring him near enough to the body, and if it bleeds . . . well, then, that's your man."

"One of your superstitions?"

"How else would you explain that, Mr Day?" Rose pointed to Oliver. "Is that somethin' you've seen before?"

"No," Day said. "But I don't pretend to know what it means."

"I do know."

"Be that as it may, give me your rifle. You people called us here, asked us to investigate this. Give us a chance to do that. If you shoot Sutton Price, I'll have to arrest you for murder. Is that what you want?"

"Do it," Rose said. "The people here are different. This isn't London. We follow the old ways."

"But it's London you'd be going to."

"What do you mean?"

"I mean, the instant I arrest you, you'll be on a train to London, where you'll face proper justice."

"That ain't how it works."

"It works however I say it works." Day glared down the barrel of his Colt at the innkeeper. He saw the rifle begin to waver as Bennett Rose lost his resolve, but Day was careful to hide the relief he felt. He kept his expression stern and his eyes steely and he tried not to shiver with cold. He hoped he looked the part of the London lawman, despite his ragged clothing and his disheveled hair.

Finally, Bennett Rose nodded and handed over the rifle. "This isn't the time, is all. I can wait. Justice will be served the Black Country way." He pointed at Sutton Price and sneered. "You hear me?"

Day didn't wait to find out whether Sutton Price had heard the innkeeper. With his right hand, he slipped his revolver back into his jacket as he took the rifle from Rose with his left hand. He gripped the rifle by its barrel and shoved it back hard at Bennett Rose's ample midsection. The innkeeper toppled over backward with a grunt and fell against the wall behind him. He slid down the wall, holding his abdomen.

"Stay there," Day said. "Stay on the floor." He swung the rifle around and pointed it at Calvin Campbell. "Drop your arm, sir, and be careful of my sergeant when you do it."

Campbell sized Day up and gave him a slight smile. "You're someone to reckon with, aren't you, Inspector?"

"I've had a rough day."

Campbell lowered his fist and clapped Hammersmith on the shoulder. He pulled Hester Price away from her husband, turned her toward him, and gathered her in his arms. She collapsed against him, her face buried against his broad chest, her arms wrapped around his waist. Day could hear her muffled weeping. Campbell closed his eyes, one hand stroking Hester's hair.

"Will you take Sutton Price back to London, then?" Campbell said. He kept his eyes closed when he spoke.

Day looked at Oliver's father. The miner stood like a statue by the bed, still staring at his son's body. He hadn't moved when Hester had beat her fists against him or when Rose had shot at the ceiling, hadn't seemed to notice any of the drama happening around him. He simply stood. Day imagined he might stand there until he died.

There was much about police work that Day didn't feel he was particularly good at, but understanding people, even criminals, knowing their motives and behavior, that was something he felt confident about. None of the people in the little room with Oliver Price's body acted like a murderer. They had found the missing people they'd been sent to Blackhampton for, but there was still much that Day didn't understand about it all.

"Not yet," he said. "Mr Campbell, I need my doctor and I don't think I can spare Sergeant Hammersmith. Would you do me the great favor of bringing Dr Kingsley here just as quickly as possible?"

"I would rather not leave Hester right now."

"I understand, but Hester needs to know what's happened to her child, and Dr Kingsley is best qualified to tell us."

"Send Rose."

"Mr Rose's behavior is . . . unpredictable. He's already caused a great deal of trouble and I would prefer to keep an eye on him here."

"Surely I'm a suspect. What's to keep me from leaving Black-hampton?"

"I don't think you'll leave her."

Campbell looked down at Hester, at the top of her head. "No," he said. "You're right about that."

Hester pulled away from him and looked up at his face. The room was dark, and lamplight from the corner table caused silver hairs among her yellow tresses to sparkle. The corners of her mouth were lined with hard experience and her eyes were rimmed with red. Day looked past the evidence of the years and saw how beautiful she once was. And he looked past the traces of her grief to see how lovely she still was. She reminded him, in some small and in-definite way, of Claire, and he understood Campbell's devotion. He felt something well up in his own chest, but he swallowed his em-pathy. He was careful not to look at the little boy lying on the bed.

"Go, Calvin," Hester said. "Bring the doctor and come back fast."

Campbell nodded. "You won't have time to miss me."

"I'm finished with Blackhampton now," Hester said. "Do you understand? There's nothing for me here."

Campbell nodded again. Without another word, he turned and left the room. Day heard his footsteps on the stairs and then heard the inn's front door open, heard the wind raging through, and then heard the door close. Suddenly the room was very quiet.

49

The American had not lost his way (he never lost his way), but the journey from the woods to the train depot, while a straight line, was difficult. He wore a good pair of brogans, but they were old and worn and the seams leaked. His woolen socks were soaked through, and he couldn't feel his toes. He had known too many soldiers, in the old days, who had lost their feet to frostbite. He didn't want the same for himself. But there was nowhere to rest. The few outbuildings he saw along the outskirts of the road had lights on in their windows. People were inside, cozy and dry by their fires. He knew from hard experience that if he went to their doors they wouldn't let him come inside. One look at his face would be enough to ensure that. But he simply didn't have the heart to kill a family just so he could enjoy the warmth of their home for an hour.

And so when he found the two horses, hitched to a carriage, he counted *it as a blessing from above. They were standing in the field, only a few yards to the west of him, as still as some statue built to depict a brave and patriotic journey through the storm.*

He veered in their direction, mildly worried that the horses were frozen in their tracks, dead already. He was nearly dead with cold himself. If the horses were dead, he would lie down in the carriage and, he imagined, people would come along someday and find him there and wonder how an American had come to be driving a carriage across the English countryside in the middle of an unseasonable late storm.

But the horses weren't dead. The younger one—he could tell by her size and energy—stamped her feet at his approach and snorted. The older one stood in her tracks, but followed him with her black eyes. He approached them slowly, and not only because he didn't want to scare them. He couldn't have moved quickly if he'd wanted to. He reached out a shivering hand and patted the younger one's muzzle, stroked her, and whispered nonsense until she calmed. It didn't take long. She was cold and hungry and tired. The older horse wasn't a problem. She wasn't going to last a lot longer, no matter what happened, and she knew it. Horses had small brains, but they were even more conscious of their mortality than humans were.

He pulled himself up into the carriage, slipping on the step and recovering, trying not to jolt the thing too much and scare the poor horses. The reins hadn't yet frozen, and he scooped them up in his stiff hands, gave an experimental snap. The horses obeyed, dug in and moved. He snapped again. The wheels gritted against the packed snow and spun, and then miraculously found purchase and rolled.

He pulled the reins and the horses slogged around, slowly, painstakingly, blinking their big dark eyes at the snowflakes that landed on them, and finally they were facing in the opposite direction and he began to steer them toward the train depot, where he was certain Campbell was waiting.

He had no idea what he might do if he found himself alive and well in Blackhampton tomorrow, but he had no other life or purpose but to finally enact his revenge upon Calvin Campbell.

50

Jessica Perkins was wiping sweat from Heath Biggs's forehead when Calvin Campbell burst through the doors of the church for the second time in an hour, his hair frosted white, his face raw and pink. He stopped at the back of the sanctuary long enough to glance around, located Dr Kingsley, and ran down the center aisle to him. An hour ago, Campbell had taken Hester Price from the vicar's room, and they had left the church. The children had not seen their mother. She had hurried past them and was gone so quickly that even Jessica wasn't sure what she'd seen. Now Campbell was back, but without Hester. Jessica dropped her cloth and glanced over at Peter and Anna, who seemed to be deep in conversation with little Virginia, then hurried over to where Campbell was gesticulating wildly at Kingsley. Campbell grabbed Kingsley's shoulder, but the doctor pulled away from him. Even before she was close enough to hear what they were saying, she recognized the tension in their voices.

"I have an obligation to these people," Kingsley said.

"He's a baby," Campbell said.

"From what you've told me, there's nothing I can do to help the baby. I can help the people here."

"It was your man, Day, who sent me to fetch you. I'm not going back without you."

"Good. Then you can lend a hand here."

"A baby?" Jessica said. The men stopped arguing and looked at her. "Did they find little Oliver?"

Her voice broke as she asked the question, and she realized she didn't want them to answer. But Campbell was wild-eyed and uncaring.

"Yes," he said. "Oliver is dead."

Jessica gasped and clutched the lace at the throat of her dress as if the air were attacking her. "Oh, no," she said. "I had so hoped . . ."

"I must get back to Hester. I haven't time for this."

"Hester?" Jessica said. "Then that *was* her. I thought it was. You've found the children's mother."

"She's at the inn."

"Is there word of Mr Price?"

"He's there, too."

"You must take the children to their parents."

"I'm not here for that," Campbell said. Jessica thought he sounded cruel, uncaring, but realized that he was completely focused on something else. He seemed to be barely aware of her next to him in the cavernous room full of Blackhampton's sick and dying citizens. "Come with me, Dr Kingsley, or I will carry you back to the inn."

Kingsley's eyebrows shot up with surprise, and he took a look over his shoulder as if determining whether he had room to run. Henry, Kingsley's massive assistant, materialized at his side. Jessica wasn't sure where he'd come from or how he managed to move so quietly.

"If the doctor wants me to," Henry said, "I will make this man go away."

Henry sounded utterly sure of himself, and Campbell reared back, sized up the other giant. Jessica wondered who would win in a contest between them. They were the two largest men she had ever seen. But Kingsley laughed, and it was enough to break the tension.

"I'm sure that won't be necessary, Henry," Kingsley said. "But thank you."

"He should be careful how he talks to you."

"I think Mr Campbell is upset and simply forgot himself."

"Yes," Campbell said. "I'm afraid I've spent too much time alone over the years. I sometimes forget my manners."

Henry nodded. "Doctor's teaching me manners. He could teach you, too."

"The children should be with their family," Jessica said.

"If the doctor will come with me, I'll come back for the children. The storm's too much right now for them." But there was something in Campbell's eyes that made Jessica think he was lying. He had no intention of coming back for Virginia, Anna, and Peter. He was right; he had spent too much time alone and that also meant he hadn't learned to properly lie without giving himself away. She had no idea why he wouldn't want to reunite the children with their parents. Maybe he wanted to spare them the sight of their dead brother. Maybe he had his own agenda in Blackhampton and they weren't a part of it. But whatever the case, she felt certain the children were strong enough for the brief trip to the inn.

"I'll go," Kingsley said. He looked around at the pews full of patients. "I'll go, if it means that the case will be finished. Then Day and Hammersmith can come back with me and help."

"I'll come with you," Henry said.

"No, I need you here, Henry. If we all go, these people will have nobody."

"I don't know medicine yet."

"They don't need medicine. They need a watchful eye."

"I have two of those."

"Indeed you do." Kingsley turned to Campbell. "Take me there. Then bring me right back here."

Campbell nodded and led the way. He waited impatiently in the foyer while Kingsley fetched his bag and buttoned his overcoat, then the doctor hurried up the aisle and allowed himself to be escorted out into the blowing wind and snow.

Jessica didn't waste a second. She knew that the men's tracks would quickly fill with snow. She grabbed the children and bundled them into their coats, slipped their overshoes on their feet, and hustled them out of the church, ignoring their questions. She carried Virginia.

Outside, footprints were still visible, pressed down into the snow, two or three inches deep. Two sets, Campbell's and Kingsley's. She pulled her hat down over her forehead, hitched Virginia higher on her hip, and set out in the direction of the inn, putting her own feet in the men's tracks. She could only see two or three yards ahead, and snowflakes caught in her eyelashes, forcing them closed. They wanted to stay closed, to crust over with ice. The village was completely silent, white and womblike. She and the children might have been the only people left in the world.

"Hold each other's hands," she said.

Peter and Anna held hands and followed her away from the church, into the swirling veil of white snow.

51

D ay broke the silence. "Mr and Mrs Price, I believe it's time you told me what's been happening here."

Hester Price sat back on the edge of the bed and looked at her son and said nothing. Sutton Price seemed to be in a daze. He stared at his wife. Bennett Rose sat upright on the floor. "I told you what's happened," he said. "Sutton Price killed his own son. You saw what happened. Oliver bled when his father came near to him. The dead boy's had his say and told us who did the deed."

Without warning, Sutton Price roared as if every ounce of energy left in his body had found an escape route through his throat. He fell on Rose, bearing him back against the wall. Rose grunted as his back hit the plaster and the breath went out of him again. He batted Price about his head and shoulders, using his forearms and elbows, but Price seemed not to notice. He pounded his shoulders into Rose in a steady rhythm, over and over, as if rocking a baby. Rose couldn't breathe. Day dropped Rose's rifle and leapt on Price. He pulled the grief-stricken father off the innkeeper and pushed him toward the center of the room. The fight immediately left Price and he staggered back toward the wall for support. He stood dumb, looking off into the middle distance as if nothing had happened. Day checked Rose, who was breathing steadily, but was mercifully unconscious. It was for the best. Day had, quite frankly, heard enough from Bennett Rose for the moment.

Day straightened his jacket and picked the rifle back up, holding it down at his side, relaxed but ready. He sniffed and looked out the window. The wind didn't seem to be blowing as hard now, but visibility was still bad. Puffy white flakes drifted swiftly past the glass, some of them piling on the outside windowsill, joining the mound there.

He had just decided to arrest everyone in the room and let a magistrate sort it out later when Hester Price began to speak. Day held his breath, scared that any distraction might halt the flow of her words. She looked down at Oliver's little body as she talked, running the tip of her finger back and forth along his cheek and under his chin as if soothing him to sleep, as if telling him a story.

"You have to understand," Hester said. "He killed a man for me. It's the most anyone's ever done for me, and I could never . . ." She hesitated for a moment, but her finger continued to trace its pattern on her son's face. "I was younger then. I was a pretty girl, and graceful, and he loved me. I lived in West Bromwich, where I grew up. Four sisters, and I was the youngest. They were all married, all except me, and my mother found suitors for me, hoping I might find a husband before I turned twenty. I didn't want any of them, though. My sisters had their houses and some had children already, two of them did, and they knew their lives, everything that lay ahead of them. I can't say what it was that made me think I was different, but I did think it. Youth, maybe. Maybe that's all it was. But one day there was a stranger at the pub, a man no one had ever seen."

"It was Campbell," Sutton Price said. He leaned back until he was touching the wall behind him and then he slid down it and sat on the floor next to Bennett Rose. Price draped his arms across his raised knees and buried his face in the crook of an elbow. Day couldn't tell if he was still listening or not, but Hester Price kept talking.

"I helped out at the pub. My sister's husband, one of my sisters' husbands, owned it, and so I spent an hour or two there in the evenings, washing mugs and picking up and trying to be of use, biding time until my mother found the proper gentleman for me.

"After a time, she thought she had found the right man. He was respectable, perhaps twenty years older than I was, maybe more. A grocer. My parents invited him to our house for dinner and left us to walk in the garden. His name was Mr Stephens, and he was not interested in walking in the garden. He didn't want to listen to me when I talked, and he didn't care what I wanted in life. The things he wanted from me, I won't speak of them. But he was insistent and I had no other suitors left, and when he proposed marriage, I agreed. You understand, I didn't want him. There was hair growing out of his ears and his breath smelled of fish and onions, and he talked and he talked and nothing he talked about was of any interest to a foolish little girl.

"But when the stranger began to come to the pub, it was as if a door had opened in my life. He was big and strong, but he was quiet. He had long hair, going grey, but he didn't look old, at least not terribly old. Not like Mr Stephens. But he looked tired and he looked like he had seen a lot. And I had seen nothing. West Bromwich was my whole world. His name was Calvin Campbell, and he was the most exotic creature I had ever encountered. I stayed longer every night at the pub, did chores that didn't need to be done, tried to do things that might make him notice me. And, finally, he did. He told me that he was only going to be in West Bromwich for a week. That he was on his way somewhere else, but he never said where. I felt like he wasn't going somewhere at all, he was going away from something, or someone.

"But he stayed. A week went by, and another week, and Calvin didn't leave. I began avoiding Mr Stephens and spending time with Calvin instead. We took long walks and we talked for hours. He had been to America and had been to war. He told me very little about his time there, he was quiet about those years, but the mere fact that he had survived their civil war and their prison camp made me admire him all the more. And he listened to me. Nobody had ever listened to me. He asked me questions about my silly little life in my silly little Black Country village. I must have seemed like the most boring person he had ever met, but he never made me feel like it.

"Like I say, I was pretty then.

"It was all so deliciously exciting, but Calvin didn't know about Mr Stephens, and Mr Stephens didn't know about Calvin.

"And then, suddenly, Mr Stephens did know. Someone must have told him, because one day, as I was waiting for Calvin by the banks of the stream outside of the village, Mr Stephens came out of a copse of trees. He had been waiting there, waiting for us. He didn't say a word to me, just pushed me down and covered my mouth before I could cry out. I remember his hand tasted like salt and shit. His other hand was under my skirts, exploring me with his dirty fingers, and he was smiling at me with his yellow teeth, and I couldn't scream. I couldn't do anything.

"But then, from where I lay in the grass, it appeared Mr Stephens had suddenly learned to fly. He took to the air, and in a moment I saw Calvin behind him, holding Mr Stephens by the nape of his neck like a rabbit. Mr Stephens made the most horrible squeaking noise, and then Calvin swung him around and smacked his head into the trunk of a tree.

"He kept hitting the tree with Mr Stephens's head, and I didn't look away. Mr Stephens's head mashed like some kind of fruit, bright pink juice running down Calvin's arm."

Hester finally looked up. She ignored Day, but stared at her husband, her brow creased with concern. "Do you understand?" she said. "He did that for me."

"He went to prison for it," Day said.

Hester turned her gaze to Day and she nodded. She opened her mouth to say something else, but stopped. They all heard the door open downstairs.

52

Day left Hammersmith to watch over Bennett Rose and the Prices. He bounded down the stairs and found Dr Kingsley stamping his feet on the mat. Kingsley was covered with snow, from head to foot.

"Thank God you've made it, Doctor."

"That man practically carried me the entire way or I *wouldn't* have made it."

"Campbell, you mean?"

"Yes."

"Where is he?"

Kingsley looked around as if he might find Campbell hiding behind the coatrack. "I don't know. He was right with me when I came through the door."

Day pulled the front door open and stuck his head out. The wind had died down a bit, but the snow was falling just as quickly, already filling in the three sets of footprints outside. Day could see where Campbell and Kingsley had approached the inn together, but the third set of prints went away from the door, around the side of the inn. Campbell had left the doctor and fled. Day briefly considered giving chase, but then thought better of it. Campbell had served his time for murder, and there was no evidence that he had committed a crime in Blackhampton. The worst he had done was to help hide Mrs Price, and Day wasn't sure he wanted to arrest anyone for that. He was certain she hadn't killed her son, which meant Campbell wasn't an accessory to a murder. Day pulled his head back in and slammed the door shut.

"I'm told you found the little boy," Kingsley said.

"He was at the bottom of the well."

Kingsley pursed his lips and removed his hat. "There's never anything sadder than the death of a child."

"I'm afraid I still need to know how he died."

"Of course," Kingsley said. "Bring me to him."

Day led the way up the stairs. Bennett Rose was on his feet, but Sutton Price hadn't moved. Day wondered if the miner had fallen asleep. Hammersmith nodded a greeting to Kingsley.

"How are you, Sergeant?" Kingsley said.

"I'm just fine, sir."

"No weakness? Fatigue? Shortness of breath?"

"All of those, but I'll recover."

Kingsley shook his head. "Lie down and rest a bit, would you?"

"I will the moment we're on the train back to London."

Kingsley shook his head again and snorted. He looked past Hester Price at the body of Oliver on the bed. The boy was a pale lavender color, purple veins feathering up under the collar of his shirt and across his face. His skin was swollen and distended from his time in the water, his eyes puckered holes. His legs bulged against his trousers. His left arm was missing at the elbow, lost somewhere in the bottom of the well. His shirt was tattered across the front, torn and open, exposing pale white-and-blue mottled flesh that showed the evidence of deep puncture wounds. One shoe was missing and the other had been stretched by Oliver's expanding foot so that the seams had burst. Dark liquid crusted his lips.

Day watched Kingsley's face, but there was no expression there. The doctor had surely seen atrocities that Day couldn't imagine.

"He bled," Day said. "I mean the body bled, not long ago. We all saw it. You can still see it there."

Kingsley leaned down, his face inches away from the face of the dead baby.

"How is that possible?" Day said. "A miracle?"

Kingsley shook his head and made a quiet sound that only Day heard. "No," Kingsley said. "Nothing about this is miraculous. Did anyone touch the body before it bled?"

"His father."

"Pressed in on the boy's chest, did he?"

"Yes."

"He squeezed out the remains of this little fellow's decomposing organs."

Hester Price gasped, and Kingsley straightened up. He turned and glared at the people gathered there in the room. "So much for superstition," he said. "Now go. I need privacy."

"Of course," Day said. He held his hand out to Hester Price, but she ignored him. Hammersmith stepped closer and took her arm, helped her up off the side of the bed, and walked her out of the room. They waited in the hall. Day followed Hammersmith's lead by taking Sutton Price's elbow. He helped Price to his feet and motioned for Bennett Rose to precede them out of the room. Day looked back and saw that Kingsley's satchel was on the bed at Oliver Price's feet. The doctor had already removed his jacket and was rolling up his sleeves, preparing for the grisly work ahead of him. He glanced up at Day and let out a long breath. His eyes were sad, pink-rimmed.

Day took a last look at Oliver's delicate little body before he shut the door. There was a part of him that wanted to scoop the boy back up in his arms and carry him away from that cold, unhappy village.

53

"Give her some time," Bennett Rose said. "She can have this room."

He turned the knob and swung open the door of the room across the hall. Day would have liked to put more distance between Hester Price and the room where Kingsley was performing his dreadful work on her son, but he appreciated that Bennett Rose was making an attempt to be useful again. He stuck his head in and looked around the room. It was nearly identical to his own room at the other end of the hall, but the view out the window was of the woods behind the inn, a dark shape rubbed into the horizon by a giant thumb, obscured by layer upon layer of thick snowflakes.

Grey upon grey.

He motioned to Hammersmith, and the sergeant led Hester into the room and helped her sit on the edge of the bed. The three men left the room, joined Sutton Price in the hall, and shut the door on Hester.

"Someone should be stationed up here in the hall, in case the doctor needs something," Day said.

And, he didn't say, to keep an eye on Hester Price. Hammersmith would understand. One never knew what a grieving parent might be capable of doing.

"You can handle . . ." Hammersmith waved his hand, taking in Bennett Rose and Sutton Price.

"We'll be fine."

Hammersmith nodded and went to the door of the room where Kingsley was presumably working. He leaned against the doorjamb and folded his arms, patient and ready. Day wondered how much the sergeant had recovered. He guessed not at all. It was very like Hammersmith to ignore himself until he collapsed. But the case was nearly finished. By tomorrow they would be back in London, and Day would recommend that Hammersmith be relieved of duty for a week, maybe two. Make the man rest, whether he liked it or not.

Sutton Price stood where he had been left in the hallway. Day prodded him in the back, herding him toward the staircase and down. One of the fires had died. The great room was dim and, all at once, musty, as if the place had been shut up for years. An open window might have cleared away the fustiness, but the storm outside demanded that everyone remain shut away from the world.

Then the door opened and the stillness was shattered as Jessica Perkins bustled in with the three Price children. She was carrying the littlest, Virginia, and dropped her on the inn's floor, collapsing against the front door as it closed. Virginia saw her father and ran to him.

"Father!"

He stooped and picked her up. The two older children were more shy. They hung back and edged their way closer to Sutton Price. He took three quick steps toward them, with Virginia clinging to him like a monkey, went down on his knees, and scooped Peter and Anna into his arms.

Bennett Rose disappeared and came back with a stack of thin blankets. He handed two of them to Day and took one to Jessica Perkins, who used it to dry her hair. Day took his blankets and draped them over the shoulders of Peter and Anna. They appeared not to notice him or care.

Day gave them a few moments and then cleared his throat. "Your stepmother is upstairs," he said. "Would you like to see her?"

Nobody spoke, but Anna shook her head. *No.*

"Come, children," Jessica said. There were dark bruises under her eyes, and her shoulders were slumped and rounded with weariness. She hung her blanket on the coatrack and held out her hands. "You should say hello to her."

Sutton Price drew back from the two older children and set Virginia down next to them. "Go," he said.

"We don't want to," Virginia said.

"Don't worry. I'll still be here when you come back. I have to talk to the policeman, but I won't leave you again."

The three children went reluctantly to Jessica, who took them to the stairs and up.

Rose busied himself with the embers in the colder of the two fireplaces, while Day led Sutton Price to the largest and most comfortable of the armchairs positioned at the hearth of the other. There, the fire still blazed cheerily and the mustiness of the room gave way to a strong ashy, nutty odor. Price sank heavily into the chair and sighed.

"You have questions," he said.

"A few," Day said. "I hardly know where to begin."

"I'll do my best to answer."

Day gathered his thoughts. He could hear Jessica Perkins upstairs, in murmured conversation with Hammersmith, but couldn't make out their words.

"You were down in the tunnels?" Day said.

"Hester had disappeared. And little Oliver . . ." Price looked away, into the fire, waiting for the ability to speak again. Day gave him time, let him work his emotions into something bearable. "She took him," Price said at last. "At least I thought she had. But where could she go? You must understand, I came home, early in the morning. Hester and Oliver were gone. They had left me. That's what I believed. I knew in my heart that she had finally left, and that she had taken our son." He stopped again, but only for a few seconds, swallowed hard, and continued. "I always knew she would leave. She never loved me, always a part of her waiting for him to come and find her."

"Him?" Day said.

"Campbell. I didn't know his name until he arrived here in the village. He actually did come for her when he was released from prison. After all this time. But Oliver is mine. Was mine. Not Campbell's. That was my son, and they couldn't have him, damnit."

"Why the tunnels? They might have been anywhere."

"Where else? A mother and child in the woods? Risking wolves and badgers and the weather? Whatever else she might be—and she was not a good wife—she loved that boy. Didn't care one whit for the other children. They weren't hers, you know, and she made them know it. But she loved Oliver. She wouldn't carry him into the woods. She hadn't taken his belongings, so she couldn't have been on her way somewhere else, couldn't have taken the train anywhere. At least, not yet. She was not well-liked in Blackhampton. Where would she go? Put yourself in my place and think as I thought."

"Below ground."

"And so that's where I went."

"But she wasn't there."

"No."

"She was being hidden from you. I think she was at the church. Why would she hide from you?"

"I don't know." But Sutton Price avoided Day's eyes. He looked away at the dancing fire.

"You had threatened her?"

"Never."

"Hurt her?"

"No, never." Price looked back at Day, this time with conviction. "I would never raise a hand to her."

"And yet she feared you, didn't she? I believe she was able to persuade the vicar that she was in danger, and so he hid her away from you."

Price shook his head back and forth, but said nothing.

"Why stay in the mines?" Day said. "Why not come out when you didn't find her?"

"There are miles of tunnel down there. Miles of them."

"Who killed your son, Mr Price?"

"He did it!" Bennett Rose said. "He did it! You saw that he did it. The body bled."

Price bounded from his chair. Day leapt forward, but not quickly enough to get between the two men before they grappled. Rose landed a solid fist on Price's ear, and the miner bellowed and kicked out, catching the innkeeper's shin with the steel toe of his boot. Then Day managed to insert himself in the mix and push the men apart. It wasn't hard to do. The fight went out of them instantly.

Day heard a door close upstairs, and then Hammersmith was pounding down the steps. He stopped at the landing and grabbed the banister, sought Day out in the cluster of men by the fireplace. His expression was panicked. Jessica crowded onto the landing behind him, and Day could see the three children farther up at the bend in the stairs.

"Sir," Hammersmith said. His voice rasped quietly, but could be easily heard over the hard breathing of Price and Rose. "She didn't answer when we knocked at her door. We gave her a moment, and then Miss Jessica went in. But Hester Price has left. She's gone out the window."

Day went to the front door. He heard Hammersmith come down the stairs behind him.

"I looked out the window," Hammersmith said. "She's nowhere in sight."

Day pulled the door open and a swirl of snowflakes entered the room in a mighty rush. Cold air settled along Day's shoulders and crept down the collar of his waistcoat.

"I think I know where she's gone," Day said. "Watch them. They don't seem to get along." He gestured at the room, indicating Sutton

Price and Bennett Rose. He didn't anticipate any trouble from Jessica Perkins and the three children, but the men remained tense and dangerous. Still, there was little they could do, and the storm would keep them inside. If they decided to resume their fight, Hammersmith could handle them. The miner and the innkeeper seemed geared for short bursts of manic energy, but they had no stamina.

Day pulled on his torn and useless overcoat.

"I'm going with you," Price said.

"No, sir, you stay with your children. They've had a difficult time of it and they need you."

With that, Day stepped out into the snow and pulled the door shut behind him. By now he could make the trip to the church with his eyes closed. The wind had died down and visibility had improved, but the road was buried under a foot of ice and powder. Day moved as quickly as he could, plodding through drifts. He tried to run and realized he must look ridiculous lifting each foot high and pushing out and down through the thin hard cover that had melted and refrozen into the soft snow beneath, then the next foot, like a duck with a tall hat. One foot, two foot, one foot, two foot. But he kept going. There was no one to see him.

His nose went numb first, and he found himself wishing his ears would follow suit. They burned and stung. His eyes watered and he wiped the tears away, worried they might freeze on his cheeks.

He tromped around the bend and saw the outline of the church ahead, still too far. The end of the road. He put his head down and watched his feet, concentrated on the up-and-down motion, ignored his stinging ears and hands and toes, and tried hard not to think about the distance, just move through it, decrease it, step by agonizing step.

And then he was there. The grey stone façade stretched up and out in front of him, and he tripped over the invisible first step of the wide front stoop. He used the momentum and controlled his fall, pushing through the front doors and arriving abruptly in the foyer. He caught his balance, spun on his heel, and shut the doors.

Inside, the church was cold, but compared to the frozen landscape just outside, it felt snug and toasty. Day stamped his feet a few times, both to get the snow off his shoes and to circulate his blood. His ears began to ping painfully as they warmed up. He clapped his hands over them to speed the process and left the foyer.

He entered the sanctuary at a trot and hurried down the center aisle for what was to be his last time, looking neither left nor right. He couldn't afford to be stopped or slowed, and the sight of Blackhampton's sick and dying was of no possible help to him. He noticed Henry Mayhew as he passed him, but didn't acknowledge the friendly giant.

The vicar Brothwood stepped out in front of Day as he reached the pulpit, but Day walked past, ignoring him completely. He heard Brothwood follow him as he pushed through the door and into the private room at the back of the church.

Day went straight to the small fireplace and found the smooth round stone in the surround. He tried turning it, but it was too slippery, there was no purchase. Brothwood put a hand on his shoulder and reached past him, pushed the stone hard. It slid back under the mantel, and Brothwood hooked a finger under the edge of the newly recessed area and pushed something else there that Day couldn't see. The floor of the firebox dropped down at the front, beneath the level of the room's floor, and a section of the hearth slid suddenly and silently out on what Day imagined was a well-oiled set of casters. There was a narrow staircase, not much more than a ladder built into the rocks, that led down into the dark beneath the fireplace.

Brothwood smiled and led the way down the stairs. Day reached into his pocket and found his gun. He kept his hand there, ready, and followed the vicar. It occurred to him that he might have been wise to bring Henry Mayhew along.

Day's eyes adjusted quickly to the dim candlelight under the floor. He ducked his head and stepped off the last rung and onto a solid slab of stone, roughly six by six feet. The ceiling was made of the floorboards of the room above and was only about five feet high. Day had to stoop as he followed Brothwood out into the tiny underground room. He and the vicar stood side by side, bent over, their shoulders braced hard against the ceiling, their necks bent uncomfortably. Day was several inches taller than Brothwood, but the room wasn't built for either of them.

It was a priest hole. Exactly what Day had expected to find. Built centuries ago, when the church was an inn and Catholic priests were regularly put to death. Many towns like Blackhampton had built secret chambers in public buildings, sometimes ingeniously hidden, where a priest could hide from questing soldiers. A priest hole only needed to be large enough to conceal one man for a few hours at a time.

There wasn't much to see. The room was abandoned, but there were still signs that someone had recently lived in it. There was a candle, just a stub that had burned down to the ground and wouldn't last more than another hour. A bedroll in one corner, hastily abandoned, a round scorched spot on the stone where countless fires had been built, and a small wooden box. Day hunched himself past

Brothwood and looked in the box. It held a few dry biscuits and a tin cup, half full of cider. Day sniffed. The musty odor of sex lingered in the air, and Day was reminded of Campbell's secret visits to the church. He looked at Brothwood. The vicar's features danced and melted in the flickering light, but it seemed to Day that his smile was warm and genuine. It was probably a relief to have his secret exposed and finally lifted from his shoulders.

"How long was Mrs Price hiding here?" Day said.

"The night she left her husband, she came here."

"Why here?"

"Where else would she go? Her husband certainly never came to church. He knew where he was destined to go. He wouldn't have thought to look for her here."

"What do you mean? Where was Sutton Price destined to go?"

"To hell, sir. For what he did to his first wife."

"What did he do to her? What do you know about that?"

"I know nothing. But I believe what everyone else believes. He murdered Mathilda Price. She never left this village alive."

Day made a face. If Sutton Price had murdered his first wife, then their nanny, Hester, the second wife, might have had something to do with it. Blackhampton was a viper's nest of rumor and innuendo, none of it proven or provable.

"Why hide her at all?"

"Because Sutton Price kills his wives. I believe I saved Hester's life that night."

"And what of her children?"

"Had she brought them, I would have hidden them as well."

"But weren't you worried? You say he kills his wives. Who's to say he wouldn't kill his children?"

"Who would kill a child?"

Who indeed? Someone had killed Oliver. Maybe it was Sutton Price, maybe it was Hester Price, but neither of those options felt right. There was another solution, something else that nagged at the back of Day's mind, but it made him uncomfortable and he avoided thinking about it directly. In any case, the vicar Brothwood hadn't killed anyone. He had, at worst, been guilty of poor judgment.

"Why not go to Constable Grimes for help?" Day said.

"What could he have done? He's a good man, but he's not competent. He even had to bring you here to help him."

"Where is Grimes now? Do you know?"

"I'm sure I wouldn't have the slightest idea."

Day shook his head. "Thank you for your time, sir," he said.

He didn't wait for a reply, but took the rungs back up to the surface two at a time and emerged in the vicar's room. He wondered again how the man and his wife could both occupy that small space, and wondered, too, about the nights they had spent with Hester Price directly below them, huddled against the bare wall on a thin bedroll. Had Calvin Campbell been down there with her? How much had the vicar overlooked in his zeal to do the right thing?

Day left the room, didn't bother to close the door behind him, and drifted down the center aisle of the sanctuary, wondering about his next move. In fact, though he hated to admit it to himself, he was probably avoiding the storm. The longer he lingered in the church, the longer he remained warm.

Calvin Campbell and Hester Price were out there somewhere, together and probably freezing, away from the warmth and safety of the church and the inn. Day didn't know where else to look for them.

"Mr Day." Henry Mayhew came up the aisle toward him, moving with purpose. "Did you come to help?"

"Hello, Henry."

"Hello."

"You're helping the sick here?"

"Yes, sir. And a lot of them."

"You're doing good work."

"Not really, sir. Nothing much I can do for them."

"I'm afraid I feel the same. There's a murderer in Blackhampton, and I seem to be out of ideas. Nothing feels right to me."

"Is the murderer at the church?" Henry looked around with such an exaggerated expression of unease that Day almost laughed aloud. He stifled the impulse, recognizing that it would hurt the gentle giant's feelings.

"I don't think so, Henry. I came looking for Hester Price or Calvin Campbell, but neither is here."

"They've probably gone to London."

"What makes you say that?"

"Because that's where I would go. I want to go there now. I don't like this place at all."

"I don't, either."

"They probably already got on the train."

"The train's not running. The storm, you know."

"It will sometime, won't it?"

"I suppose it will. It had better. I plan to leave tomorrow."

"Let's both leave. We can wait at the depot, and when the snow stops we can get on the train and go away from here."

Day rubbed his jaw. He had neglected to shave, and his chin

rasped against his dry fingers. "Henry, my good fellow, I think you may be on to something."

"We'll go, then." Henry ran down the aisle and disappeared among the rows of moaning villagers. He emerged again in a moment with two lanterns and the small wooden box. He ran back to Day and presented the box to him. "I took good care. See?"

Inside, the baby magpie was moving about in a way that seemed very healthy to Day. The inspector grinned at Henry Mayhew.

"Henry, he's better than ever, isn't he?"

Henry smiled and looked bashfully away. "I tried my best, sir. Took good care of the baby all day long, just like the doctor and me did these sick folks."

"Good job."

"Thank you, sir." Henry held out the box tentatively, with a pensive frown and a furrowed brow. "He's yours, sir. You can take him back, if you want to."

"I think he still needs you, Henry. Better leave him with you until he's big enough to fly."

Henry nodded, quite serious. "I'll get him big enough."

"I'm quite sure you will."

"Let's go, sir."

"I suppose the train depot is as good a place to look as any."

"Look for what?"

"For Hester Price and Calvin Campbell."

"Oh, was I right? Are they leaving, too?"

"I think they might be. Given Hester's frame of mind, I can't think of anything that would be keeping her here anymore. She said as much, but I thought she might return here for her things."

"She had things here?"

"Not really, no. She was living like a prisoner, waiting for her son to be found. And waiting to leave this place."

"And she's gone now?"

"On her way."

"Then we'll all go together."

Henry led the way up the aisle and through the foyer. He pulled the doors open and took a moment to close the wooden box and stow it away beneath his enormous long overcoat. Day could still hear the bird chirping somewhere deep in the folds, but he imagined that it was warmer than he was and he wished that he was small enough to fit in a wooden box within a giant's coat, ferried safely through any storm. He wished that he felt the way he had as a child, secure and trusting in the sound judgment of everyone larger than he. He knew that Oliver Price had felt that same thing and that the boy's faith had been misplaced, and for a brief moment before plunging into the storm behind Henry Mayhew, Day wondered how any children ever made it to adulthood when they so blindly placed their trust in adults.

The moment his foot broke the thin icy surface of the church's stoop, the earth beneath him rumbled and shook and he was thrown backward into the foyer.

He landed hard on his left shoulder and braced himself, both palms flat against the floor, waiting for the church to collapse around him. But the sound died and the shaking stopped and the calm of the snow resumed.

From somewhere behind him, back in the sanctuary, he heard the frightened cries of sick villagers and he wondered how far the church had sunk into the tunnels below, whether the priest hole was still intact, and what might have happened had he still been down there beneath the vicar's room when the tremor struck.

Henry reappeared at the church doors, covered with white powder. He took a step into the foyer and held out his hand, helped Day to his feet, then stuck his hand into his coat and drew out the little wooden box. Day was touched by the anxiety on Henry's face, the pure worry for his tiny charge. Henry opened the lid and peeked inside, and Day heard the bird chirp once. Henry smiled and closed the lid again and put the box away.

"Oliver's all right," he said.

"You named the bird Oliver?" Day said.

"I did, sir. I heard a lot of people saying that name since we came here, and I like the sound of it."

Day smiled, but couldn't think of anything to say that wasn't impossibly complicated and unnecessary. The smile seemed like enough of a response.

"I think we'd better hurry, sir," Henry said.

"Yes," Day said. "I'm afraid Blackhampton is collapsing beneath us." He moved past Henry and jumped into the snow and trudged away as fast as he could, Henry right behind him, sheltering the living bird that had been given a dead boy's name.

54

H ammersmith waited until he was certain the inn had stopped trembling on its foundation before he released his grip on the banister. Across the room, Jessica was sunk deep in the cushions of an armchair before the fire. She had slept through the tremor. And the remaining members of the Price family at the inn had also withstood the tremor with little sign they had noticed it happening. They were, of course, much more used to their sinking village than Hammersmith was.

Sutton Price was holding his three children in a big loose hug as they spoke to him. Virginia leaned in close to her father, and Hammersmith read her lips as she whispered the words "I know a secret" in Sutton's ear. The other two children tensed and began trying to distract their father, but Sutton calmed them and smiled indulgently at Virginia, who began to babble at him. Price had spent days separated from his children, but now he seemed utterly attached to them, listening carefully to his daughter. Hammersmith tried to read Virginia's lips to make out what she was saying. He squinted and leaned forward, but the little girl's long hair was in the way.

Peter and Anna Price broke away from their father and Virginia. They scurried over to Hammersmith as if by some prearranged agreement between them, took him by the hands, and began to lead him toward the dining room.

"I'm hungry," Anna said. "Let's find something to eat."

Bennett Rose was there at his bar, polishing the surface with a dirty rag. He stopped scowling at Sutton Price long enough to scowl at Hammersmith instead.

"There's your man," Hammersmith said. "Why don't you ask Mr Rose for a bite of something?"

"We want you to come," Peter said.

"For heaven's sake, why?"

"We like you," Anna said. "We'd like to spend more time with you."

Hammersmith pulled away from them and stopped in front of Rose. "The children are hungry," he said.

Rose nodded and left his rag where it was, wiped his hands on the legs of his trousers, and sulked through the door, headed toward the kitchen. Anna shook her head. "You come, too," she said.

"I'd rather stay near your father."

"It's no good if you don't come," Peter said.

"I'll be here when you've finished. Go with Mr Rose."

"I'm not hungry, after all," Anna said. "Let's have a chat."

"Yes," Peter said. "Let's have a chat."

"I'm sorry, children. I'm a bit run-down at the moment. Perhaps we can talk later." Hammersmith walked rapidly away from Peter and Anna, but he could hear them scurrying after him. They seemed terribly nervous.

As he drew near Sutton Price, he stopped, surprised by the expression on the miner's face. Or rather, by the expressions, because Sutton's features reflected a kaleidoscope of horror, shock, grief, pain, and anger. He picked up his youngest daughter by her shoulders and shook her. Her feet flopped back and forth almost comically, dancing in air. Hammersmith rushed forward, ignoring the two other children behind him.

At that moment, the floor shook again as another tremor hit the inn. Hammersmith was running, his head and shoulders too far out over his feet. There was no possibility of regaining his balance. He saw a flash of light as his jaw smacked hard into the planks of the floor.

He blinked hard and, just as his vision began to return, he saw Sutton Price, weirdly distorted, tall and out of perspective, stride confidently toward him, perfectly adapted by decades of experience with tremors, able to walk without a trace of difficulty. Price had Virginia by one arm, dragging her along after him. Hammersmith raised himself up as Price approached and opened his mouth to speak just as Price pulled back one steel-toed boot and kicked Hammersmith squarely in the forehead.

There was another flash of light, brighter than the first, and then there was darkness and, strangely, a sharp whiff of sulfur as the world shuddered away from him.

From far away, he heard Peter Price yell, "Father, no!" And then there was nothing.

55

Jessica woke with a start, and it took her a minute to get her bearings. She had heard Peter shouting, but associated his voice with a dream she had been having in which children were climbing up the walls and across the ceiling of the schoolroom, calling out to one another as they jockeyed to get into position above her head, planning to drop down on her like spiders. There had been a dark figure watching from the corner of the schoolroom, an evil man with a hideous face from a children's rhyme. Despite the crackling fire in front of her, she was still shivering. She rubbed her goose-bumped arms and yawned.

She craned her neck to see over the chair back behind her and saw Sutton Price, his daughter Virginia tucked up tight under one arm, march out into the snow, leaving the inn's door wide open behind him. Peter and Anna followed their father as far as the threshold, but stopped there, reluctant to brave the storm again. Sergeant Hammersmith lay facedown on the floor, unmoving.

Jessica jumped out of the chair and ran to Hammersmith. He was bleeding heavily from a scalp wound, but he was breathing. She strained to roll him over and shouted over her shoulder at the children.

"Close the door!"

Peter jumped as if he'd been burned, and then hurried to obey. The wind didn't seem to be blowing as fiercely now, and the door shut with a bang. Bennett Rose came running from somewhere at the back of the inn. He was holding a small ceramic pot of groaty dick, with a pewter spoon sticking out of the top of it. He set it on the bar top and scuttled over to Jessica's side, where he easily flipped Hammersmith over. He untied his apron, rolled it up in a ball, and stuck it under the sergeant's head as a makeshift pillow. He used a corner of it to dab at Hammersmith's wound, but that was clearly ineffective.

"Anna," he said, "go bring me a rag. And be quick about it, girl."

Anna opened her mouth as if to object, but changed her mind and ran to the counter where the fragrant groaty pudding steamed. She reached underneath and rummaged about a bit before producing a handful of rags. Jessica wondered whether they were clean, but decided it wasn't the right time to be choosy. Anna brought the wad of threadbare fabric back to Rose, who pressed it tight to Hammersmith's head.

"I don't think it's as bad as all that," Rose said. "Heads bleed horrible bad, and I've seen my share of 'em every time something goes bad at the mines."

Jessica nodded. Of course she'd seen her share of head injuries, too, many of them fatal, but she appreciated the innkeeper's optimism.

"Too bad Dr Denby's not here," Jessica said. "He might . . ." She broke off and smacked herself in the forehead with the palm of her hand. "I'm not especially clever today, am I? Anna, run upstairs and fetch Dr Kingsley. He'll know what to do."

Anna bobbed her head and ran to the staircase. She turned back when Hammersmith moaned and she stood on the bottom step, watching as he sat up and grabbed his head. Blood soaked through the wad of rags and trickled out between his fingers. He didn't seem to notice.

"Where?" he said.

"Price?" Rose said. "Did he hit you?"

"Where did he go?"

"He left," Jessica said. "He took Virginia. I don't understand."

"I'm afraid I do," Hammersmith said. He wrestled himself up off the floor and stood, swaying slightly. "I'm afraid Mr Rose was righter than we knew."

"Come to the fire," Jessica said. "Sit." She glanced at Anna, who still stood watching. "Anna, what are you doing? Go. Get the doctor."

Anna scampered up the steps, turned the corner at the landing, and hurried out of sight. They could hear her footsteps on the floor above.

Hammersmith lurched toward the door. He grabbed for the knob, missed it, and fell against the jamb. Jessica pulled at his arm gently, physically suggesting that he listen to her, but he shrugged her off, found the knob, and wrenched the door open. An icy wind rushed into the room, and the fire wavered, flickered, protested.

"Get word to Inspector Day, if you can," Hammersmith said. "Tell him . . . Tell him I've gone to the seam."

"Why the seam?" Jessica said. "Sutton won't go back there now."

"Where else would he go?"

Hammersmith waited for a second, as if hoping she might have an actual answer, then he grabbed the side of the door with his free hand and propelled himself out into the storm. Jessica watched as he was swallowed by the snow and disappeared from sight, then she shut the door and leaned heavily against it as another tremor hit the inn and the air filled with a groaning sound, echoing down through the chimneys, shaking the air, and sending a shower of sparks into the room.

Jessica heard something thump hard against the floor above her.

56

D r Bernard Kingsley stood back up and looked down at the body of the little boy. Three tremors in the last few minutes had knocked him down, but he had spent long minutes staring at the boy, and he couldn't blame the trembling earth for his hesitation.

The boy's mouth was a delicate pink bow, pursed as if about to smile, and his fine pale hair swept gently across his high forehead. His eyes had been dulled by the water, but Kingsley could imagine them in life, wide and flashing with curiosity as Oliver tottered about, learning to walk and to talk. But, of course, he would not learn anything more, would not grow up to take his proper place in society. He would be a child forever.

It was Kingsley's job to deal with corpses, and yet he was still shocked and dismayed every time a little one came across his table.

(The most exacting portion of his mind offered up a correction: The boy was lying on an unmade bed, not a proper sterile table.) He thought of his own children, his two daughters.

There was a soft rap at the door and he turned, pulled a sheet up over the boy's body before speaking. "Yes?"

The door swung open slowly, an inch, two, three. Finally a little girl's head poked through the narrow opening. "Are you the doctor?"

Kingsley stepped away from the bed and pulled the door open the rest of the way. He did his best to compose his expression, erase the sadness he felt must show there, and smiled down at the girl. "I am. My name is Dr Kingsley." He held out his hand.

The girl brushed her fingers delicately against his palm, barely touching him, in lieu of a handshake. "I'm Anna. Your policeman was kicked in the head by my father."

"I see." But Kingsley didn't see. Had no idea what she meant.

"It's bled quite a lot, but he can talk and move about like anything. I believe he may have gone."

"Does someone need my help, child?"

"I don't know. I don't think so."

Kingsley frowned. He looked around the room and located his satchel, checked it to be sure he had the basic necessities if someone had been injured. He wasn't sure what had happened, but there seemed to be a possibility that either Hammersmith or Day had been kicked in the head, and a head injury was never a thing to take lightly. He smiled at Anna again and went to the door, but the girl stepped farther into the room, her gaze fixed on the shape covered by the sheet.

"Is that Oliver?" she said.

Kingsley nodded. "Did you know Oliver?"

"He was my brother."

Kingsley moved back into the room and took a tentative step toward her. Hammersmith or Day, whichever had been injured, could probably wait a moment. The girl hadn't imparted any real sense of urgency. He set his satchel down on the miniature round table by the door, but didn't know what to do with his hands. Living, grieving people were much more complicated to deal with than the dead. He assumed the girl needed to be comforted, but wasn't sure how to go about that tricky process. His wife had tended to their daughters' emotional lives. He had always concentrated on the relatively simpler tasks of teaching.

"I shouldn't say that," Anna said. She spoke to the dark corner of the room above the boy's body, and Kingsley couldn't see her face. "He wasn't really my brother. Not properly. He only came along after my mother left. What did that make him?"

"I'm not sure," Kingsley said. "Did he live with you as a brother?"

The girl nodded. Her hair bobbed and swung, heavy and clean and still slightly damp from melted snow.

"What's your name again, child?"

"Anna. Anna Price."

"The boy shared a name with you."

"Yes."

Kingsley waited, looked nervously at the black bag on the table, aware that time was passing and that someone might be bleeding downstairs. But he was loath to interrupt whatever Anna was experiencing and equally uncomfortable about leaving her alone in the room with the body of her brother.

"He could talk a little bit," Anna said. "Only some words. And he could walk a bit, too, but he fell down a lot. He said my name. But he was sick. He coughed and he cried too much. He said my name when he was crying, but I didn't help him."

Kingsley reached out and laid his hand lightly on her shoulder, and she turned and buried her face against him and he felt her small body convulsing with grief. He hugged her and felt his throat constrict with the memory of Fiona, sobbing, inconsolable at the death of her mother. He had felt useless then and he felt useless now. Anna said something, but the folds of Kingsley's waistcoat smothered her words.

"What did you say, Anna?"

She pulled her face away from him and looked up. Tears streamed down her cheeks and snot coated her upper lip. Her eyes were bright pink, bloodshot and swollen. "I put him there," she said. "Peter and I did that."

"Put him where, child?"

"In the well. We threw him into the dark, and he never liked being in the dark. But we did it anyway. He was gone already and we didn't know what to do."

Kingsley pulled back, horrified and confused. He put his hands on the girl's shoulders and pushed her away, held her at arm's length and looked at her livid eyes. He opened his mouth to speak, to try to understand what she was saying, but then the world opened up and collapsed around them.

The roof broke open with an earsplitting roar, and the wind and the snow and the ice banged into the room and filled it, and the spidery black sky came crashing down. Anna was torn from Kingsley's grip as something hit him hard in the back and sent him stumbling across the room. He heard her screaming from somewhere nearby. He hit the wall and spun around and gasped as a tree thrust itself at him too fast for escape.

Icy branches punctured the plaster wall all around him and pushed through into the next room, and Anna Price stopped screaming and the world became curiously silent.

57

━━━⊂∞⊃━━━

It sounded like a freight train bearing down on him, and Hammersmith was half turned, off balance, when the tremor reached him and threw him face-first into a drift. It buried him completely as snow shook loose and caved in over him. It was womblike under there, but cold crystalline light filtered through the white blanket. Hammersmith panicked and windmilled his arms, pushed himself up, and shook himself off. The handful of bloodstained rags that Rose had given him lay partially buried at his feet. Hammersmith touched his fingers to his head. They came back clean. No fresh blood. The wound was healing already. Or was frozen stiff. He turned and tried to see the inn with its giant protective tree through the falling grey sky, but it was invisible. He was alone.

It was possible that something had happened at the inn. The

majority of the noise had come from that direction, not far behind Hammersmith. He remembered what he'd been told, that the villagers routinely shoveled snow off their roofs in the winter before their buildings became dangerously heavy. Nobody had done much shoveling in the past two days. He shook his head and turned and continued on the way he had been going. He left the rags in the snow, the red turning to pink and slowly disappearing under fresh snow.

Somewhere ahead of him was the killer of Oliver Price. He was sure of it.

Vicar Brothwood threw himself upon the altar as the entire church tipped and dropped several inches into a tunnel.

The building weighed nearly three hundred tons, a fact the vicar wasn't privy to, but he had known for years that it was only a matter of time before the ground gave way under much of the village. It was, after all, a coal-mining village. What could one do except trust in the Lord and pray for the best?

The pews, which Henry had hastily put back in place, now slid across the center aisle and tapped against the pews on the other side of the sanctuary. The latter pews were fastened to the floor and held their ground against the heavy tide. Brothwood counted three sick men who had been knocked to the ground. The others, perhaps a hundred people, had stayed in place, even as pews and candlesticks and bibles skated smoothly past them. Brothwood smiled to see that a handful of people had slept through the disaster.

He ran to help the three men back onto their pews and sent up a silent prayer of thanks. Then he crossed his fingers, hoping the building would stay put just a little while longer, just until the people of Blackhampton were back on their feet.

A small tree, bigger than a sapling, but not more than five or six years old, had fallen across Day and knocked him into the snow. Its trunk was as big around as his leg, and he lay there, catching his breath. Henry reached down and grabbed the tree, flung it aside, took a fistful of Day's torn overcoat in his massive paw, and pulled the inspector to his feet.

"Thank you, Henry."

"What happened, do you think?"

"This village. They've dug tunnels all under it, chiseled out the coal in the ground. Everything's sinking now. There's nothing to hold it all up."

"That tree didn't sink; it fell."

"Its roots weren't anchored. It was top-heavy."

"Other trees fell, too. Look."

"Indeed."

They had left the road, cut cross-country toward the train depot, hoping to make better time, but the snow was deeper here and it had been a hard, slow slog. Day had lost count of the tremors they'd felt, but the tree line was a shaggy crosshatch of felled trees, their roots now exposed to the air like some other hidden forest made suddenly visible and vulnerable.

"Look." Henry pointed through the grey at the village on the other side of the road, not far, but in another world, on the distant horizon, made so by the storm.

Day squinted and saw a fuzz of smoke. He galumphed along through the snow hoping for a better view. "Henry, is that the inn?"

"It's a tree, sir. A big one."

"But under the tree, Henry?"

"Under the tree, that's a house, but it's all gone now, isn't it?"

"Henry, that's the inn. Nevil's in there! And Dr Kingsley!"

Day galloped ahead, sending sprays of powder up on either side, but not moving very quickly despite the energy he was expending. Henry opened his overcoat and checked the little box inside. Baby bird Oliver looked up and chirped, snug in his nest, warmed by Henry's body heat and the tangle of straw in the box. Henry closed the box again, made sure it was securely tucked away, buttoned his coat, and then strode along easily after Day.

58

Sutton Price helped his daughter down the rungs, took a lantern that hung from a hook on the wall, and lit it. Opened the shutter and grabbed Virginia's hand. He pulled her into the black mouth that led to the warren of tunnels and away from the active seam. He moved along, slow and steady, matching her pace. She seemed unperturbed by the darkness, the damp, the strange echoes of their footsteps that faded away from them under the earth.

At least here it was warm.

Neither of them spoke until they reached a place where the tunnel widened out and formed a sort of unnatural cavern, roughly ten yards around. No digging had been done there in a generation, but it had been inhabited. There was a bedroll, unkempt and dirty, kicked against one wall, and evidence of a recent fire in the center of the room. A thick coil of rope, a stout wooden crate, and three jars of water kept the bedroll company. The entrance to another tunnel across from them led to more tunnels. Between the coal and ashes of the campfire and that other tunnel mouth there was a mound of settled dirt. The mound was six feet by three feet and rounded across the top. Two short sticks had been lashed together in the shape of a cross and stuck into the cavern floor at one end of the mound. A trench had been dug next to the mound, also six feet by three feet. An upright shovel rested against the wall, its blade biting into the dirt floor.

Virginia followed her father around the room by the wall without taking her eyes off the mound of dirt.

Sutton set the lantern on the floor, leaned against the wall, and eased himself down onto the bedroll. He crossed his legs and beckoned to Virginia, and she came to him, sat in his lap. She turned her head so that she could see her father's face in the flickering lamplight. He smiled down at her, and she smiled back. But there was sadness in his glittering eyes, and Virginia's forehead creased with worry.

"What's wrong, Father?"

He stroked her hair and grimaced. Shook his head.

"Is it what I told you?" Virginia said.

"Yes," Sutton said. "Tell me again what you did."

"He was coughing, Father. And crying. Keeping everyone awake."

"Was he?"

"Oh, yes."

"Is that why . . ."

"Well . . ."

"Tell me, Virginia."

The little girl frowned and turned away from him. She scratched her nose. "It's dusty in here."

"You get used to it."

"I don't want to get used to it. I want to go home and I want you to come home, too."

"I don't think we're going to go home."

"Don't be silly, Father. We can't stay here. It's filthy."

"Tell me again."

"What's that?" She pointed at the mound across from them. At the tiny cross that marked it.

"It's there because of a mistake I made."

"And what's the hole next to it?"

"That was for me, but I was too much of a coward to lie in it."

"It would have been fine for Oliver."

Sutton breathed out heavily through his nose and rubbed his forehead. "It's my fault. All of this is my fault."

"Oh, no, Father. Don't say that. It's all Hester's fault, really."

"What about Oliver?"

"Well, of course it's his fault, too, but he's only a baby."

"What did Hester do?"

"She took Mother away and she made Oliver. She made everything wrong. And then I saw her leave that night with the other man and I knew it was my chance to make things right again."

"Make things right." There was no emotion in his face.

"If only you'll come home," Virginia said, "then Hester will leave and we'll be a happy family just as we were meant to be."

"You can't have done what you said. You're lying. You saw something happen and you've made up a story about it."

"I practiced first," Virginia said. "I took Mr Baggs's smallest pig, the runt that he was going to kill anyway, and I took it to the woods, and it followed me just exactly like Oliver did."

"A pig."

"Yes. And really, Father, the pig was so much harder than Oliver, because it tried to run away from me, and then I got blood all over my best dress. Oliver did just what I told him to, but he was coughing and coughing and so I had to do it to him faster and he got blood on me, too."

"You murdered your brother."

Virginia snorted. "He isn't my brother at all."

"And you put him in the well. Like rubbish, you tossed him aside."

"No, Father. He was too heavy for me. Peter and Anna found us and they put him in the well and they said not to tell anyone." She smiled at him and put her tiny hand on his arm, her knuckles dimpled into the chubby flesh. "But I can tell you because I did it for you."

"No," Sutton said. A single tear turned his pale cheek pink and lost itself in his beard.

"Now you don't have to be with Hester anymore."

"Stop talking, Virginia."

"I know it was bad."

"Stop now."

"You're not too terribly angry with me, are you, Father?"

Sutton closed his eyes and reached for his daughter. He pulled her to him, and she snuggled against the warmth of his chest. He wrapped his arms around her and stroked her hair and put his lips against the top of her head.

"Shhh," he said. "Quiet now, my princess."

59

Peter Price was shouting, and so she eventually opened her eyes to see what he wanted. The first thing she saw was a billow of brown and white, and she blinked hard, refocused her eyes, and saw that she was in the top of a tree. But she was lying on the floor of the inn, and gravity seemed to be all wrong. She blinked again and now the top of the tree was above her, and the world spun and righted itself around her. Or rather, her perception of the world righted itself.

The ceiling was only partially there. Above it, the top floor seemed to be gone and had been replaced by the very old tree that had always stood beside the inn. Branches of the tree, each of them as big as any normal tree she had seen, had invaded every nook and cranny of the inn's many rooms. At least, all of the inn's rooms that she could see from her position on the floor, and she could see a surprising number of them. Snowflakes and errant brown leaves fluttered down and about, and already there was a fresh skin of snow everywhere inside.

Of course, inside no longer seemed to be quite so inside as it usually was.

Peter Price was still shouting. Jessica sat up and checked herself for injuries. Aside from a multitude of scrapes and scratches, she seemed to be fine. The tree had apparently pushed her down and across the common room without doing her much damage.

Next, she looked around for Peter. He was pinned against the far fireplace by a tangle of strong and flexible branches. He was waving at her, his eyes wide and frantic.

"Are you okay?" he said.

"I seem to be fine," Jessica said. "How about you?"

"My arm hurts." She looked through the massive wooden nest and saw that Peter's arm was twisted strangely. Possibly broken.

"Can you move?" she said.

"No," he said. "And I think it's on fire."

It took her a moment to figure out what was on fire, but then she saw the tendrils of smoke weaving their way around the boy and realized that the tree had inserted part of itself into the fireplace.

"Wait there," she said, then realized it was a ridiculous thing to say since Peter had already admitted he couldn't move. But it did seem to calm him.

The roof had slowed the tree's progress through the building, but it had been moving fast. Thin, strong wooden limbs had thrust their way through her dress, just missing her legs, and into the floor. She broke through them with her wrist. Quick jabs. She looked around for her missing left shoe and found it under a lot of brown.

She grabbed it and stuck it on her foot. She took hold of a bigger branch above her and pulled herself up, groaning with the effort, then looked around for the next big branch between herself and the fireplace.

"Where's Anna?" she said, shouting to be heard over the rushing wind.

"She's upstairs. You sent her there."

Jessica looked up. There was no upstairs.

She hiked up her skirts and straddled a branch that was as big around as her body, swung her other leg over, and hoped Peter wasn't looking her way. There was no time for modesty. Her feet touched the floor and she gauged the distance to Peter again. Closer, but it was going to take a while to navigate through the sudden thicket, and she was worried about the smoke forming behind the boy. She considered kicking off her shoes. She could move faster that way, but the floor was covered with splinters, some of them huge, jagged, dangerous. Bare feet would quickly become a liability.

"Peter!"

"Yes?"

"Look around you. Look for a fireplace poker or a stout stick."

She watched him swivel his head around, then he disappeared from view as he bent from the shoulders to look at something. She heard him stifle a gasp of pain. He must have wrenched his bad shoulder even more. She continued to make her way toward him, but too slowly. Her hip still hurt from her fall at the Price home, but it took her weight.

"I found this." Peter's head popped back up into view and he raised his good arm. He was hefting a long flat iron bar, twisted nearly in half, with wicked hooks set at regular intervals. It was the mount for the inn's fireplace tools. It had been securely bolted to the mantel, and Jessica wondered at the force necessary to wrench it loose and bend it. She nodded, excited.

"Yes, that's brilliant. Can you use it to lever yourself loose?"

"I don't know."

"I can't see what's pinned you down. I can't help."

"Come closer."

"I'm trying, but there are too many branches in the way. I'll be there as soon as I can, but you must try to help yourself."

The boy swallowed hard, and his head disappeared once more as he bent to his task. He could only use one arm and he wasn't a heavy boy. He didn't have a lot of upper-body strength to put into the effort. On the other hand, he was skinny enough that she hoped he might be able to slide out from behind the tree limbs if he could create just a little more space for himself.

"Peter," she said. She pulled herself up onto a limb and balanced, teetering there for a second, looking for a place to put her other foot. "Hurry, Peter."

"It's a little bit loose now," he said. She still couldn't see him and she held on to a solid branch beside her, going up on the toes of one foot, the other foot still dangling in the air. The smoke was denser now where Peter was, but it had thickened imperceptibly. She hadn't realized that she couldn't see the stones left from the crushed fireplace until they were gone. She couldn't tell if Peter was standing or was still bent over his task. Then she saw shuddering orange tongues flicking in and out of the smoke. The great broken tree was on fire!

"Peter!"

"I'm loose!"

"Move!"

"Which way?"

"Toward my voice!"

"I can't see where you are!" Then, softer: "My arm hurts."

"Peter, listen for me and follow my voice."

"I can't!"

The air in the room wavered as flames licked out toward Jessica, and there was a rending sound as if two trains had gone off their tracks in unison, locked in combat. She lost her grip on the branch and slipped, fell hard against the trunk of the tree, and the breath went out of her. She shook her head and sat back up. Her leg was bleeding.

"Peter!"

No answer. Her leg didn't hurt much. No broken bones. She'd live. She pushed aside the smallest branches near her, and a bird's nest fell out of them and rolled to a stop at her feet. It was empty, useless. She kicked it aside, and it bounced off an oddly shaped bundle trapped in the branches three feet from her. She made her way to it and reached out, touched it. It was white and soft, like a pillow. Like a pincushion. Bennett Rose was on his side, resting on the floor of his inn, his apron pulled up over his head. Countless thin branches, none of them any bigger around than Jessica's thumb, had skewered him through his chest and abdomen and throat. Blood, more than she had imagined could be in a person's body, had trickled, was still trickling, down his body, pooling on the floor, shiny and black. She rolled him over, the branches resisting her, and pulled the apron from his face. One scraggy branch had been driven through his eye, and something clear oozed from the corner of it down the side of his nose. His other eye rolled and looked up at her and she screamed.

Rose twitched his hand as if to reach out to her, then he went slack by degrees. His legs never moved, but his hands fell loose, then his arms, then his upper body seemed to relax and his head lolled on his neck and the scraggy branch plucked its way out of his eye socket and whipped a spray of blood at Jessica.

She backed away and bulled her way through the top of the tree, headed toward the murkiest part of the room, the smokiest, where she thought she had last heard Peter. The tree had settled and shifted, rolled slightly to one side, and she no longer knew where she was in relation to anything else, but the smoke was her guide.

The inn had never seemed so large to her before.

She pushed on a branch and it sprang back at her and struck her across the eyes. She cried out and felt tears welling up, running down her cheeks. Where was Peter?

"Miss Jessica?"

She turned at the sound of his voice and looked up. Peter was balanced on the huge branch she had fallen from. He was practically hanging there, his good arm wrapped around an overhead tree limb, shirtless and grinning down at her with his hair wild and smoky, his face and his furrowed chest smudged, like some wild boy from the jungle. His shirt had been tied around his neck and made into a sling to support his damaged arm.

"Peter? How did you . . . ?"

"He sent me for you. Because I'm smaller. It's easier if you go this way. The branches are more broken over here."

He grinned again and scampered along the giant limb. Jessica followed him and, gradually, the branches did thin out and she began to smell fresh air. She hadn't realized how warm she was until she felt a lovely cold draft against her wet cheeks.

And then she was outside.

The far wall of the inn was completely gone, vanished under the crushing weight of the centuries-old tree, buried in a tunnel somewhere beneath her. Peter ran past her, his feet bare in the snow, and stopped at the side of a man who stood with his back to her, slightly stooped under a weight. The man turned and she was relieved to see that it was Dr Kingsley. He was cradling the small still body of Anna Price. He looked at Jessica and then down at Anna and he smiled.

"She'll be all right," Dr Kingsley said. "We were lucky the tree knocked us out of there before it did its nasty work on your inn."

"How did . . . ?"

"The branches really are somewhat sparse over there. I was able to get to young Peter, but he was very brave to find you."

"He made this out of my shirt," Peter said. "My arm feels better."

"Is anyone else still in there?" Kingsley said.

Jessica shook her head. She didn't know whether Peter had seen Rose's body and she didn't want to say anything out loud. The children had already been through enough.

Kingsley nodded. She watched his breath drift away on the breeze. "Well, then," he said, "the boy has no shoes and the girl has had a shock. We ought to find shelter for them. And quickly."

There was another tearing sound from the inn and some part of the tree invisible to Jessica crashed down, sending a shower of sparks into the night air. A portion of the wall caved inward, and fire sprang up to take its place.

"The fire will take this whole road," Jessica said. "Everything on it."

"The detective will help," Peter said. He beamed at her, his eyes glittering in the firelight, and Jessica did her best to smile back. Then she saw what he was pointing at. Two shadowy figures struggled toward them holding lanterns aloft.

"Hallo!" Inspector Day said.

Jessica gave a great sigh of relief. Her legs disappeared from under her and she toppled into the snow. Before she lost consciousness, she heard the inspector shouting out orders.

"Henry, can you carry the schoolteacher? I'll get the boy. Good gracious, he has no shoes."

60

Hammersmith trudged forward through the snow, driven as much by the nothingness behind him and all around him as the desire to catch Oliver Price's killer. He passed through his own exhalations, his warm vaporous breath freezing in his eyelashes, gluing them together and threatening to drag his eyes closed. His mouth was sealed shut by a crust of snot. He could not have opened it if he tried, but he didn't try. He thought of nothing.

The Black Country was different than Wales had been, and they did things differently here, but a coal mine was a coal mine and Hammersmith looked without thinking for the familiar signs. He did not think of his childhood, not of the ponies clopping through the long, dark tunnels, not of the rats crawling over his legs, not of the silence or the loneliness. He simply followed the depressions in the snow of Sutton Price's boots and looked for the dark shape of a pit.

And, eventually, there it was, a snow-covered mound, a scabbed-over black maw that had recently been scraped open. The snow around it was trampled and had been smoothed back over by a fresh accumulation. Hammersmith ducked and entered carefully. He listened, but heard nothing. He backed slowly down the wooden rungs and into the mouth of the seam. It was warmer here, and he sank down, rested with his back to the dirt wall, gave himself a few minutes.

He was in no shape to deal with a murderer and he knew it.

61

The train depot had sunk five inches into the tunnels beneath Blackhampton. Each tremor had driven the small
building another inch into the ground. Calvin Campbell
and Hester Price were inside when the first tremor hit, moved out
into the snow before the second tremor, but had stayed inside since
then. The building was solid and unadorned, and there was nothing
inside to fall on them, except the ceiling. There were no shelves or
statues or lamps, just three squat benches bolted firmly to the planks
of the floor. And so they sat inside and listened to the earth tremble
and the wind howl. Hester nestled against Calvin and he put his
arm around her, and they stayed like that through three successive
tremors, riding the depot as it sank.

"The train should have come," Hester said.

"It's the storm," Calvin said.

"Will it still come tonight?"

"I don't know. I hope so."

He took his arm back and stood, stretched, and went to the tiny window, the glass shattered and crunching underfoot, snow piling up on the sill. There was nothing out there, no sign of an oncoming train. Only snow.

And, somewhere on the periphery of Calvin's vision, a glint of metal.

The old horse was dead. Frozen solid, standing upright in its tracks. The American steadied his Whitworth against its back and took aim at the tiny black square in the front wall of the depot. The horse was already cold, and the fingers of the American's right hand were stiff and tingling. He rubbed them against the leg of his trousers, but the friction only made them sting. He lowered the rifle and turned toward the young horse. Its black eyes followed him as he reached out and put his hand against its warm belly. It snorted, but didn't stamp its hooves, didn't move. Maybe it couldn't. He supposed the beast was warmer on the inside and thought about cutting it open, but he needed that horse to get away from the village once Campbell was dead.

His fingers were limbering up a bit. They still stung, but he could move his trigger finger easily and that was all he needed. He withdrew his hand from the young horse's belly and set the Whitworth back across the dead old horse's back, pointed it at the depot, hunched down, closed his eyes, and made himself still. He opened his eyes and stared down the sight at the depot's window and saw the blank white face of Calvin Campbell staring back at him.

The American pulled the trigger.

———

Another tremor hit the depot and the boxlike building bucked and swayed just as Hester Price rose from her bench in the middle of the room and approached Calvin Campbell. The big Scotsman was staring hard out the window and, when the building began to sink into the earth, he grabbed the windowsill. Hester heard the crinkling of broken glass and she drew in a last sharp breath, worried that Calvin had cut himself.

There was a whistling sound and then a faint pop from somewhere far away, and Hester's knees gave out and she fell.

Calvin heard the distinctive whistle of a hexagonal Whitworth bullet and ducked, though he knew it was too late. If you heard the whistle, you were already dead, you just didn't know it yet. But the tremor was shaking the ground hard, and he hoped that might be enough to throw off the shooter's aim.

He let go of the windowsill and turned and saw Hester falling, the top of her head open like a bowl full of gore and Calvin fell, too, fell toward her, reaching out, trying to put himself in the path of the bullet that had already passed him.

He went down on his hands and knees and scrabbled across the floor, grabbed Hester up in his arms, leaving some essentials of her behind, and crabwalked with her to the wall. He didn't cry out, didn't make a sound, but his mouth opened and closed, opened and closed, as wide as it would go. His throat was tight, unrelenting, and it kept his grief bottled in his chest. He cradled

Hester, protected her, and waited for Grey Eyes to come and finish the job.

Waited for his death and welcomed it.

The American immediately understood that he had missed. The bullet had passed right by Calvin Campbell and on into the building. He tried to adjust for the next shot, but the ground was shaking under him and he couldn't hold the rifle still.

The young horse whinnied behind him, and he turned just in time to watch it disappear, pulled all at once down into the ground. The old horse toppled toward him and he tried to move, leapt to the side, but he wasn't fast enough. He hit a high drift, sending spumes of snow into the air, and the horse fell against him with a loud whuff, *pinning his leg and hip.*

He couldn't tell if anything was broken; there was no sensation at all, he was so cold. He pushed out against the old horse, but stopped and turned his head at a wrenching sound nearby. The back wheels of the carriage sank into the ground, and then its long wooden tongue lifted up and the entire thing tipped back and rolled away, out of sight somewhere below.

The American panicked and hit the old horse, beat his fists against it, reached for the Whitworth and smashed its butt against the horse's back, but the beast didn't budge.

He was surrounded by a roaring sound, as if he had stumbled into the fast-moving stream of a waterfall, plummeting blind through the churning foam, and then he was actually falling and the horse was falling with him and the world went dark around him and the sky receded.

He hit the floor of the shaft below him, hit it hard, and the horse came

*a second after. It landed heavily on his right foot. The foot jounced vio-
lently to the side, twisted like something strange, some inanimate thing
that wasn't connected to him, and there was a crunching sound and a
blinding flash of pain that ended deep in his right shoulder.*

*He looked up and saw a mountain of ice and snow and dirt funneling
down at him, on top of him. His open mouth filled with it, and his eyes
shut automatically.*

62

Day was worried about the boy's bare feet. He had taken off his tattered gloves, shoved them on the ends of Peter's feet, but he doubted they did any good. Still, it had made the boy giggle to see that he had monkey paws, and he had not complained about the cold.

Dr Kingsley also seemed to be struggling, carrying the girl through the snow. She hadn't awakened yet, and that worried Day, too. Henry was the only one of them who seemed to be doing all right. Jessica had woken up and asked to be put down, but Henry had refused. He trudged along with her, polite but stubborn, his large body hunched over the schoolteacher as much as possible to protect her from the blowing snow.

The tremors hit them hard. Both Day and Kingsley fell down, dropping the children. Day heard a rifle's report, but the crack of it echoed back and forth around them and he couldn't locate it. He motioned to the others to stay down. Henry stood where he was, unaffected by the tremor, sheltering Jessica with his arms.

The girl, Anna, woke up, sat in the snow, looked around at them all. She opened her mouth to speak, but Peter shushed her, watching Day's face to see what he should do next. Day smiled at the boy and listened for another rifle shot.

But there was no other sound and the tremor stopped. Day nodded at Peter and the boy crawled over and hugged his sister. He helped her to her feet. Jessica pressed a hand against Henry's chest, and he finally let her down. Day gave his lantern to Jessica, held out his hand to Kingsley, and pulled the doctor up. They stood, looking into the distance, seeing nothing.

"We need to get the children inside," Kingsley said. "Someplace warm. Or, at least, out of this wind."

"I still think the depot's in this direction," Day said. "We must be close."

"I can see the fire there," Kingsley said. He pointed to an orange glow on the horizon where the inn blazed away, still busy cremating the bodies of Oliver Price and Bennett Rose. "Which means you're right, I think. If we just keep going . . ."

"But there's someone shooting out here."

"Surely not at us."

"Whoever they're shooting at, it can't be good for us. We don't want to stumble across something. Not with the children."

"We'll be fine," Anna said.

"You let us be the judge of that," Kingsley said.

"No, thank you," Anna said.

"Anna!" Peter said.

"We've done very well on our own, so far."

"That may be," Day said. "But we're all in this together now and we need to rely on each other. You know this place much better than the doctor and I do. We'd very much appreciate your help in finding the train depot or we'll freeze to death."

Anna looked at Peter. He raised his eyebrows at her. Day worried that if the boy stood in the snow much longer, with nothing but gloves on his feet, he might lose his toes.

Anna sighed. "Very well," she said. "I think it's this way." And she marched off into the night, expecting the rest of them to follow. They did.

Jessica caught up to Day and touched his arm. "You're very good with children," she said. Her voice was a whisper, barely audible.

"Thank you," Day said. "I'm expecting my first at any moment."

"I know. You'll do well, I think."

He grinned at her. "I do hope so," he said.

Then he fell into a chasm and disappeared from sight.

63

Hammersmith staggered through the tunnel, stopping every few feet to rest and to make sure he was still following the tracks in the dirt. He didn't have a lantern, and so he had to strike a match every time he checked the ground under him. He had four matches left and was just beginning to worry when he saw a dim yellow glow coming from somewhere ahead. He put the matches away and leaned against the wall for a minute, waited for his vision to clear. The blow to the head had affected him more than he'd imagined it would. He'd assumed he'd shake off the effects and be fine, and maybe under other circumstances he would have, but since arriving in the village he had hardly eaten, he'd fallen ill, and had even been drugged. He was afraid the omen of the owl had been more than a silly superstition. That Blackhampton would kill him if he spent another day here.

He took a deep breath, pushed off the wall, and moved toward the light.

Four minutes later, he stepped into a large chamber dug out of the rock below the village. The space was lit by a lantern on the floor, and later he would have time to look around and would notice the bedroll, the shovel, the remains of the fire. And he would notice the two dirt-covered mounds against the far wall.

But when he entered the chamber, the first thing he noticed was Sutton Price, swinging by his neck from a wooden support beam that ran across the length of the cavern's ceiling. A crate had been upended two feet away from Sutton's feet, and it was instantly clear that Price had thrown the rope over the beam, tied his knot and stood on the crate, then kicked off and swung free. Sutton's feet were still moving, kicking sullenly at the air beneath him.

Hammersmith hurtled across the chamber to the hanged man and grabbed his legs, hoisted him up, creating slack in the rope above. Sutton Price thrashed like a fish in the bottom of a boat, and his voice rasped down at the sergeant. "Keh . . . Kawh . . ." A broken bird.

"No," Hammersmith said. He gasped and held on tight to Price's struggling legs. "Stop fighting me."

Price laughed. The sound forced up through the swollen furnace of his throat, burning the air. "Glad . . . glad you're here. Hear my confession. Last confession."

Hammersmith stretched out his right leg, angled his foot, trying to hook the box and drag it over, but it was still inches out of his reach. "I'm not a priest," he said.

"Not . . . I'm not Catholic," Price said. "You'll do."

Hammersmith struggled to keep his feet under him, balancing

the hanged man above him. He felt weak and suddenly very tired of everything and everyone. "What is it? What do you want to say?"

"Don't blame her. Virginia."

"Where is she?"

"She was lost."

"I don't know how long I can hold you up. Tell me where your daughter is. Which tunnel?" He was panting, spitting out short sentences like a mockery of Sutton Price.

"Mathilda. I hit her. Ended her. Buried her here."

"Your first wife?"

"There."

Hammersmith looked at the far wall of the chamber, at the two mounds, one packed down and settled, the other fresh and high. "You buried her here."

"Played out."

Hammersmith understood. "This tunnel. The seam's played out here. You brought her here and no one ever found her."

"She was good. A good person."

"But you wanted the nanny."

"Hester. So beautiful." The words forced out of Price as if by a bellows. "But she loved another. Another man. I knew she did. But I did it all anyway. I did everything."

"The other grave?"

"It was in her."

"Who?"

"My wickedness. All my fault. Don't blame her."

"Who, man? Tell me before I fall and let you dangle."

"She killed Oliver. My responsibility. Done now."

Hammersmith realized who was buried under the mound of

earth, had realized it as soon as he saw the two piles of dirt, but had refused to acknowledge it. His stomach flopped over and he cried out. Price kicked at Hammersmith and the sergeant lost his footing for a second, but regained it, used the swaying man to right himself. He planted his feet again and pushed up, but he could already feel his arms starting to give out.

"Put me next to them," Price said.

"My inspector will come," Hammersmith said. "He'll help me. We'll get you. Get you down. And you'll pay for your crimes properly."

"Am paying."

"This isn't the way."

"My way."

"No. By order of Her Majesty, I'm placing you under arrest. For the murder. For the murder of Mathilda Price. And for the murder of Virginia Price, too. Damn you."

Sutton Price chuckled. The deep harsh sound of sand shaking through an hourglass.

"I can wait. Policeman. If you can."

Hammersmith closed his eyes and gritted his teeth. He wrapped his arms tighter around Sutton Price's dangling legs and steeled himself, prepared for a long wait. Price began to talk again, but his voice was gone, nothing but rasping, and Hammersmith didn't try to listen. He held on and concentrated on breathing, on staying awake, on rooting himself to the ground. He held on and he waited for help.

64

I'm all right!" Day said.

The others couldn't see him.

"Stand back," Henry said. He cupped his massive palms around his mouth and hollered into the chasm made by generations of miners. "I'm coming down!"

"No!" Day said. "Don't! We'd both be trapped!"

Kingsley put a hand on Henry's chest and shook his head. "We'll find rope," he said.

"Where?" Henry said. He looked back and forth through the snow, pantomiming a search.

"I'm in a tunnel! I can feel air moving! It must lead outside!"

Kingsley knelt at the edge of the hole. "You could wander forever down there!"

"There must be a way out!"

Peter Price squatted down next to Kingsley and peered into the darkness. "I've been in the tunnels! I can help you!"

"Yes!" Day's voice didn't sound like he was very far down there, even if the others couldn't see him. "Any advice would be good! I think I should go . . . I can't tell one direction from another!"

"Look up!" Peter Price said. He jumped into the hole before Kingsley, or anyone else, could stop him. A half a second later there was a loud *whoof* as Peter landed on Day.

"Oh, my God!" Jessica said.

"I'm all right!" Day said. Again.

"So am I!" Peter said. "It's warmer down here! You should come down!"

"No!" Day said. "Please don't!"

"I hurt him!"

"He didn't hurt me! But please, don't anyone else jump on me!"

"Can you see anything down there?" Kingsley said.

"It's very dark!" Day said.

"Take one of the lanterns!"

"Don't throw it!"

"No!" Kingsley said. He stood and looked around. "No, that wouldn't do, would it?"

"I have an idea," Anna said. She squatted like Peter had at the lip of the chasm. Kingsley and Jessica both reached out and grabbed her shoulders. "I'm not going to jump in there. I'm the smart one. Peter's the impulsive one." She cupped her hands around her mouth and shouted down at Day and Peter. "Stand well back! I'm going to try something!"

She stood and walked back from the fissure and squatted again, putting her arms out in front of her, bent at the elbows so that her forearms were straight across her face. She moved forward, pushing the snow ahead of her, using her arms as a plow. By the time she reached the hole in the ground, she was sweeping a high pile of snow. It went over the edge and fell into the dark with a soft *plush*.

Kingsley grasped what she was up to and grinned. "Come, Henry. Let's help her." He blew out the fire in his lantern and set it next to the hole to cool, then he and Henry moved out into the drifts of snow. They mimicked Anna, who was already pushing another heap of snow toward the chasm. Jessica followed them, knelt in the snow, and plowed it ahead of her just as the others were doing. After a few minutes, they stood and brushed themselves off, blew warm air into their cupped palms, and returned to the hole.

Anna peered down at her invisible brother and the inspector. "Did it make a cushion down there?"

"It did!" Peter said. "Good job! It must be a yard high at least, but I don't think we can climb up it! Too soft!"

"Soft is good!" Anna said. She took the cold lantern and clicked her tongue at it. "I'm afraid we may lose some of the oil."

"What?"

"I wasn't talking to you!"

"What are you doing?"

"Stand back and let me just do it!"

She lay on her stomach and crawled out as far as she dared, then dangled the lantern over the edge and let go of it. It landed like a whisper somewhere below. A moment later Peter's voice drifted up to her. "Got it! Brilliant!"

"Did it leak?"

"I don't think so! Not very much!"

"We need to get matches for you now!"

"I've got matches!" Day said.

She listened to a rustling sound in the dark, and then there was a small flash of light and the sound of metal on metal as the lantern opened and was lit. And all at once she could see her brother and Inspector Day, standing in the snow and looking up at her. Their faces were yellow in the lamplight, and their bodies faded out into nothingness below their chests. They looked almost close enough to touch.

"Henry might be able to reach you," Kingsley said. There seemed to be no need to shout anymore, now that they could all see one another.

"I don't think so," Day said. "It's farther than it looks."

Henry reached out anyway, reached his long right arm far down into the ground, his fingertips still far above Day and the boy.

"It's okay," Peter said. "I can lead us out. I know the way. I think I do." He seemed eager to please, and Anna understood why. Both of them had a lot to make up for.

"We'll be okay," Day said. "It really is warmer down here than up there. You lot must be freezing. You look wet."

And, suddenly, they were freezing. The initial rush of adrenaline had faded and they weren't moving, just kneeling in the snow. Henry reached into his overcoat and found his little wooden box. He opened the lid a crack and squinted inside it, then closed it again and held it over the chasm.

They all heard a piercing *peep*.

"Henry!"

"Catch," Henry said.

"Henry, no!" Day said.

"He can help you, little Oliver can."

"How is that?"

"Like a canary. It's a coal mine you're in. They take canaries into coal mines to protect them, don't they?"

"That they do," Day said. He doubted whether Henry understood why miners carried canaries, that the birds' deaths were meant to warn men of gas leaks and pockets of poison in the underground air. "Thank you, but I doubt it's necessary. You need to keep Oliver safe with you."

Henry frowned, but tucked the bird back into his coat.

"Right," Kingsley said. "We'll head on to the depot and see about warming up. You get out of there and make your way to the depot, too."

"Or somewhere," Day said. "If we can find a safe place, we'll wait for daylight. I'll find Sergeant Hammersmith. Or Constable Grimes."

"The train will come once the storm lets up."

"We hope."

"We do indeed."

"I want to send the sergeant home as soon as we can."

"We will."

"Peter," Anna said, "take care."

He nodded up at her, the lamplight catching highlights in his hair and a glint in his eyes. She knew he understood her. She didn't want to spell it out. She needed him now. She had a horrible feeling that they had no one else left.

65

---

ell," Day said, "lead the way, young man."

Peter bit his upper lip and preceded the inspector down the long black tunnel. Day held the lantern high, and shadows bounded ahead of them over the craggy walls and the beaten-down floor, the ceiling with its rough timbers meant to keep the village from crashing through and failing miserably at that task.

"How is your arm? Does it hurt much?"

"No," Peter said. "Perhaps it's the cold, but I can't feel it at all now."

The boy trotted along barefoot, his arm in a sling made from a torn shirt, his hair plastered to his head. He and his sisters had spent days on their own, wild children, their father stalking these same tunnels and their mother hiding in a tiny hole under a church. Peter Price had been attended by a housekeeper and a schoolteacher, but he had gone without a parent, had most likely taken the role of parent for his sisters' sake, and there was something new awakening in Day as his wife grew larger, as their baby grew larger inside her. He was a father, or would be very soon, and he was astonished by the depth of feeling that this simple fact inspired in him. He wanted to be an example for his child, whether that child finally presented itself as a boy or a girl. And, like generations of men before him, he also wanted to take a train in the other direction and never set his eyes on that child. Granted, this latter emotion was a false one, gnarled and stunted, a poisoned apple offered up by a part of himself he had never listened to, but it shamed him and he aimed that shame at Sutton Price, who had actually left his children to fend for themselves while he hared off after a woman who didn't want him, and who didn't want to be a mother to Peter and Anna and Virginia.

"You won't be left alone again," Day said to the boy's filthy back as they hurried along. "I won't leave until you're safe."

The boy didn't react, but his back stiffened and he jogged faster, his bare feet slapping against the dirt. They both moved along silently after that. Day felt mildly uncomfortable, as if he'd said something wrong, but he was glad he'd said it anyway.

At last, Peter stopped and bent his head and peered forward. "Do you see that?"

Day looked down the length of the tunnel. He squinted. "Is the wall yellow there?"

The boy nodded. "I think so."

"Is it gold? Did we find a gold mine?"

"I think it's a light, sir."

"Yes," Day said. "It looks like lantern light to me."

"Should we go on?"

"Let's," Day said. "But if you don't mind, I'll take the lead."

He passed the boy and quietly reached into his coat. He drew out his Colt Navy and, comforted by the weight of it, crept forward and around a slight curve in the narrow abandoned tunnel.

He stopped again when he ran into the back of a horse.

66

As it happened, the train depot was only a few yards from where Day had fallen into the chasm. It was over a rise that had been piled high with snow, and as soon as the four of them—Dr Kingsley, Jessica, Anna, and Henry Mayhew—topped the ridge they saw it, half digested by the landscape, listing to one side deep in a chasm of its own. They ran to it, lifting their feet high and bounding forward as if they still had energy, even though the place was dark and empty-looking. Even tipped up on end, it was better than the limitless tracts of nothing they'd been wandering through.

Henry wrenched the front door up and open and lifted little Anna through, lowered her down. They all heard her gasp, but Henry lost his grip and was unable to pull her back up. So he jumped in after her, careful not to land where he thought Anna must be. He slipped and slid down the inclined floor, but caught himself with a paw on the broken windowsill. Kingsley lowered their remaining lantern down to him and Henry raised it up, peered into the gloom.

There were no furnishings. Just three benches tilted at an odd angle, bolted to the floor. In the lowest corner of the room, Calvin Campbell looked up and glared at the sudden light. He was hunched over something that resembled an old blanket, discarded there where nobody would think to look. When Henry brought the lantern closer, he saw that the blanket-thing was a woman and that the woman was missing the top of her head. The wall behind Campbell was painted with a black swath of liquid that ran and dripped and spattered, all of it pointed directly at the big Scotsman and the dead woman.

"Henry," Dr Kingsley said.

Henry looked up at the rectangle of black sky behind Kingsley's head. Kingsley was half in the room already, straining with worry. Behind him was the silhouette of Jessica's upper body, leaning forward over the doctor.

"Henry, is the girl all right?"

"She's dead, Doctor."

"Oh, no!" Jessica shoved Kingsley out of the way and tripped forward through the door, falling into Henry's arms. He held on to the lantern by its wire, and its swaying bulk swung crazy shadows around the room, into every corner. Anna sat on a bench, perched on the arm of it, her hand on Campbell's arm. When she saw Jessica with Henry, she pulled herself up the bench toward them. Jessica pushed herself out of Henry's arms and met the girl halfway as Kingsley dropped down next to Henry.

"You said she was dead," Kingsley said.

"I meant the other girl," Henry said. "The big one. I'm sorry."

Kingsley patted the giant's shoulder and moved forward, past Jessica and Anna, who were crying, holding each other, neither of them looking at the grisly tableau against the tilted baseboards. Campbell looked up again as Kingsley came near and he let go of Hester's body. He stood, balancing with one foot against the wall.

"It's too late," Campbell said.

Kingsley nodded, his shadow self trembling across the walls, its head stretched out across the ceiling that wasn't properly a ceiling anymore. "I see that."

"My fault," Campbell said. "It's my fault."

"You killed her?"

"I brought all of this here. All the death, all the evil. It's all mine."

"That's something for the police to determine, Mr Campbell."

"I'll go quietly. There's nothing here anymore."

"There's whoever did that," Kingsley said. He pointed at the body of Hester Price. "This place doesn't seem particularly safe, but we should guard against that person's return." He waved to Henry. "Check outside, would you?"

"He has grey eyes. The one who killed her. He takes the people I love."

Anna broke away from Jessica and went to Campbell, put her hand on his back. Campbell looked down at the girl, his expression unreadable.

"You knew her," he said.

"I didn't know her well enough," Anna said. "I'm sorry."

"She was good. Too good for me. But she waited all those years."

"Who's the grey-eyed man?" Kingsley said. "Who did this?"

"An American," Campbell said. "I never knew his name. He's stalked me for years."

"But where is he now?"

67

The American listened as they struggled to get past the carriage that was stuck in the tunnel. The horse whinnied and bucked, and when they got around it they still had to climb over the carriage. They weren't quiet about it. It sounded like there were two of them. He had plenty of time to prepare for them, but he didn't see much that he could do beyond loading the Whitworth. He was sitting with his back against the opposite wall from the tunnel mouth where they were making all the noise. His foot was twisted in a way that made him sick to his stomach when he looked at it. He had peeled back his stocking and had seen bone. He set the rifle across his knees and waited.

The man entered the chamber first, his arm held out, keeping the boy safe behind his own body. The American recognized the man. He had been on the train from London and had followed Campbell around the woods. This was the plainclothesman. The American's eyes flicked over to the other London policeman, the one in uniform in the middle of the chamber, then back to the detective. Both he and the boy looked as if they'd had a rough time of it recently. The detective's clothes were in tatters and the boy was barefoot, smudged with ash. They both peered around the chamber, taking in the scene. The boy gasped when he saw the American's face, and he gasped again when he saw the dead man hanging from the ceiling. "Father!" He ran forward, but the detective caught him and held him back, eyeing the rifle, the American holding it loosely but with his finger ready on the trigger.

At the boy's voice, the uniformed policeman stirred. He was on his feet, but had slumped against the hanged man, held upright by that swaying weight and an apparently boundless reserve of stubbornness.

"I'd like to check on my sergeant," the detective said.

The American nodded and swung the Whitworth up, pointed it at the detective. "Go ahead. He was here when I got here. Both of 'em like that."

The detective pushed the boy back in the shadows of the tunnel and whispered something. It sounded like the boy wanted to argue, but the detective stood his ground. He left the boy there, out of the American's sight, and walked cautiously to the middle of the chamber floor. His eyes flicked here and there, taking in the two shallow graves, one old and one fresh, the signs of a campsite.

"My name is Day," the detective said. "Inspector Day of the Yard."

The American shrugged. It didn't matter to him.

"And this is Sergeant Hammersmith."

Day reached out and felt for a pulse in Hammersmith's throat. He gently pulled the sergeant away from the dead man, and Hammersmith's knees buckled. He fell against the detective and came awake. "No!" He scrambled back and tried to lift the dangling body up, but it was too much for him. He gazed upward at the swollen face of the dead man, ignoring the American and his rifle. "I thought I could . . ." He turned on the detective. "What took you so long?"

"I didn't know," Day said. "How could I have known?"

"You couldn't have saved him," the American said. "Not on your own."

Both policemen seemed startled by the realization that the American was still there. He smiled his too-wide smile, amused that they had forgotten him.

"I saw you in the woods last night," Day said.

"That you did."

"I'd feel better if you'd point that rifle somewhere else, sir."

"Bet you would." But the American kept the rifle aimed at Day's midsection. He weighed his options. The Whitworth held a single shot. The smart move would be to kill the detective right away. Then he could use his knife to finish off the boy and the other policeman. Sergeant Hammersmith didn't look like he could do much at the moment. The man was barely able to stay on his feet, leaning heavily against Day.

But the American thought of that bone sticking out of his ankle. He couldn't maneuver well and wouldn't be able to chase down anyone who ran.

And he didn't have any grudge against these police. They'd only met Campbell the day before, and their behavior toward him, although viewed at a distance through a rifle scope, had seemed cool. They had no way of knowing about anything that the American had done over the course of the day and a half he'd spent on the outskirts of Blackhampton. And they might be able to help him find his way out of the tunnels.

He could always kill them later.

He stood carefully on his good foot and set the Whitworth upright against the wall, within easy reach. He extended his hand. "I apologize, mister. Used to being alone. Makes a man rude."

Day shook his hand, clearly suspicious, but polite down to his bones. Trying not to stare at the American's face. He loved the English and their good manners.

"Hope my cheek don't bother you."

"Not at all. Are you quite all right?"

"Old wound. Healed up, just ugly's all."

"I meant your foot. It looks painful."

"I've suffered worse."

"We need to cut him down," Hammersmith said. He was still looking at the hanged man, still ignoring the American.

"Of course," Day said. He looked around the chamber. "I have a knife, but I don't think it's up to the task."

"Got a good one here," the American said. He pulled his hunting knife from the sheath strapped to his thigh and held it out. For just a second, he considered plunging it into Day's throat, using the element of surprise, and then taking his time with Hammersmith, but instead he flipped it around and offered the handle to Day. The detective's eyes were narrowed, suspicious. As if he had somehow seen the American's murderous impulse.

The American grinned at him, trusting his mutilated face to throw Day off, and it did. Day averted his gaze and took the knife.

"Help me lift him, would you?" Day said. "I mean, can you? Your ankle . . ."

The American didn't answer. He hopped forward and grabbed the dead man by the legs, hoisted him up until the rope went slack above. He heard the slap slap slap *of bare feet on the packed soil behind him and let go of the hanged man, swiveled on his good foot in time to see the boy lift the Whitworth in one hand, balancing it by jamming it against his shoulder, his other arm useless in a sling.*

"*Rawhead and Bloody Bones!*" The boy took aim and fired before the American could move. The chamber filled with a piercing whistle, and his chest blossomed red and pink and grey. He tried to take a breath, but nothing happened. He grinned at the boy, showed him it wasn't so bad. Showed him all those teeth arrayed behind his butchered flesh, and then toppled facedown at the detective's feet.

"He killed my father," the boy said. "And he killed Oliver."

The American tasted dirt and felt rough hands turning him over, saw the detective's stricken expression, and wondered who the hell Oliver was.

And then he died.

68

They took the carriage apart.

Day used the shovel to break the axles, took off the uprights, and reduced the bed of the thing to about half its previous size by smashing through the planks all along its length. Hammersmith helped, as much as he could, but had to stop frequently to rest.

After Day took the rifle away from Peter (he gave it up without protest), the boy gentled the horse who had been frightened by the gunshot, while Day lashed the wide litter, all that remained of the carriage, to its harness.

Day left the boy and the horse to care for each other and he cut Sutton Price down from the ceiling. He had trouble loosening the rope, which had buried itself deep in Price's flesh and had dislocated his skull, but he managed to cut it away with minimal additional damage to the corpse. He covered Price with the remnants of Day's own ragged overcoat.

He and Hammersmith dug up the two graves.

The dirt that covered the fresh grave was easier to dig through, and they found little Virginia's body quickly. Her lips were blue and her head lolled on its broken spine. Her hair and dress were streaked with dirt, and they both recognized a kinship between the tiny ruined gown she wore and the blood-spattered dress Hammersmith had found in the woods, but neither of them spoke as they carried her to the modified bed of the carriage and laid her there next to her father. Day did his best to distract Peter from the sight of his sister, but the boy saw her body and didn't react. He looked away and turned his attention back to the horse, petting its muzzle. His lack of reaction bothered Day, but he had no idea what to do about it. Perhaps, given enough time, Peter would grieve and heal.

Gravity had worked its magic on the soil of the second grave and it was harder going. Hammersmith's legs finally gave out—Day marveled at the fact that the sergeant had stayed on his feet as long as he had—and he sat down to rest. Day removed his jacket and dug, slow and steady, and eventually began finding bones, scattered through the dirt three or four feet down. There was a dress, well-preserved and nearly intact, and a cloud of light brown hair. Day used pieces of the carriage's bench and leftover nails from its bed and fashioned a crude box that he used to collect the pieces of Mathilda Price, Sutton's first wife. All the pieces he could find.

He lashed the three bodies—Virginia, Sutton, and the unnamed American—and the box of Mathilda's bones to the homemade litter and hitched the horse to it. He put Peter on the horse, made him lay forward and hug its neck so that he wouldn't scrape the low ceiling of the tunnel, and he led them away from that dark chamber. Hammersmith trudged behind, and they made slow progress.

After a long while, they came to the mouth of the mine.

Peter finally began to cry when they left the horse and the bodies behind and climbed up into the evening light. Day held the boy tight against him, half carried him through the high drifts.

The snow had stopped falling and the wind had stopped blowing. A sliver of pale moon showed through a seam in the colorless sky.

Day uncorked his flask and took a long draught from it. Far in the distance he heard the low whistle of the train from London.

EPILOGUE

⸻◦◦◦⸻

The train was warm and largely devoid of passengers, and so Inspector Day had commandeered it. The tracks didn't appear to have been affected by the tremors of the previous night, but the engineer was taking his time examining them and the train sat quiet and ready. Dr Kingsley announced his preference for a sleeping car for the children and for Sergeant Hammersmith, but there wasn't one, so he made do, temporarily curling Peter and Anna up across from each other on the long seats of one compartment, where they fell instantly asleep. Extra cushions were brought and another compartment was made up like a sultan's seraglio, pads and pillows covering the floor and the seats. Hammersmith was swallowed up by the space, but once he settled in, he looked almost comically comfortable, and Day realized he had never seen Hammersmith at ease.

Day ushered everyone out of the sergeant's opulent train compartment, enduring Dr Kingsley's scowl of disapproval and his admonishment: "He needs rest." Day cleared off a small portion of the edge of one seat and perched there. He uncorked his flask and swirled the amber liquid in the bottom of it, frowning. He took a sip. Hammersmith blinked up at him from his well-lined nest.

"The doctor's given me something," Hammersmith said. "I'm having trouble staying awake."

"Drugged, yet again," Day said.

"I do seem to have a knack for it."

"You've earned some rest, Nevil. You're lucky to be alive."

"I am?"

"Well, that owl did land on your chair." Day smiled and winked.

"Nobody died. At least, nobody who was in that room when the owl flew in. That disproves the superstition, doesn't it?"

"Bennett Rose died. He was there. And it's true you were sitting on that chair, but it belonged to him. The owl actually landed on Rose's chair."

"I say we should call that a coincidence. Anyway, there's still work to do. The bodies we left in the tunnel. That poor horse."

"They've been tended to."

"When?"

"You weren't entirely conscious, I'm afraid. The village men pulled together. Watching them bring up that horse was something to see."

"Was Constable Grimes there? I haven't seen him all day."

"Funny," Day said. "I thought he was with you. I suppose he'll turn up."

"What will we do with the children?"

"I've spoken with Jessica Perkins. She's going to assume responsibility for Peter and Anna when they finally wake up. We'll find a way to make it official. By the way, Jessica asked me to tell you good-bye. She seems rather smitten with you."

"She is? I hadn't noticed."

Day shook his head. "You're blind, Nevil."

"But shouldn't we arrest them? The children, I mean."

"Neither of them killed anyone."

"But they helped hide Oliver's body in the well, didn't they?"

Day sighed. "Peter has had a hard time of it. Both the children have. He finally broke down and told it all. Virginia Price led Oliver to the woods and stabbed him to death after first practicing on a pig. I can't imagine anything more horrible than that. I have no idea what seeing such a thing would do to the fragile mind of a child. Peter and Anna were protecting their only remaining sibling, and I don't think I'd feel awfully good about myself if I consigned them to prison or to a London orphanage."

"I suppose not," Hammersmith said. "You know, while he was hanging there, Sutton Price told me that he was responsible."

"Did he say . . . Do you think it's possible that Virginia saw him kill his first wife, Mathilda? That she learned her behavior from her father?"

"Place the ultimate responsibility on him, after all?"

"He did claim it," Day said.

"If only Hester Price had cared for her stepchildren. So much might have been avoided."

"I believe the only person she cared for was Calvin Campbell."

"And little Oliver, of course," Hammersmith said. "She stayed in Blackhampton, waiting for Campbell to find her baby. Do you suppose they really thought they could run away together? As a family?"

"That's what Campbell says. True love, he says."

"Will he stay now? The village will have to be rebuilt."

Day shook his head. "He's already gone. He disappeared from the depot after we brought Hester's body out. Took the horse, so I suppose I ought to arrest him for that if we ever see him again. When poor Freddy recovers, he'll miss that horse." He stared out the window as if he might be able to see the row of bodies—Hester Price and her husband, and Virginia Price, and the mysterious American—laid out in the snow by the ruined outbuilding, but they were on the other side of the train.

Bennett Rose and the tiny body of Oliver Price had been destroyed in the fire at the inn. Day supposed their remains might eventually be found once the site cooled off enough that the village could rake the ashes.

Hammersmith began to softly snore. Day drank the last of the brandy in his flask, corked it, and put it away. He covered his sergeant with a blanket. He left the compartment as quietly as he could and slid the door shut along its well-oiled track. Kingsley was waiting for him in the hall. Day held a finger to his lips and led the doctor a few feet away.

"He's sound asleep," Day said.

"He ought to be," Kingsley said. "I gave him a little something to help with that. The man fights against sleep."

"He does prefer to get things done."

"Yes. You should get this train moving, get him back to his own flat and let him rest for the next few days."

"You make it sound as if you won't be going with us."

"I won't be. They need me here. Half the village is sick, and the other half is underground. There are injuries to tend to."

"But what of Claire?" Day was alarmed. "She's due to give birth soon."

Kingsley chuckled. "She'll have that baby whether I'm there or not, but don't worry. She's got plenty of time yet, and I'll be back in London by early next week. I might even get there before she returns from her sister's."

Day took a deep breath and shook his head. "I do wish you'd reconsider."

"I'll leave Blackhampton as soon as their doctor is back on his feet. I want to show him a few things about proper medicine. He's still using leeches. Probably boils potions in a cauldron. He needs a bit of training."

Day smiled, despite his worry. Kingsley laid a hand on his shoulder.

"Are you sure you're all right?" Kingsley said.

"Of course. I never drank the water here."

"I meant . . . Whoever that deformed American fellow was, you'll have to live with the fact that you killed him. That's not always an easy thing."

"I had no choice."

"I'm sure you didn't."

Day looked away from Kingsley's probing gaze. He wasn't comfortable with deception, but now that he had committed to the lie, he intended to stick to it. He wouldn't be blamed for the killing, and Peter Price had been through enough in a week. The boy didn't need to be labeled a murderer on top of everything else. Day wanted him to have a chance at a good life.

He changed the subject. "What about Henry?" he said.

"He's decided to stay on with me here for a bit."

"But he seemed so anxious to get back home."

"Well," Kingsley said, "it's entirely your fault for giving him that little magpie."

"How is that?"

"Henry says the city is no place to raise a baby."

ACKNOWLEDGMENTS

My agent, Seth Fishman, and my editor, Neil Nyren, for their guidance, patience, and good humor. Ivan Held and Marysue Rucci for showing that first crucial bit of faith in me and in this book. Claire Sullivan, Kate Ritchey, and everybody else who had to go through this and fix my most glaring mistakes. Alexis Welby, Kelly Welsh, Lauren Truskowski, Victoria Comella, and Kayleigh Clark for making me peek out of my shell a time or two. All the other wonderful people at Putnam and the Gernert Company.

My early readers and experts, who were gracious with their time and showed great kindness while tearing my prose to little bits: Roxane White, Alison Clayton, Melanie Worsley, Brandy Shillace, Whitney Lyn Kalin, and Arnold Hermansson, DDS.

The many booksellers and readers I have been fortunate enough to meet. I hope to see you again soon.

My father.

My wife and son, without whom there would be nothing important.